Blue Tide

By: Jenna-Lynn Duncan

Blue Tide

ISBN: 978-1-63422-212-9
Cover Design by: Marya Heiman
Typography by: Courtney Knight
Editing by: Cynthia Shepp

content disclosure

For more information about our content disclosure, please utilize the QR code above with your smart phone or visit us at www.CleanTeenPublishing.com

TO MY PIRATE CREW,
JEYLANI, ALIYA, AND ZAYDAN.

Chapter One

"The sea never sleeps, and in the sleeplessness of the sea is a consolation to a soul that never sleeps."
—Jubran Khaleel Jubran, 1883-1931

Water here and water there.
Sailing around to who knows where.
With nothing to do, I sing this tune.
E'ryone died but me 'n you.
There's only one man to blame,
Thanks to Asmodeus, we're rich but insane.
Lands destroyed—now we rule the seas.
We'll take what we want and do what we please.

MAKE IT STOP. I CRINGED, MY HEAD THROBBING FROM the off-key voice. It was a song most people would sacrifice their firstborn to never hear. Most who heard it never lived to hear it twice. Because of all the dangers of the sea... Nothing was worse than pirates.

Water here and water there.

Damp, musty-smelling wood filled my senses. I was lying facedown in a small boat. The half-moon offered little illumination in the dark sky. I must have blacked out because I had no memory of this—the boat, the swaying ocean, or why my head felt like a

1

pounding island drum. Blinking away the fog of sleep, I pushed myself up on shaky feet and adjusted my dress.

I rubbed my temples, fighting nausea, the stench of fish making it worse. The contents of my stomach bubbled hotly and saliva pooled in my mouth. Willing myself not to throw up, I concentrated on breathing. *In, out, in, ou*—something sharp and deliberate poked at my back. I hissed at the sudden jab, and flung my head around to glare at the pirate who'd poked me. My jaw dropped at the scene behind him. *Not good.*

A large ship towered next to us. In the distance, a line of people stumbled up a wooden gangway onto it.

Lands destroyed—now we rule the seas.

We'll take what we want and do what we please...

The man with the slurred voice herded people onto the next ship, and the islanders in front of me all shared the same hopeless saunter. I imagined this was how cattle looked being sent to the slaughterhouse. Except there were no slaughterhouses anymore. There weren't even any cattle.

Water here and water there.

The man came down the line toward me, his voice growing louder as he approached. *Please make it stop.* Pinching the bridge of my nose with my thumb and forefinger, I paused. I just needed a minute to think.

E'ryone died but me 'n you.

I was the only prisoner left. The man's cold, dirty hand pushed me, and I slunk away from his touch. "Touch me again and I'll gut you!"

His round face and droopy mouth fell before it scrunched together. "That's hardly language for a girl."

His words struck a chord inside of me, as it was something I already knew to be true. I'd once been a refined young lady, one who always left the gutting to Leif when we went fishing. It had to be the stress that made me snap. I'd been *so close* to getting what I spent the past five years longing for. Now, in the midst of pirates, that life was further away than ever.

The throbbing got worse, and I closed my eyes, finding small relief in pressing my forefingers into my temples.

"Ey. It's you again." His eyes lit up with recognition.

I dropped my hand from my face and studied him. Familiarity screamed at me, but my brain couldn't function beyond the pain. All I needed was to get back to shore so I could finish what I was doing and put this mistake behind me. I could use my position as a mayor's daughter—act as if we had a hundred ships and an army ready to come to my defense.

A cunning smile spread across my face. "Yes..." I nodded and spoke in a slow voice. "You know who I am, don't you? There seems to be some sort of mistake, you see..."

His pinched expression caused me to pause. "I ain't slow, and I don't give a damn who you are. You been disobedient once already, and if I hear one more peep outta you, you'll wish I killed you with that blow I gave ya earlier. Now move!"

Ah, so this rude man was the reason my head felt like my brain had been removed, scrambled, and then replaced. My jaw clenched. He didn't understand whom he was dealing with. I tilted up my nose and said, "My name is Lux Rayan Aiello. I am the daughter of the *Mayor* of Sirbiad. If you bring me back now, you will not be punished."

His lips curled and his bulging eyes—or rather *eye*—gave me a once-over. His eyes freaked me out. One didn't move. I thought it might be fake.

"Send her overboard!"

"Excuse me?" I put my hands on my hips.

His crooked eyes never let me out of sight while

he signaled to someone behind him and turned away. Sticky hands grabbed me, and the air was once again filled with fish and copper. The men pulled me away, their uncut nails searing through my arms, my skin straining.

Images of the creatures in the waters below came to mind, as did the many people who had been eaten by them. "Wait," I pleaded. "We can pay you."

The men paused.

One-eyed's broad shoulders stiffened. He was a short man with stocky legs, but his burly arms and barrel chest promised pain.

"My father will trade with you if you return me." I should have swallowed my pride and said that from the start. Obviously, I had chosen the right words that time because he turned back.

"What makes you think I want any kind of payment?" He took a quick step toward me, his sweaty, fishy scent sending me backing up into the pirates restraining my arms. Reaching out, he coiled his plump hand around my entire wrist. I dug my teeth into my bottom lip, refusing to scream, but then he twisted my arm. The cry I held back came out in a harsh exhale.

Hushed whispers spread before a commanding voice rose over the rest. "Stop."

I glanced at the second ship. Tall, leather boots stomped down the plank.

The man groaned and released my arm, shoving me to the deck. I smacked into the slippery planks, breaking my fall with open palms. A splinter bit into my flesh.

"Sir, this one was being disobedient. I was gonna send her to the fish."

I got to my knees, picking the wood out of my skin, even though such a cut was the least of my worries. But for something so small, it really hurt.

"No, you weren't, Sokum. You were trying to keep one of *his*, weren't you?" He approached, and I lifted my head. Along with his boots, he wore leather pants with a belt full of weapons and a chest covered in armor. *Holy*—I flinched, wondering what kind of battle I just found myself in the middle of. I swallowed and continued studying him. His face was covered with a gray scarf that billowed behind him like a dark sail. A sliver in the wrapping revealed a pair of icy blue eyes and thick, dark brows. His clothes were clean and finely made, and he stood with poise rather than slumped over like the Neanderthal next to me. I didn't know whether to place him in a ballroom or on a battlefield, but he definitely didn't belong on a pirate ship.

"N-no, Captain. She—"

Captain. This mysterious man was the captain? Finally, someone civil to negotiate with. There was hope. Surely, *he* would—

Craaack!

My head shot up in time to see the captain's fist come away from Sokum's face. Sokum missed crushing me by inches as the force propelled him to the floor.

The captain bent over and pulled him up by his collar. I blinked. The man moved like a tiger, beautiful to admire from afar, but frightening beyond all measure when he pounced. Sokum looked so meek under the towering form of the captain, cowering from his cocked-back fist. I winced at the thought of him receiving another blow.

"Don't!" The word escaped my lips, surprising me as much as everyone else.

That set of chilling eyes burned into me, narrowing with suspicion before easing and turning back to his victim. He drew his fist back farther.

I released a quivering breath, preparing myself for more violence. The captain's eyes darted to me again. To my surprise, he dropped the fist. "Don't *ever* disobey me again." He released his grip on Sokum, as if it was beneath him to even touch him.

Racing to a stand, I wiped the ocean slime from my dress with little success. The captain towered over me. I shuffled back a step.

"You defend him even though he just tried to have you killed?" He quirked a brow at me, waiting for an answer I couldn't give. I suppose Sokum deserved it after he tried to have me thrown overboard, and it wasn't as if he would have done the same for me. But there was that moment right before Sokum was about to be hit again when true fear flashed in his eyes. No matter how many sparring sessions they put me through on the island, I detested violence. I couldn't watch anyone suffer at the hands of someone who wasn't his equal.

The moon caught my attention when it reflected on the captain's armor. Dawn was quickly approaching. I was running out of time. It was imperative I get back to shore before anyone knew I was missing.

"My name is Lux. I am from Sirbiad—"

"Lux... of *Sirbiad*?" He indicated my sundress with a nod. "You hardly look Sirbiadian." Despite his dark and foreboding demeanor, his eyes danced with amusement and held a promise that his veiled-mouth was smirking.

I clenched my fists. *Let him laugh, Lux, you'll have the last one.* Ignoring his insensitive comment, I attempted to add the much-needed confidence to my voice. "Based on the Maritime Codes, I demand you take me back immediately."

He tipped his head back and laughed. "And which

code is that?"

"What?"

"To which code are you referring?"

I straightened my posture, shoulders back and chin high, even though I felt very small inside. In truth, I had never read the laws created by Asmodeus before. The only allegiance I had was to the US. I would do anything to make it back to shore, and if that meant using a dictator's laws to suit me, then so be it. "580." I spoke the first number that came through my mind.

His dark eyebrows arched.

I swallowed. *580? Dumb, Lux. Might as well have guessed three million.*

"And *who* put the Maritime Codes in place?" His smooth, muffled voice contrasted the harsh, mocking tone

My forehead creased. If he noticed I was bluffing, he made no indication of it. But what was with the inquisition? I tilted my head and answered. "Asmodeus."

"And *that's* exactly whose orders I'm following."

He's following Asmodeus' orders? That didn't make sense. As far as I was concerned, Asmodeus was evil with a capital E—a dictator of the third degree. But my dad still brokered with him. Asmodeus fed our island. *Was he the one behind our villagers' disappearances?*

He glanced over me from head to toe, as if truly seeing me for the first time. My stomach fluttered at his scrutiny, but I glared back, refusing to let him intimidate me. His ocean blue eyes contrasted starkly with his dark eyebrows and lashes. Night and day in one tall, dark, and cruel package.

"Take her to the ship. We depart immediately." At his orders, everyone dispersed except for Sokum, who wore the same baffled expression I imagined I wore.

My lips parted, but the words caught in my throat.

"You broke my nose," Sokum shouted nasally, cupping it as if it were a priceless artifact. *Pretty sure it already looked broken before.* "And sir, she was being disobedient. There must be consequences!"

Snapping my head in his direction, I narrowed my eyes. I was really starting to regret telling the captain to stop.

The captain glanced back. "Your mouth broke your nose." Still refusing to meet my eyes, he added, "She appears strong enough for labor. Now do as I say, or I'll impose the consequences on *you*."

"Please, I have to go back." It made my flesh crawl that I was begging a pirate. Possibly the same ruthless pirate who was responsible for the disappearances of our villagers for years, but it was my last chance to be returned to shore while we were still anchored.

"You belong to Asmodeus now. There's nothing I can do." His voice was as hard as the iron rigging of his ship, and he turned away before I could register his words. I was left openmouthed and speechless as he crossed in perfectly measured strides onto the next ship, disappearing in a thick, salty fog that crept in with the morning air.

A grunt sounded behind me, and I whipped around.

"Move it," a bald-headed giant roared.

A sudden knife of panic slipped through my gut. I shook my head. This was not happening. I *had* to get back to shore, or I would lose my one chance to—

The bald pirate shoved me toward the gangplank. I stumbled, ducking under his arm, wanting to be far, far away from the very narrow plank that was the only solid surface between the boats and the dark, deep water below. But when I came face to face with more pirates, the water looked like the better option, despite the certain death lurking there. I turned in every direction, a blockade of criminals surrounding me. It was hopeless. The bald pirate turned around, his face scrunching together.

He stepped toward me again.

"No, no, no." I twisted and pulled at my dress. "I *need* to go back." Prickles covered my scalp as I shot sidelong glances at the pirates advancing on me.

How could I let this happen? How could I let myself be kidnapped when I was so close to getting the only thing I've wanted for the past five years? Dizziness consumed me, and I was starting to hyperventilate. "I won't go!" I tried to dodge past them to the smaller boat.

Someone caught me, and I let out a scream.

"Wait just a sec now, boys."

I held my breath in hope, but the voice that spoke was nasally. I turned to find Sokum still holding his nose trickling with blood.

"I'll take care of this one." Sokum's eyes shined with a vindictive twinkle. When he drew a long sword, the moonlight glinted off the razor-sharp blade.

"Sokum, you heard what the captain said." The bald man's voice sounded lower than humanly possible.

"I *said* I got it from here." Sokum turned his fish-like eyes back on me. "Now you're gonna walk across to the other ship like a good little girl, and we're not gonna have any more problems with you, are we?" He gave me a confident smile, all the while holding the sword as though it was an extension of his body.

If he straightened that elbow, I could knock it from his hand. Could show him how well trained Sirbiadians really were.

He raised his cutlass, bringing the tip dangerously close to my neck. I tipped my chin up, exposing my throat. Should I be worried that it was irritation, not fear, that clawed at my insides?

The deep voice of the bald man whispered Sokum's name in warning.

There was no way I would be able to make it back to shore. I couldn't argue my way through this one. "Do it," I egged him on in a moment of recklessness. He wouldn't really kill me, would he? The pirates' loyalty seemed to draw beyond their fear of disobeying the captain, and he did make it seem like he desired me alive. *For the time being.* But the look in Sokum's dark eyes told me he was more than capable of taking my life.

"You wanna die, girl, or are you gonna move?"

My mouth opened to speak, but words escaped me as I was scooped up by the bald man. He held my arms and legs tighter than a fisherman's ropes. The scream I let out burned my throat.

"I said I was handling it," Sokum complained from behind us on the gangplank.

"Enough time wasted." The bald man's clipped response rumbled against my back as I wiggled like an angry octopus.

My stomach rolled when I was carried over the threshold of the next ship. I stopped fighting the iron hold the pirate had on me now that my first plan of escape had been crushed.

The new ship towered over the measly one that brought us to it. Looking around took me back centuries. It was like the old ships I'd seen in movies back home. Based on the materials, it had to have survived from the Floods five years ago.

Despite numerous snowy white sails, the ship was dark and screamed power—just like its captain. Fascinating to see, but teasing with the promise of danger. There was no doubt in my mind that this was *his* ship.

Sensing I was no longer a flight risk, the bald pirate none too gently set me down. As I stumbled across the deck, the teak beamed in the moonlight. The work and time it must have taken to build such a vessel was unimaginable. I continued to stare up at the sails with a mixture of fascination and contempt. The bald man pushed me below after I had taken too long at the top of the stairs.

"Hope the accommodations are to your liking, *Your Highness.*" He shoved me into a small prison in the belly of the ship, his deep laugh echoing through the close quarters. Lanterns offered the barest illumination to the row of makeshift jail cells. They were small despite the size of the ship. People were jammed in them like sardines.

The smell of bilge water was strong, but manageable, and not at all like Leif described ships to reek of. In my opinion, the ship was clean, and the gleam of the brass showed its crew took pride in it. Only the faint stench of urine and sweat remained, reminding me the cells must be well used. The one they put me in was the most crowded. My vision tunneled as I squeezed past my fellow prisoners. *This isn't real. This has to be a nightmare!*

There were rumors on our island as to why pirates kidnapped people. As the stories of cannibalism played through my mind, my only consolation was hearing I would be a laborer and not an entree. *For now,* my mind taunted.

Chapter Two

LEIF... HE WAS WITH ME LAST NIGHT. WHAT HAPPENED to him? I had to remember, but the lump on my head throbbed in protest. How could I have let this happen? What went wrong? I tried to think of when Sokum might have appeared, if I could've done anything differently, but my memory was still murky. I'd have to start earlier.

I navigated through the others sharing my cell, needing somewhere quiet to think. Closing my eyes, I put myself back into my hammock on Sirbiad...

⁓⌣⌣⌐

A star shimmers through a hole in the roof. The blazing red dusk of the sunset has long ago passed, along with the firelight from the islanders' huts. My jittery foot kicks off the sandy floor, swinging my hammock to the rhythm of my father's snoring. My parents are sleeping just ten feet away beyond the fabric partition in the other section of our tent. They've been out for a while now, but I'm waiting for the perfect moment to escape. I can't risk getting caught. Not tonight.

My rucksack lays inconspicuously under a blanket next to me. I've smuggled the most dried fish and canned water I could find.

My swinging slows to a stop. Ready or not, it's time. Ignoring the coconut-sized lump lodged in the back of my throat, I sit up and swing my legs over the hammock as I have countless times before. I lurch forward... and fall face-first onto the ground. When I lift my head, grains of sand stick to my lips. I turn my ear toward my parents' side of the tent and listen. Father inhales sharply, and his snoring stops. My hands clench fistfuls of sand. If he wakes up, it's all over. He will never let me leave. All the hard work over the past months would have been for naught. All the waiting I've done—pointless. All the longing for my family and friends back home—permanent.

With a snort, my dad turns over and resumes his noisy breathing. I release the breath caged in my lungs, and the blood rushes back to my face.

My gaze narrows at the blasted hammock as I struggle to free my tangled foot. I stand, brush the sand from my dress, and then glare at the pile of rope I've been sleeping in for the past five miserable years.

I steal to the entrance, the cool sand muffling my footsteps. Pausing, I risk a glance back toward my parents. An unfamiliar burning in my chest sends my world spiraling. Horrible thoughts fly into my head. Oh God, what if I'm not making the right decision? What if I die like the others who've tried? I scrunch my eyes closed as if I can squeeze these thoughts away. No, I have to stay focused. I have to remember why I am doing this. Opening my eyes, more determined than before, I whisper goodbye to my parents.

Parting the flaps, I step into the tropical night air. Each sense our tent subdued comes roaring to life. The lapping of the waves against the shore, the brilliance of the moon, the buzzing of cicadas, and the faint, sweet smell of hibiscus. I allow a small sigh to escape. I've managed to make it past the first obstacle.

I wrap a wool cloak around me, tucking my long, sun-bleached hair into the hood, hoping no one will catch the Mayor of Sirbiad's daughter sneaking out at night. Retrieving an oil lantern from beside our hut, I dash around the embers still burning in the community fire pit, straight toward the rainforest.

Pausing at the edge, I peer down the shadowy foot-path. Of course, the moon offers no illumination where I actually need it, but there's no way I can take the shoreline around to the other side of the island at this time of night. The fishermen are there, risking their lives to catch nieneti. I'd be angry, but the stupid nocturnal fish are the island's main food source. Mom and Dad have to eat, so I dart away.

The path dumps me onto a secluded beach, and I head toward a small cave under the cliffs. The jagged onyx rocks hide the boat I've been building since the day I received a map back home.

I rub the back of my neck, studying the third-quarter moon. It gives us only twenty days to get to Fiji, which according to the new map, has a small population surviving on their sole remaining island. I chew on my thumbnail, debating the accuracy of the map in terms of distance. I hope I've given us enough time to get there and settle in before the next full moon.

Anxiety and excitement sends me rushing into the cave. I gather our tools and the canvas for the sail, taking it out to the beach. A shadow appears in my peripheral.

I am no longer alone.

When I spin around, the hemp satchel tumbling out of my hands, I find Leif, my only friend on the island, yawning.

I let out an exaggerated sigh. "What took you so long?"

"Sorry 'bout that." Leif shrugs. He speaks nearly perfect English, his brown eyes heavy with sleep. I crane my neck to look up at him. The lamp he holds illuminates the sun streaks in his brown hair. The color transforms to a molten gold that would make any girl jealous, including me. With a smirk, I shake my head and go back into the cave to pull out the boat.

I drag the bulky contraption from the cave, and then stand, beads of sweat trickling down my back. Wiping my forehead with the back of my hand, I do a double take. Leif still standing next to his lantern, looking every inch a Sirbiadian warrior: tall, strong, and tan. We couldn't be any more opposite. Our only similarity is we are both seventeen. He is capable of doing everything in training I struggle with.

Since the first villager disappeared years ago, every Sirbiadian, upon reaching sixteen, had to train. I roll my stiff shoulders. My muscles still ache from this morning's session. The only reason I gritted through was because I knew I would only have to put up with it a little longer. Soon, I'd never have to hold a katana again.

I throw off the smothering cloak, sweat and wool itching my skin. Leif is still staring off into the distance, oblivious that I just brought the boat out. "What are you doing? Get busy." I toss Leif the satchel. "Remind me again—how long do you think it will take?" That doesn't seem too desperate, does it? Leif has no idea we have any sort of timetable...

"With tonight's wind, a week, maybe less."

That gives us plenty of time to get there before I set sail again on the eve of the full moon. A tingling courses through me, stealing a portion of my breath. "We're actually going! I can't believe it." I grin at him, bouncing from foot to foot.

"Yeah, it's—it's great." His head hangs, his concen-

tration on the bag as he sifts through it.

My smile falls. "What's wrong?"

"Nothing. I'm very excited. Really." He glances at me, as if on cue, and forces a smile.

I cross my arms over my chest and smile in disbelief. "You liar!"

His eyes widen. Leif has probably never been called a liar in his entire life, but since I'm American, my outspokenness is usually forgiven.

Usually.

Why did I start? We're about to set sail; we can't spend the whole night debating again. Last night, it was about if the tide was right. The night before, it was about how much food to pack. The night before that—

"I just have… apprehensions." Leif still avoids looking me in the eyes.

"Apprehensions?" I drop—no, throw—a mallet into the sand. "Apprehensions about what? About leaving?"

"Yes, don't you?"

"No!" I choke on my disbelief. I can't wait to leave. "You've had a month to bring this up. We've been losing sleep, working our tails off. I've traded nearly everything of value I owned for the materials. And you say this now?" I squeeze my hands into fists, running the pads of my fingers over the calluses, scars, and splinters that resulted from building this stupid boat.

He takes a step toward me. "Lux, I'm not like you. You want—I don't know—adventure, I guess. But I'm just an island boy. You… you're like a princess." He nods at my sundress, so different from the earth-toned kimono-like tunics Sirbiadians wear. No, thank you.

My hand reaches up my neck, seeking out my charm necklace, idly toying with the small compass attached. I used to dream of how it would help navigate me home. A memory flashes through my mind of my father giving it to me before we sailed to Sirbiad, and I clasp the necklace protectively to my chest. My clothes may hold a soft spot, but the necklace is the only thing left I own of real value—and my only real reminder of the Old World.

The anger slowly seeps out of me. I shouldn't have gotten so angry with him for not wanting to go. If he doesn't want to travel on dangerous waters to an unknown destination in a boat we built ourselves, who could blame him?

I counted on him coming back to Sirbiad to explain everything to my parents. Hoped to send him back with something great to present to the island and help alleviate what I'd done. I was only thinking of myself. Now, I have no one to go with me.

I look up at the moon. No matter what, I am going. I've been dreaming about this since I was twelve, since the world I knew ended. This map in my hand tells me there are other surviving islands. It breathes new hope into my dream of finding answers about what happened to my home and my people. When Leif and I started building this boat, started talking about our future, that dream became a reality. All along, he didn't share my dream, but I was too focused on my own desires to think about his.

I frown, rubbing my chest with a fist. If he can understand my need to leave, I should be able to understand why he wants to stay.

When I look at Leif, the moon reflects his tear-glistened eyes. I think about his father who depends on him. His ailing grandmother who only seems to smile when Leif is around.

Leif's eyebrows pull down in concentration, and a sad smile comes across his face. Without warning, he pulls me roughly into a side hug.

Crushed under the strength of Leif's arm, I feel my heart warm.

"I won't make you come with me, Leif."

"Stay with me."

"I can't." I shake my head. I need to tell Leif the whole truth. Isn't that what I've demanded of everyone else? Truth has become my obsession. There are too many unknowns in my life to tolerate lies.

"I'm leaving, Leif. Not just to Fiji, but to the US. Remember when the traveling fisherman came? Not only did he give me the map, but he also spoke of an expedition to my home. I made a deal to go with him. On the eve of the full moon, I have to be in Fiji, or they will leave without me."

"I had a feeling this trip was something more than just getting supplies for our island. You need to move on, Lux." Scoffing, I roll my eyes as he continues. "Do you feel guilty for surviving? Is that it? The Floods were inevitable. It wasn't anyone's fault."

How can he say such a thing? I spin around to face him, my nostrils flaring. "It was! If Asmodeus had warned our country, we could have prepared."

Leif shakes his head, trying to understand. It's nearly impossible for someone whose culture is rooted in mysticism and destiny. If only I could be like everyone else in Sirbiad and never dwell on the past, I wouldn't be in my current predicament.

I reach for the hatchet in his hands, but he pulls back.

"These waters are dangerous. This boat wasn't built for you to go alone. You don't have as much sailing experience as I do. And what if nothing is out there? What if the fisherman lied? What if you can't come back?

"It doesn't matter. I have to try."

"Then it is my duty to accompany the mayor's daughter."

"I know all too well what if feels like to be taken away from your home. I won't let you do that. I'm going alone. Consider that an order, if you have to."

"I can't just leave you out here. You know why no one goes out to the shore at night." He uses the same hushed tone as the elders do when they tell the tales, but I'm not scared of the island's boogey monsters anymore.

"Just leave, Leif."

"But—"

"Leave!" Hot tears pool in my eyes, but I hold them back like always. No one on the island has ever seen me cry. And they never will.

The hatchet slips from Leif's hand and falls into the sand with a muted thump. With a stony expression unmarred by the disappointment he surely feels, he turns and jogs back to the path through the rainforest.

A vacant stare blurs my vision, and I plop into the sand. All my previous motivation evaporates—replaced with this icky feeling I can't pin down or shake. I pinch my lips together.

The snap of bamboo from the jungle behind me sends an initial tremor of fear down my spine.

Leif? I fight a smile, but I have to remain firm. I won't let him convince me to stay. Standing, I say, "Leif, I'm going, and there's—" Before I can turn around, everything turns black as a scratchy, dark cloth is slipped over my head.

Leif's warning fills my panicked thoughts. No one goes to the shore alone at night...

Cold, calloused hands grab my bare neck. As hard as I can, I jab my elbow behind me. It digs into a squishy stomach and causes my attacker to let out an oompf. His hold eases just enough for me to break free and run, but the sack blocks out the moonlight. I stumble and fall into the sand. Yanking the cloth off, I attempt to stand, but the chilling hands catch my waist again. He calls me a dirty name. I kick his shins. Squirming as much as I can, his cruel grip tightens.

"Come on! Let this be a fair fight," I blurt out.

"A fair fight, eh?" A rumble of laughter follows a deep burr. "Okay, I accept your challenge." He spins me around to face him and then releases me.

My eyes run up the length of him, and I gulp. Okay, maybe I hadn't elbowed his stomach earlier. He blocks out the moonlight, so I can scarcely make out his features. All I see is his shaved head towering over me, his bulging muscles, and a belt full of weapons. He breathes through his mouth, his angry breaths smelling of fish and copper.

A fair fight? What was I thinking? Even with my katana, I'd hit no higher than his elbows.

He cracks his neck mockingly and holds up his fists. Knobby hammers with rings brighter than any gold I have seen. A nervous laugh slips out of my mouth. I hold up my own measly fists and try to remember my training.

Then I run.

So the running away isn't a part of training, but I'm not about to test the elders' theories about brains being much more important than brute strength. Easy to say when you have both.

So focused on the sheer size of one man, I forget to consider that he might not be working alone. A fist flies out, striking me on the side of my head. Pain explodes across my temple, the force knocking the breath out of me. I blink back stars.

Falling to my knees, I fight unconsciousness.

The sand kicks up behind me. "Why'd ya have to ruin my fun, Sokum? I was so looking forward to a fight." My eyes flutter as the dark cloth is thrown back over my head.

"'Fraid it wouldn't have been much of a fight anyway," the brute who hit me replies.

I can smell them on either side of me before they each grab an arm, lifting me off my knees.

I whimper and try to twist away, but their grips are relentless. They drag my limp body across the beach, the top of my feet and shins scraping on rough, damp sand. The sound of the waves becomes louder. My feet meet cool ocean water, and I inhale sharply. As we move deeper into the sea, my heart jumps in my chest.

"Where are you taking me?" I scream until my head throbs. With the last of my strength, I struggle against the arms that hold me, as well as the dizziness from the hit to my head. Somewhere, someone starts singing a pirate song...

~ ᴗ ᴗ ᴗ ⌒

So *that* was why Sokum and I weren't on the best of terms. It also explained his recent limp. I smiled— until I looked around at where it got me.

A sickening thought occurred to me, and my heart dropped into my stomach. My hands slid clumsily to my chest where my necklace still rested safely around my neck. *Oh, thank God.* I closed my eyes, tipping my head back. It could have easily gotten lost during the scuffle or, worse, stolen by those pirates while I was passed out.

Anger erupted like poison in my veins. *Pirates.* Complete savages. And who did that arrogant captain think he was? *He worked for Asmodeus.* I clenched my teeth until they ached. My muscles bunched, and I longed to destroy every pirate on this dreadful ship. I uncrossed my arms, shocked at the violent turn of my thoughts. But if there was anyone I hated more than pirates, it was Asmodeus.

Chapter Three

IF SOMEONE COULD HAVE PREDICTED THE FLOODS, THEY could have either saved a lot of people or become the most powerful person in the world. It turned out someone could. That man was Asmodeus, and he chose the latter, sending nearly three-quarters of the population to their deaths so he could control the surviving islands. It was only by chance that my parents and I were on one of them. Asmodeus' army with all their modern resources oversaw everything, except for the rogue pirates who haunted the waters around us. All this time, they were one and the same? Where were we going? What did they need us for?

It didn't matter; I wouldn't stick around to find out. The belly of the ship offered no windows, but somewhere out there, the rising sun meant I had lost one more day.

I sank to the floor of the cell, pulling my legs against my body. Slinging my arms over my knees, I studied the people locked away with me. Men and women, all with varying degrees of desperation. A woman hugged herself, resting her chin on her chest. She looked familiar. *Wait—I know her.* She worked with the night fisherman, using her special recipe to jar and preserve fish.

My jerky gaze searched the crowd. I knew the girl my age who stared blankly, dragging her nails down her cheeks and the elderly man who trembled with fear. I knew them. These people were from my island. They had cooked for me, cared for me, and took my family in when we thought our home was destroyed. I swallowed. I wasn't even sure I could escape, let alone with a whole group of people.

No.

I had to stick to my plan of escape. If—when—I got out, I could tell someone. *They* could rescue them. It was our best option.

The air expanded in my chest before I forcibly sighed. If it was the best option, why didn't it feel that way?

"Y-you... you're Lux?" a small voice next to me stuttered, bursting me out of a dozen dreary thoughts.

I lifted my head, and my chest tightened at the glossy eyes looking up at me. It was a child. A young girl who couldn't have been older than nine. She was shaking. I shifted on the hard, uncomfortable ground. "Yes?" I softened my tone.

Her arms dropped from their hold on her legs, and she straightened. I knew that look. She was hopeful. "Mayor Aiello's daughter? The mayor of Sir... Sirbiad?"

I whispered, "Yes, but—"

She flung her arms around my neck, the coolness of her skin jarring. Poor girl—she was freezing.

Everyone around watched us, and I gave them a weak smile.

The girl eased her grip and spoke the words I dreaded. "We're saved!"

I grabbed her arms to quiet her. "Wait—"

"The mayor's daughter is onboard!"

My face burned hotter than the midday sun. How

was I going to explain that we weren't saved? The pirates couldn't care less who I was. Just as she got the possibility in her head of seeing her family again, I would have to take it away. But I didn't have to.

A middle-aged man wearing the robes of a shaman stepped forward, parting the bodies and fixing his eyes on the girl. "Leave her alone; we're all going to die anyway."

A woman cried out from somewhere in another cell, and the girl trembled beside me. I scowled at the man. *I see Shaman Tamati hasn't lost his flair for the dramatics.* He might be right, but he was *not* helping the situation. I rubbed my hand across my face. First, a child was on board, and now Shaman Tamati? How did that happen? Shaman's were highly regarded in their culture and never had to go out at night. Only the night fisherman risked their lives by going out to shore to hunt one of the only food sources we had left. "They're not going to kill us; I heard the captain say we'd be laborers," I amended.

"They're pirates! As soon as they be hungry, some of us will start disappearing," another man murmured from the back of the cell.

I craned my neck to see who had spoken. "Those are just rumors…"

"No, it's true." The shaman pointed a finger at me. "I've heard stories about him. We may be going somewhere to work, but perhaps he doesn't need all of us."

"The captain dumped a body overboard as we came on deck. I saw it with my own eyes. He's getting rid of the weak, I tell ya," an elderly man added, wringing his hands together.

"But he's just a boy," a woman's shrill voice interjected.

Just a boy? Were we talking about the same person?

24

"Say that when he flogs ya with a flagrum. It will be a slow, painful death when your flesh is torn from your body."

Yep. Same person.

I turned to the little girl next to me, whose eyes had widened at our conversation. I needed to stop a panic before it happened. "Enough," I called out, throwing my hands up. The whispering died down. "Speculating isn't going to help us."

"She can save us. Her father is a *mayor*." The girl spoke up. All at once, she was hopeful and oblivious to the others who could see that I wouldn't be able to save them. I wished she were right, but what could I do? I wasn't positive I could save myself.

The man turned up his nose in anger. Or was it contempt? "*She* cannot save us, you child! Don't you see where she is? Locked in here—just like the rest of us."

I scoffed in indignation. Sure, he was right. But to hear it from him was a challenge. My fists dug into my sides. "We have to do something! There is a child on board."

None of the prisoners had answered my plea. Studying the rusting metal bars of our cells, I thought about a new course of action. I wouldn't leave without them. If I was going to get myself back to Sirbiad, what were a few more people? I could get us back safely *and* make it in time to finish what I started on the shore last night. Right? *Oh, God...*

What would my father do? If he were in this situation, he would probably rally everyone together. I wished now more than ever that I could be like him. He could cure people on the inside. I was more like my mother, the healer. If she were here, she would be tending to their scrapes and ailments. I could do that; I could manage physically mending people.

It's not about what's on the outside, but on the inside.

The voice in my head sounded suspiciously like my father's.

The people in my cell came from Sirbiad. Were the other cells filled with more of us or had they come from a different island? Everyone appeared unharmed, but they all shared the same grim look. I looked back at the girl. Her arms gripped her legs and her eyes glazed over.

Oh, darn it. My father was right. I knew what I had to do. I took a deep breath. *What did I have to lose?*

"He's right. I'm a prisoner, too." I stood up. The man's eye darted to the sides, but he hesitantly nodded. "But that doesn't mean I won't try to get each and every one of you back to your families. I have a plan." I paused, deciding not to spread more panic by telling them Asmodeus was behind it all. "Whatever they want us for, I think they need us alive. There are a good number of us here. If we come together, we can overpower them and sail back home!"

Most heads turned in disbelief. A murmured, "It's hopeless," came from the crowd.

A wave of déjà vu came over me. This was just like all the other times that I had "big ideas" that ended in disaster—building a treehouse in a palm tree, having a crab for a pet, the 'indoor' plumbing fiasco... They all said those ideas wouldn't work either. But I thought things through this time. I singled the man out. "Why not? What's wrong with my plan? Isn't this what we've been training for?"

"You know we never fight without being provoked." He shushed me. "And they're pirates! Did you see their modern weapons? Do you want an early death?"

"We are locked in a cell." My arms stretched out,

gesturing around me. "I would say that's *very* provoking. I think you're just afraid. Did you even try to fight when they came and kidnapped an innocent child and a shaman?"

"But..."

Shaman Tamati raised up his hand to demand silence. "We are here for a reason. This is where our path has led us, and we must follow it." He looked at me as they always did on Sirbiad when I did something outside of their customs, like giving thanks before meals.

Everyone sighed, slumped down, or turned. What had I expected? That people would pump their fist in the air and shout 'For Sirbiad'?

Yes.

Because they would have if it were my father's speech.

I guess a mutiny against the crew is out of the question. As I leaned back against the bars of the cell, the metal cooled my exposed skin. I squeezed my eyes shut and nearly collapsed to the floor.

The ironic part was that I wouldn't have been taken if I hadn't been on the beach, and I wouldn't have been on the beach if I hadn't been trying to leave Sirbiad. A stab of guilt lay buried in my chest. Maybe helping them would be one step toward atonement. Maybe I could finally be as much like them as I always pretended. Maybe...

"I believe in you."

My eyes shot open, and I turned to the girl next to me. The hope returned to her eyes. Giving up wasn't an option. I had to convince them to fight, and I had to do it quickly. I had no idea where the pirates were taking us or how long it would take to get there.

"What's your name again?" I whispered. Her beautifully angular eyes were Sirbiadian, but her hair—

curly and sun bleached—was unusual and stuck out among the straight, golden-brown hair of most of the population.

"Lilou," she replied with a yawn. I inched toward her until our arms touched. Her body relaxed as she fought another yawn. Lilou sank into unconsciousness and her drowsiness unwantedly spread to me. My body ached, my head throbbed, and I urgently wished I would wake from this nightmare. It wasn't much longer before the movement of the boat lulled me to sleep.

What seemed like seconds later, metal clanking and feet shuffling woke me. My head still pounded, and I rubbed my face with my hand to force myself awake. As I blinked through the fogginess in my vision, people were standing up, filing toward the door. A rattle of keys pulled me further from my slumber, followed by the squeaking of locks.

They were letting us out.

I became aware of the warmth pressed against my side. Lilou still slept, her head slumped against my shoulder. I shook her shoulder gently with my free hand.

"Lilou, wake up." Her moon-shaped eyelashes that rested against her cheeks fluttered.

She rubbed the sleep from her eyes with her fists. "Mama?" Her innocent brown eyes focused on me. "Oh." Her expression fell. "What's going on?" She glanced around at the people being freed from the prison.

"I'm not sure; I think we're far enough out they're letting us on deck." I stood up, holding my hand out to her.

Her bottom lip curled into a pout at my confirmation that we were not being rescued. I silently cursed myself. *Please don't cry.* I couldn't handle crying.

"That means we'll probably get something to eat." I added the positive news as soon as I thought it.

"I have to go to the bathroom."

I paused to take a resigned breath. "I'll take you." Her lips straightened and she grabbed my hand, a little bounciness left over from her former self.

We emerged from below deck, greeted with a blood-red tinted sky. The smell of fish wafted in with a salty breeze. I turned my head away from the big, ruby ball rising from the horizon and took in the cloudless sky. The clearness made it impossible to tell where the sky ended and the ocean began.

Prisoners gathered on the main deck, standing orderly with their eyes cast down. I frowned at their lack of assertiveness. We shouldn't stand for this. We should be fighting. But then I took in my surroundings. Around us, pirates worked with disciplined efficiency—there were hundreds of them. Their clothes had Middle Eastern influences—traditional pieces of armor and wide-legged pants, although many were bare-chested. More of them worked in the rigging, obeying orders shouted from below.

A pair of boots pounded the plank floor. The rhythm of their movement held a note of arrogance that could only belong to the captain. Crossing my arms over my chest, I surveyed him. In the light, his appearance was dangerous. He still wore his dark armor. Something told me he didn't own anything that wasn't black, other than the silver scarf wrapped around his face, revealing nothing but those clear blue eyes. I imagined the rest of his face must be so hideous he kept it concealed, and I was a little pleased by that thought.

He turned on his heel toward us. "As many of you

may have already concluded, *I* am the captain." His voice was velvet, yet uncompromising, with a slight accent that unfortunately added to its appeal and left me wondering where he originated from. "For those of you who've heard I am a merciful captain, I'm here to tell you, you've heard wrong." His eyes remained cold and impassive. The crowd tensed with every word. "As long as you do exactly as I order, you will fare well. You have been freed from the cells under the condition that you'll have chores while onboard. If you cooperate, you will be allowed to sleep in the hammocks below and have hot meals."

I scoffed, which garnered me a male hush from somewhere behind me.

No wonder the ship was in such pristine condition. It was easy when the only thing you had to do was shout orders.

The captain's menacing eyes scanned the crowd to make sure he held everyone's attention. He didn't look at me long enough to satisfy my need to glower at him. Once he finished, his dark eyebrows arched in a way that said *please* -give-me-a-reason-to-kill-you. "I don't think I need to elaborate on your alternatives, hmm? We'll just say that the cells will remain empty— whether you decide to cooperate or not." Without a backward glance, he turned and was gone.

The arrogance! Stubbornness and false courage bubbled inside me. I could scarcely contain my temper. It was enough he kidnapped me—us. Now he just expected us to slave away on his ship without a word of protest, without knowing if we would live or die

"And what's exactly to become of us, *Captain?*" I probably shouldn't have been so condescending when I spat out his title. *Oh well.*

He stopped walking, his head cocked as if he were unsure he had actually heard a prisoner speak. Then, all at once, he whipped around. His eyes searched the crowd, his furrowed brows not as angry as they were satisfied, as if he was thinking, *"Oh, good. I get to kill you now."* I wished I hadn't spoken at all, but I couldn't think straight when I was angry. It usually took me until the next morning before the regret settled in.

His steel-blue eyes landed on mine, as if he located me with magic. *How did he know it was me?*

"That's none of your concern."

Again, he spoke as if I were beneath him. Anger coursed through my veins hotter than before, and I let out an unladylike snort. "Isn't my concern? I'd say it's the only thing we have to be concerned about!"

His eyes turned even colder. "I had *one* rule—"

"Cap'n!" one of his men shouted, running toward us. The captain's attention turned toward him. I couldn't decide who he was more enraged with—me for challenging him or the crewman for interrupting. "Captain," he repeated between pants.

"What is it?" he snapped, not taking his eyes off me. He stepped to the right, partially blocking my view of the crewman.

"Please, it's urgent. Kamran was in the storage hold when a crate toppled over. The wood—I think it severed his leg." The man paled. *"So much blood."*

I gasped, but remembering I was under scrutiny, returned my composed gaze to the captain. What I found there surprised me. His eyes had changed. His glare was gone, replaced by something like worry. *Ha! As if a pirate would care about someone losing their leg!*

The captain took a moment to recover before inquiring, "Have you sent the doctor to him?"

"The doctor? Have you forgotten, Cap'n? You got r-r-rid of him..." the pirate stuttered.

The captain turned on the crowd, his fists

clenched at his sides. "Is anyone a healer?" It was more than a shout; it was a warning. Everyone, including me, took a step back.

I searched the faces in the crowd, waiting to see if someone would speak up.

No one did.

I spotted Shaman Tamati. He had basic medical knowledge at the insistence of my mother. His head was cast down, lips sealed together, and his expression showed no hint of concern.

A new crewman came into the clearing. "Please, Captain. Come now."

I gave the shaman a hard stare, but he never looked up. I pictured the victim withering in pain as the blood seeped from his leg, his glossy eyes becoming lifeless, an imaginary family hurting from their loss. Someone had to help him.

"Tell me now, or I'll throw all of you overboard." The captain's voice was deafening.

"I am."

There were a few gasps from my fellow prisoners. The word "treacherous" was whispered. I didn't consider that if I healed him, I may just be helping him live another day to cause harm and terror. But again, I was like my mother, and it went against every one of my instincts to not help someone. Perhaps I could somehow justify it by bargaining...

I didn't have time to process everything before the captain turned his icy gaze back to me with renewed irritation. "Come with me." He turned and started for the hatch door.

My mind reeled, freezing me in place. He stopped walking, realizing I had not followed. As he stormed back, every muscle in my body tensed. He didn't stop coming at me until he was within inches of my face. His body arched over me, his covered nose brushed mine, and I could feel the heat of his breath through the scarf. "I said to come with me."

How could I possibly move now?

He grabbed my arm and pulled me in his wake.

I wrestled my arm free. "Wait." I stood a little firmer in place.

He glared at me murderously, the fabric around his mouth puffing in and out with each enraged breath. "*Excuse me?*"

"I'll heal him, but—"

"No."

"No? You didn't even hear my request!"

"You will help him, if it's the last thing you do."

He had to be bluffing. Lifting my chin, I met his icy gaze straight on. "You can threaten my life, but there is nothing more you can take from me that you haven't already."

"Oh, really?"

He stepped forward, towering over me. *Wow, he was tall.* I resisted every instinct to cower or curl into a small ball. His hand shot out so quickly, I hardly felt the pull around my neck. My hands flew to my chest. My necklace!

The captain held up the chain, his eyes wide with victory. It was clear he was waiting for a reaction, but, except for that first jolt of surprise, I was *paralyzed.*

Everything fell silent except the slap of waves against the hull and the drum of his boots as he walked to the railing. I clutched my arms to my chest. My heart sped up so fast I couldn't tell if it was still beating. He held his hand over the side of the ship. The back of my throat ached with a pain so great I thought it would tear out.

"Stop!" One hand still clutched my chest, the other reached out toward the necklace.

"Still think I have nothing I can take from you?

There is always something, *Princess*."

Desperation replaced all courage. "Please stop. I can help him."

He shrugged.

"Wait!"

He opened his palm, one finger at a time. The gold chain slid down, dipping closer to the waters below.

"Please, I'll do anything!" I pressed my fists to the sides of my head.

He drew his fingers in, closing them around the chain. The necklace dangled safely.

I dropped my arms in relief. "Thank—"

With one slow, deliberate move, he opened his palm.

The chain slipped through his fingers.

"No," I cried, running to the railing. My necklace had disappeared into the roaring waters below. *Lost forever.*

I choked on the air I strove to inhale. "That was... that was the only thing..." The sound of my heartbeat thrashed in my ears before every emotion was washed away. Every muscle in my body tightened and my eyes twitched as they narrowed. I turned mechanically to face the heartless brute. My face expressionless, my feelings numbed. *He would pay for what he'd done.*

"You are in no position to negotiate. Make no more requests or the next thing I drop in the water will be prisoners. One. By. One." He dictated to me without one ounce of regret for what he'd just done. Turning just as easily, he shouted orders behind him. "Ahmed, bring her."

Another pirate approached me. Would I ever escape them?

"I'm sorry for what he did."

When I faced this new pirate, Ahmed. I expected

him to be tall like the others, but found myself looking straight into a deep-set pair of brown eyes that seemed familiar. I blinked. His skin, hair, and eyes reminded me of my father's. But it didn't matter where he was from—he was a pirate.

"I can see the necklace meant more to you than gold." He continued in a whisper. "I know you have no reason to believe me, but Kamran is a good man. He has a family. Will you help?"

"It's not as if I have a choice anymore." There were a dozen emotions struggling to break free. I swallowed, waiting to see if anger would reign once more. "Just take me to the patient." I let out a breath, no longer feeling rage. Just emptiness.

The surprisingly gentle-mannered pirate held the hatch door open, gesturing for me to descend first. With a creak, the ship rolled left, and I caught the rope railing on the stairs to help balance myself. When I entered the storage hold, the air became cooler. A hint of copper accompanied the musty scent. I swallowed, preparing myself for buckets of blood, wishing I'd paid better attention to my mother's instructions.

A small crowd, which included the captain, stood around the man on the floor amidst crates staked to the ceiling, piles of rope, and discarded sails. It was no wonder the man was injured. One by one, four heads turned. Finally, the captain noticed me. His left eyebrow raised a fraction before his eyes slipped back to cold and menacing. I could tell in that instant he was both enraged that I was his only hope and doubtful of my abilities. To my relief, his gaze left mine and traveled back to the man on the floor, his dark brows slanted. Why did he care so much about this man's welfare if his regard for life was so low?

As soon as I saw Kamran's condition, I took a step

back. His leg was still attached by the bone. Thankfully, one of the pirates applied pressure to his thigh. The wood might have severed his artery—which would explain all the blood—and a nicked artery would mean I'd have to close it somehow. Remembering the doubt I had seen in the captain's eyes, I asked myself if I could do it. I'd seen my mother do it before, but I had never attempted it myself. *Oh, God. What if the man died because of some error on my part? Why couldn't Shaman Tamati just have spoken up?*

A hand landed on my shoulder. It belonged to Ahmed, the one who brought me down. I didn't bother hiding the fear and reservations written all over my face. Taken from my home, robbed of my most sentimental possession, and entrusted with someone's life—my emotions had been a rain cloud, collecting water until it couldn't be contained any longer. But now, it was pouring.

Ahmed gave my shoulders a delicate squeeze, pulling me from my thoughts. "You can do it." His encouragement was spoken so no one could hear but me. Why had he shown me this kindness? "I will be right here if you need me."

He had said it so quietly, so gently, that I had no trouble believing him, because right then, I needed someone to believe in me.

I nodded and pushed my way through the crowd. "Get me something to elevate his leg." My voice seemed far away and not my own. My mind couldn't stop going over what I would do if I had to close an artery. I remembered the last time I had seen my mother do it and how I fainted from the smell of burning flesh. That was years ago; I had to be stronger than that by now.

I inspected the wound, being as delicate as I'd ever been with a patient out of fear of a foul-mannered lashing if I struck a nerve during my prodding. Thank God, the wound wasn't so bad it would require amputation, but based on the warm, sticky puddle I knelt in, he had already lost a lot of blood and, *if* he survived, he was at risk for infection. Then I did something I shouldn't have—I looked at his face. Thin lips trembled between a scruffy beard. Glossy, dark eyes peered trustingly up at me. I held still as a calm washed over me. He was no longer a pirate—he was a patient.

I looked to see if the materials I requested had arrived yet, only to find no one had moved from their previous positions. Beyond frustrated, I snapped, "Do you want him to die?"

No one moved until the captain shouted, "You heard her! Get whatever she needs."

Someone brought over a bundle of blankets, and I set to raising his leg.

"I need clean cloths and fresh water. And something to tie around his thigh as a tourniquet." Examining his leg, I tried to see if he would require sutures. I swallowed, having no choice but to touch the wound. Holding my breath, I slipped my fingers over the gash, mentally gagging at the warm, gooey feel of blood. Sharp intakes of breath came from the man whenever I moved. Once I made sure it wasn't deep enough to require stitches, I pulled my hand back and let out a whoosh of breath. "He'll be okay. We just need to stop the bleeding and watch for infection. If we were on land, I could make a salve, but here..."

"Ahmed, grab what the doctor left behind."

"Yes, Captain." Ahmed's soft voice came from behind me, confirming he had never left my side.

What happened to the last doctor? Why would he have left behind his things? I didn't like where the possibilities were taking me.

A bowl of clean water and folded white cloths appeared beside me. I washed the man's wound. I had already set aside three bloody muslin cloths when Ahmed came back with his arms full.

"How are you doing?" he whispered.

I nodded and gave him a tight smile. It was the best I could manage under the circumstances, and my hands were still covered with the man's blood.

Ahmed set a cloth wrap next to me, as well as a traditional medicine bag with marred leather and brass handles. I opened the bag, pulling out a few different sets of surgeon's blades with horror, before finding three jars of oils and salves. None of it was labeled. I unscrewed the first cap and recognized the flowery smell of Calendula. The other jar was an odorless liquid. The last one, I didn't touch. I went back to the Calendula. Poppies were in high demand. When my mother could get her hands on some, she used it to chase away infections. I rubbed the yellow cream over his wound, hoping it would suffice. After binding the bandage around it, I turned to wash my hands in the basin, but I frowned at the water turning bright red.

"Are you finished, *healer*?" the captain snapped.

I tensed at his coldness. Barely had I finished mending the man's flesh before I had to face the captain's cruelty again. I didn't voice the snide comments inside my head. The adrenaline no longer coursed through me. I was empty and exhausted. Nodding, I didn't even bother to look up at him.

"Sokum. Novo. Bring two others to help carry him to his cabin. Ahmed, get the girl fresh water."

I gritted my teeth at the way he said 'girl.' Like I didn't just treat one of his men. I flipped my head around and glared at his back as he stomped up the stairs.

Four men creaked back down a minute later. The last one locked eyes with me, giving me a curt nod. Was that... appreciation? But the moment was over and Ahmed came down, balancing a bowl with water sluicing over the sides, the roll of the ship making his task impossible. As I finished cleaning myself up, the men lifted my patient with little effort and carried him up the stairs. I tried not to watch but failed. I was a healer and a healer always cared, no matter who the patient was. The injured pirate raised his hand, and the men stopped. He beckoned Ahmed and whispered something in his ear. I watched until I was sure they had left before turning back around.

Ahmed crouched next to me.

What was he still doing here? I kept washing longer than I needed just to keep myself busy and away from Ahmed's appraising gaze.

"He told me to tell you thank you."

I scoffed, threw down a washcloth, and stood up.

I didn't need a pirate's thanks, and it wasn't as if I had a choice in treating him. But still, the expression of gratitude was surprising.

I softened a bit. "You'll need to change the bandage and reapply the ointment daily. Also, watch for fever over the next few days." Technically, I didn't have to offer this information. I'd done everything the captain asked. As far as I was concerned, my duties were complete, but remembering the trusting look in Kamran's eyes, I couldn't let him suffer.

Ahmed gave me a warm smile and nodded his thanks. I folded my arms over my chest and pivoted toward the opposite wall, anxious to escape his uncomfortable presence.

Finally, he spoke, "You're free to go above with the others whenever you're ready." At that, he left me alone. As alone as I have ever felt in my entire life.

Chapter Four

AS MUCH AS I WISHED TO STAY AND SULK IN THE QUIET, dark confines of the storage hold, I remembered my promise to Lilou. I had to go look for her. I couldn't feel sorry for myself for very long, knowing she had to be feeling even more alone.

I weaved through people above deck, ignoring the stares of crew and prisoners alike. When I tripped over a coiled piece of rope, the fisherman's wife from my cell caught my arm. "Careful, dear."

I muttered my apologies to a pair of concerned brown eyes. "Sorry, I was just looking for someone."

"She's over there."

I followed the direction of her gaze and found Lilou with her back turned, staring out at the horizon.

The lines around the woman's mouth said she smiled often. "You did the right thing, dear. A life is a life."

I offered her my thanks and walked toward Lilou. She jumped when I grabbed her hand.

"Lux." She let out a breath of relief. I could only imagine what the others had speculated regarding my fate. "I didn't know if I'd see you again." Her eyes glistened and her lower lip quivered.

Awkwardly, I cleared my throat. "Lilou, don't."

Uncertainty made my voice harsh and demanding. She began sniffling. "Lilou, look at me." I grabbed her shoulders and turned her to face me. "Please don't cry."

She nodded, but not before a tear escaped.

"Don't ever cry for me. No matter what happens, you must keep going. Understand?"

She nodded again.

I searched around, needing a distraction. "C'mon, I need to speak to someone." Lilou lifted her head with a smile. Her small hand slipped into mine, and I tensed at the contact. I squeezed her hand back, even though the attachment was the last thing I needed if I wanted to get out of here alive, let alone rescue a whole group of people.

I tugged Lilou toward the stairs where I had seen the shaman. A strong, refreshing breeze blew across the upper deck. The wind blew my long hair into my face, and I pulled it back to stare out into the horizon. Nothing but aquamarine water surrounded us, clear and smooth as glass. The ship gracefully cut through it, gliding like a massive bird. As the deck swelled and dipped beneath my bare feet, I shut my eyes and inhaled. The air didn't smell briny at all, but rather sweeter, clean and slightly salty. Gripping the cool polished railings, I appraised the pristine canvas sails. I grudgingly admitted I preferred it over any of the modern, pre-Flood naval ships Asmodeus owned. I lowered my gaze. *Stop appreciating it. It's a pirate ship!*

The shaman failed to acknowledge me when we approached him. His concentration was devoted to the water as he stood next to a group of two other gossiping prisoners.

"We need to start organizing—" I licked my lips and turned away as one of the pirate crewmen passed us by. "I will talk to the prisoners who came from the other islands and tell them the plan."

The shaman said nothing.

"Did you hear me?"

"I heard. I already spoke about this matter. I have nothing left to say."

"So you're just going to resign us to our fate despite the uncertainties lurking there?" My voice rose, but I didn't care. The anger was there to justify everything.

"Fate? Yes. Fate was when one of his men got injured, but instead, you healed him."

"That's ridiculous. I couldn't have just left him to die."

"And see how far that got you." He shook his head. "What happened was a sign, but now you've changed fate. There will be consequences. I can feel it."

My eyes darted around, trying to locate something. Trying to identify the feeling in my chest. I never really shared in their beliefs, but something about what he said stung like the salty ocean in an open wound. My beating heart was filled with panic. "I... I tried to negotiate. I tried to use it to help us."

"You are not your father." He turned and was gone.

You are not your father. My thoughts drifted to my parents, who were probably worried sick. No one who disappeared from Sirbiad's shore had ever made it back to tell the tale, but I knew my mother and father wouldn't give up hope. The three of us were all we had left. Why was I always so reckless?

I will make it back; I swear it. But I knew when I did; I would just be hurting them all over again when I left for good.

"Ahmed!" A distinguishable growl shook me from my thoughts and sent my stomach fluttering with all the dread and desperation of a butterfly stuck in a spider's web. I groaned and turned to see the captain, the very cause of my suffering. He stood dictatorially next to the pirate manning the wheel. His air of calm and self-confidence made everyone around him seem inadequate.

Ahmed strode up the stairs to address his caller. "Assalamu Alaykum, Captain. K'fahlik?" *How are you doing?*

K'fahlik? Wait, that wasn't English. That was.... *Arabic.*

Since birth, my father was insistent I learn his native tongue even if he had abandoned every other aspect of his homeland. I was fluent in it, as well as the other major Old World languages. That was when my father counted on me following in his footsteps as a diplomat. There was no use for it now. The only languages spoken on Sirbiad were English and Horous, the preferred spoken tongue of Sirbiad, similar to Japanese and Somoan. My father tried to inflict his language lessons on Sirbiadians as well out of fear it would die out, but to put it mildly, they weren't receptive to things outside their culture. Instead, I was enlisted in defense training, a daily routine for every villager upon reaching their sixteenth year of life.

I continued to eavesdrop, relishing in my sudden advantage. They would say anything, thinking I couldn't understand. My lips twitched, trying to prevent a hysterical laugh from escaping at my good fortune. Now this was fate. Maybe the shaman got it wrong; maybe doing the right thing changed my fate for the better.

"Jayed." *Good.* The captain continued speaking in Arabic. "Kamran is settled comfortably in a cabin, but have Sokum feed the prisoners immediately. There is a storm brewing, and we must prepare the decks."

"Na'am, Captain." Ahmed turned to head back

down the stairs to give the orders.

"Ahmed?" He called him back.

"Na'am, Captain?"

He continued speaking in Arabic. "Remember to keep an eye on this one. I have a feeling she will be more trouble than she's worth. Find out everything you can about her. Torture it out of her fellow prisoners if you need to. I want to know her weaknesses."

My head shot up, horrified, yet curious to know who they were talking about. Ahmed's big, round eyes turned to me. I glanced away, doing my best to pretend I didn't understand their conversation.

I lifted my head again, only to meet Ahmed's gaze. His brown eyes flickered. *They were talking about me!* He turned back to his captain and bowed his head. "Na'am, Captain." Ahmed was allowed to leave, and he scurried down the stairs as quickly as he had come up them.

How casually the captain mentioned torture just to get information about me. *That snake!* He would not break me, I vowed. I went over the conversation again in my mind as Lilou bounced out energy beside me. My eyes roamed across the sky, concluding that the captain must be insane for thinking a storm was coming.

There wasn't a cloud to be found. A storm. *Right.*

Chewing on my lip, I formulated a plan. With a new card up my sleeve, I possibly had the key to our escape. My eyes slid closed in relief, hope restored. Being able to understand Arabic changed everything. I could find out where we were going and how much time we had. Maybe discover their plans for us. I couldn't wait to tell Shaman Tamati about this, but first, I needed to keep a low profile. Certainly, the captain wouldn't let anything slip in front of a girl he was suspicious of, even if it was in a different language.

I had to let the captain forget about me. Play along so I could blend in with everyone else. No more outbursts, no more letting my anger get the best of me.

My spirits rose now that I had a plan. If I could prove the pirates were going to kill us, then maybe I could get Shaman Tamati and the others to stand up and fight. I smiled down at Lilou, who was breaking a stick from a broken crate into little pieces. When I risked a glance back to the helm, the captain had disappeared. I searched all around the deck, failing to hide my urgency, but there was no sign of him.

The smell of roasted meat wafted from below. I clutched my rumbling stomach and brought Lilou down to the main deck. Three cooks set up serving trays on a rectangular table. Prisoners congregated and formed a line on their own, while Lilou and I stood together. I was handed a divided aluminum plate filled with meat and vegetables covered in a bright yellow sauce, white and orange rice, a semicircle of bread, and a bar of a sesame sweet.

Lilou squealed in front of me. "This is all just for me?" The cook grumbled a yes, and she squealed again. "It's all mine? I get to eat it all and not have to share?" The cook didn't bother answering this time, and I directed Lilou away from the table.

"Oh, what are these green things?" She picked up a green bean, staring at it as if she had never seen anything like it. Then I remembered that she probably hadn't. She would have been no older than a toddler when the Floods started. I warmed a little at her naïveté, but a pang of remorse shot through me that she never experienced a world like I had.

Part of the control Asmodeus had over us was water and food. At first, our island rejected the Codes. We would not follow a man who committed the gravest sins against humanity. We were rebellious because we had fresh water and fruit. The plants and fruit we had on our island were plentiful at first, but as they became our sole supply, they could never reproduce fast enough. Our infertile forest soil was like a wet desert. Everything we took from it would be gone forever. Sirbiad was a fishing community, but since the Floods, fish had diminished. Catching the predators that remained was a challenge, which was why we were only successful at night. And there hadn't been livestock on the island for years. We grew weary and hungry. It was when our fresh water supply was threatened that people had wanted to rethink the Codes. We had no choice. Soon, desperation overcame principles, and people actually anticipated Asmodeus' shipments of grains and wheat.

As I tried to describe what a green bean was, Lilou and I moved along with several others and found a place to sit along the side of the ship. I adjusted myself, ironically wishing for the softness of the silica sand on the beaches of Sirbiad to sink into.

Everyone's mood had lifted since we'd been served. Most of the food sent from Asmodeus was grains, and I couldn't understand how they were able to get vegetables, which was something that had become so rare, so foreign to me. I picked up a green bean and brought it to my nose before hesitantly taking a bite. Wow, delicious. I savored the peppery taste, wondering how these pirates ate better at sea than we did on land.

I ate a few bites of roasted meat, but then a quick and disturbing image of Kamran's leg came to mind. With a loss of appetite, I handed my plate to Lilou, who had finished her own food within minutes and now licked up leftover grains of rice and sauce. She didn't hesitate to accept mine, especially seeing the nearly whole sesame bar. As I looked around at my fellow Sirbiadians, I had a lightness in my chest that had nothing to do with the foul images of Kamran's leg. Not one head was raised as they focused on their plates, their mouths full and chewing. It was some condolence to see the people from my island well fed. Some peace among the ruins.

As Lilou clapped the last of the sesame off her hands, the wind picked up. Clouds swept in, covering the sun and giving the morning sky the appearance of night. *A storm?* The captain had been right. Just as quickly as the clouds came in, more pirates surfaced. It unsettled me that, even without their weapons, we were far outnumbered. Maybe the Shaman was right. My plan was flawed. The noise increased just as fast. Boots thundered over the plank floors and sails whipped in the wind.

"Secure the rigging!" My body spun toward the upper deck where Ahmed shouted as crewmen ran by. The manner in which the ship was being secured was hectic, but appeared well practiced. The sails were taken down at a startling pace. Sensing alarm, the other prisoners stood up and took their plates below deck where I had seen hammocks for sleeping.

"Lilou, we should probably go below." As I eyed the ominous clouds, a shot of lightning sparked the sky. My stomach hollow, I replayed the shaman's words: *There will be consequences.*

"Please, Lux, just a little longer." She paused as thunder pounded. "I'm not feeling too good." Her lips had grown pale and the rosiness that had previously colored her cheeks was absent. My heart skipped. *Poison?* I looked to the empty plates we had set on a nearby crate. No, that wouldn't make sense. *Illness?*

I prayed she hadn't caught anything as the sound of sloshing water made a lantern light up in my head; the waves had gotten stronger and ferociously rocked the ship. Lilou was only seasick. I was grateful I didn't feel the least bit affected, like I was meant to be at sea, but that joy was cut short when Lilou made her way off a crate to the railing. I followed.

Uneasiness washed over me as I watched the sky. The clouds swept in farther and the sun was snuffed out. The strange, sweet smell of ozone filled the air, and the sound of pitter-patter grew as the clouds opened above us. The rain splattered across the wood and metal of the ship, creating a symphony of musical sounds. The sound gradually became louder and the top of my head became damp. Each droplet fell harder than the last.

"Lilou..." I grabbed her arm to take her toward the stairs. It was way too dark for this time of day, and the uneasiness advanced to dread in my gut. *Something bad is going to happen.* I just knew it. At that moment, Lilou vomited over the railing into the dark waters below. I pulled back her hair while she finished spitting up everything she had just eaten. A pang of sadness shot through me, knowing she would be going on an empty stomach and not knowing how long it would be until the next meal.

The waves lapped against the hull. I leaned over the railing. My eyes widened as I watched the contents of Lilou's stomach ravished by sea creatures. A three-foot-long mackerel inhaled what floated on the water before a shark surfaced, ate the fish, and then consumed what was left of the vomit. A school of fish approached, followed by a frenzy of white foam and blood. I squeezed my eyes shut and tightened my grip on Lilou. The raindrops grew thicker, soaking my hair and dress.

"Lilou, we need to go below. *Now.*" I gave one last glance overboard. The sea creatures had vanished. I scanned the dark waters, but there was no sign of them. *That's odd.* Lilou turned toward me and weakly nodded. Strands of wet hair glued to her face. I unstuck one with my pinky finger.

"I'd advise you to go below deck immediately." A male voice that was both firm and warm spoke from behind us. I turned to find Ahmed. His eyes were wide, and had his voice shaken?

"Yes, we—"A wave pounded against the opposite side of the ship. Everything pitched forward, and the deck became almost vertical beneath our feet. Lilou, Ahmed, and I fell backward, hitting the railing behind us. Water spilled onto the ship, and the smell of brine was strong. Thankfully, I still held onto Lilou. I tried to stand, but another wave, fiercer than the first, hit. I slid backward, looking toward the sky in order to see the other side of the ship. My heart raced. The next wave that hit would cause the ship to capsize! I felt just as young and fragile as the girl I was trying to protect.

"Come," Ahmed shouted, grabbing both of our arms, trying to get us to the hatchway ten yards away. Scrambling against the slimy wood, I grabbed a long rope tied to a cleat. I wrapped it around my wrist twice, not yet letting go of Lilou.

"Follow Ahmed," I instructed Lilou as the wind bit my damp skin.

She fought the slippery floor. Ahmed pulled her upright and held on. I let go, following behind them as they struggled against the wind and gushes of rain.

The ship rolled in the other direction. *Not good, not good, not good.*

"Lilou," I screamed over the rain. Before I could pull her to me, a third wave hit the hull. Lilou's limp body flew over the side like a stuffed doll. Horrified, my whole body froze, even the breath that was on its way to my lungs. A thud and distinct sound of human flesh hitting water forced me into action.

"*No*," I cried. Still holding the rope, I ran to the railing. Relief washed over me, stronger than the wave that had washed over the boat. Lilou was safe. She dangled on the side of the ship, fiercely gripping a fishing net. I searched the waters below.

Who had fallen in?

A brown head bobbed with a wave. Adrenaline pumped through my veins. Feelings of helplessness and failure spun out of control. Impulsively, I climbed onto the railing and jumped.

I slid down, the rope burning my palms. When I reached Lilou, she clung to me like a drowning cat.

"It's okay," I assured her. But I didn't know if it was. Ahmed, who had only been trying to help us get to safety, was in the water below. If he hadn't already drowned, the moment the ocean calmed, he would be food to the animals lurking there. I used the net and rope to climb back to the deck. Lilou clawed me, and it was like knives digging into my back rather than fingernails. When I was far enough up, I pushed her over.

"Grab that extra rope. Tie it around yourself and do *not* let go. No matter what," I yelled at her through an opening in the railing. I didn't wait to hear her answer. I barely had time for another breath before a new wave hit the hull.

I let go, diving into the roaring waters below.

The impact stung my face as I cut through the cool water. Underwater, I was weightless. Silence and darkness encompassed me. The saltwater stung my eyes, and I wasn't sure which way was up. Wasn't sure if I would be able to find Ahmed. Wasn't even sure if I remembered how to swim. It had been five years since I had last gone swimming. My body was not used to the salt and chemicals polluting it, but instinct took over. I kicked my legs with the need for air. Breaking the surface, I gulped in a quick breath before diving under a wave. The heavy rope in my hand made it difficult to tread water, so I swam toward where I last had seen Ahmed. I came up for air again, my search proving useless. My face tightened. The waves made it impossible to see anything. I would only be able to see him from higher above.

Without warning, a wave crashed into me and pulled me under. Saltwater filled my nose, burning painfully, the pressure suffocating. When I surfaced again, I choked on a mouthful of water. Sucking in another breath, I dove under before another wave hit. I drifted deeper and farther out. Too afraid to go up to the surface again, I stayed under, my lungs tightening in my chest, yearning for air. I kicked my feet harder. Nothing but dark ocean surrounded me. I came up for air with the worst timing. Another wave poured over my head before I could catch and hold my breath. My lungs burned for air and my instincts forced me to inhale, but I only succeeded in sucking in water. I coughed, struggling to keep my head afloat.

A flash of bronze hair appeared in the trough of a wave.

"Ahmed," I cried, my voice hoarse from coughing. "Swim toward me!" He was farther out than I expected, and my rope had grown short. Another big wave came at us, covering his head. I swam as close as I could. The rope pulled tight, out of slack. I broke the surface, using the last of the air in my lungs to call out for Ahmed again. He was facedown in the water, his body slack and rolling with the movement of the waves.

Was he dead? Unconscious? If I didn't swim toward him, he'd float away or be pulled under. But that meant letting go of the rope. If I let go, there was a good chance I wouldn't see it again. "Ahmed! Wake up," I called, spitting out a mouthful of seawater. I uttered a curse. After taking a deep breath, my lungs expanding to the point of pain, I let go.

As soon as I grabbed Ahmed, I flipped him onto his back. His body was limp but warm. He wasn't dead. At least, he wasn't *yet*.

"Ahmed." I tried to wake him. We needed to swim back to the boat or we would both drown. He didn't stir, just floated lifelessly like a buoy. The current was strong. I couldn't pull us both back. My chest shook in what could have been a cry, but I wasn't giving up. Linking our arms, I laid back and kicked. For what seemed like an eternity, I went backward, not able to stop and look back to see where the ship was. Everything darkened around me, and I knew it wasn't because of the weather. I was about to give out at any moment. My body, my limbs—everything went numb.

This is it; this is the end. I let a wave wash over us before my head bumped up against something. A barnacle scraped my forearm. I twisted to look up at the towering ship. *I did it! At least I saved Ahmed.* I wanted to cry for joy, but instead, I used the last of my energy to push him up so he could grab hold of the ship.

Then I stopped swimming.

Ahmed's body was pulled from my grasp and I stopped treading, unable to keep my mouth above the water. As my head sank under, hands gripped my body and pulled me out of the water by my arms and clothes. The calls from the crewmen grew louder as I reached the deck. There were a few cheers when Ahmed was pulled onto the deck. The men who carried me over the railing set me on my feet and left to check on Ahmed. I searched the crowd for Lilou. A languid, triumphant smile spread over my face.

Then I collapsed.

Just before I hit solid wood, someone caught my arm, scooped me off my feet, and cradled me against a rock-hard chest. My head fell to rest against a shoulder that was warm despite the dampness of the tunic. Dizzy, my eyes involuntarily fluttered closed.

Then I welcomed the darkness.

Chapter Five

I EASED BACK INTO CONSCIOUSNESS WITH A CONTENT smile. My body knew it was time to wake, but my mind was not quite there yet. The sun peeked through the porthole and warmed the bed in which I lay. Rolling around in the dry sheets that felt sinful against my body, I could smell.... What or *who* was that delicious smell?

I stretched my arms over my head only to find my muscles stiff and sore, but that wasn't surprising, considering that just hours before, I'd been drenched, cold, and weak. My body shot up. All the memories came back to me at once. *Lilou.*

Tearing the covers off, I got to my feet. Wait, where were my clothes? My hands clasped my torso with a gasp. I now wore a pair of brown pants and a tan shirt that fell below my waist. Its owner wasn't a *girl*, that was for sure. Pushing my lips together, I shook off my anger, vowing to deal with it, or rather *him,* after I made sure Lilou was safe.

"Lilou," I called as I started for the door.

"She's fine," an exhausted voice grumbled.

I turned, my heart dropping like an anchor in my chest at the discovery that I was not alone. A young man around my age sat in a chair in the corner, his legs apart, elbows over his knees. He had a tanned face and disheveled hair. Dark circles were under his familiar eyes. *His eyes!*

The captain. Unveiled. I managed not to gasp at his youth. *So, it* was *true!*

In no way was he a boy, but he had to be no more than a few years older than me. I shouldn't be afraid anymore, but, unfortunately, his age did nothing to diminish his intimidation. He was still cold and cruel. And, much to my dismay, he didn't look like the squid I pictured him to be under the scarf. Crossing my arms over my chest, I surveyed him. He was—unarmored. He still wore his leather boots, covered in yet more leather guard-like things, and leather pants. Gone was the weapon holster—my lips twitched at this realization—the other leather belt I had seen him wear, as well as his breastplate, outer coat, and the metal thingy over his shoulder. All that was left was a leather tunic with billowing white sleeves.

The opening at his chest revealed defined muscles that complemented his angular features. My gaze traveled further north. The skin on his face looked smooth, and I suppressed the ridiculous urge to touch it just as quickly as it arose. *No, Lux. Pirate, remember?*

His eyes were a bright blue. Too bold against his skin. Too light and innocent to be capable of the things he was accused of. His hair, black. Black as the night I was taken from. Black as his heart.

"W-where is she?" I demanded to know if Lilou was all right. And Ahmed. "Where's Ahmed? Are they okay?"

He dropped his arms and rose to his feet. Maybe he wasn't as young as I originally thought, because, as he stood before me, he radiated power. "They're fine. Thanks to you. Now lie down."

The blood drained from my face. I shook my head. "I don't want to lie down. I'm *fine*. I want to see Lilou." Like I would trust anything that came from his arrogant mouth. Not while I could still remember the agony of my heart shattering as my necklace slipped through his fingers into the depths of the ocean.

"Again, it seems, I owe you my gratitude. If it wasn't for you, I would have lost a crewman. Despite the fact you are a disobedient nuisance, I relinquish my cabin to you for the duration of your journey in an effort to show my appreciation. There is breakfast on a tray by the bed; you will be well taken care of."

His English was eloquent for someone who wasn't from the United States. Yet, it was different from anyone's on Sirbiad—more smooth and even, with perfect articulation. But it was his words that disturbed me. The blood rushed back to my face, my cheeks burning in fury. "Is that all you care about? That you would've lost a laborer? They're people, for God's sake. And what about Lilou? Are you not grateful she survived?"

"I'm a pirate. Do you really expect me to care every time a slave goes overboard?" He turned away as if already bored with our conversation.

Apparently not. I remembered what the elderly man had stammered about him dumping bodies overboard. "Thank you."

The sarcasm must have been lost on him as he became suspicious. His heavy brows drew together like charcoal smudges against his tan skin, and he turned back to me with renewed interest. "Pardon?"

"Thank you for confirming the fact that you are a heartless thug. It will make it so much easier for me when I have to kill you." I gave him my most wicked, condescending smile, but he just laughed like I was a kitten trying to growl like a tiger. I gritted my teeth.

Why wasn't he taking me seriously? "I've had enough of this. Now, if you'll excuse me..." With a superior attitude of my own, I held my head high and headed toward the gigantic wooden door. My hand almost made it to the iron knob. In two strides, he appeared in front of me, grabbing my wrist. "What—ow!"

He lowered his head, but he never broke his gaze. "I *said* I think you should lie down."

I pressed my lips together stubbornly as I fought his restraint. When his grip didn't ease, I straightened my back and looked straight into his smoldering eyes. "*I said* I don't want to lie down."

"I show you my appreciation and this is how you treat me?" His hand tightened around the sleeve of my shirt.

"Wait, how did I get into these clothes?" I questioned, beyond enraged. He dropped my wrist and sent me a crooked smile. My eyes widened. "If you touched me, I swear I will kill you!"

"Yes, you've spoken twice now of your intentions to kill me, but I have yet to see an attempt—or a weapon for that matter." He turned away, bored and overly confident again.

I locked my jaw and stared at him, my eyes tight slits.

He walked past his desk, his arm catching the edge of a bundle of scrolled papers. He *tsked* and straightened them before turning to face me.

"Once again, you should be thanking me for my hospitality. If I didn't get you out of those wet clothes, you would have died. But you think too highly of yourself. I had a female slave do it for me."

"And whose clothes are these?"

"Mine." But he didn't taunt me. Instead, he looked away, hiding his face.

"Agh! I'd rather die than wear the clothes of a pirate."

"Well, you have one other option, but it might be a bit chilly."

"*You—*"

The ship moved, and I grabbed onto a post to keep my balance. The captain, on the other hand, remained perfectly upright. A smile quirked his lips as he crossed the room. *Where was he going?* I wasn't going to stick around to find out. Taking it as my opportunity to leave, I took two steps toward the door. Strong, punishing hands gripped my shoulders and spun me around. My heart plunged like an anchor into the ocean.

His eyes were icy and way too close for comfort. I inhaled, smelling the ocean on him. It reminded me of the bed I woke up in. His gaze searched my face, resting on my mouth. "What a waste of beauty. If you weren't so stubborn and disobedient, I might have been tempted to keep you."

I managed to choke out a gasp at his audacity. "*Keep me?* Wow, I think someone has swallowed too much seawater if you think *you* can keep *me* against my will."

He leaned in, his nose almost touching mine. I cleared my throat, suddenly feeling parched, but I wouldn't give him the satisfaction of recoiling. He chuckled with confidence. "Oh, trust me, Princess. You would be *very* willing."

I hated that he was attractive. Hated even more that he knew it. I wanted to scream at him to put the damn scarf back on, but I pushed my parted lips together. "Like I said, I'd rather die."

He pulled back, and, just as quickly, the coldness in him returned. "You will lie down, even if it means I have to tie you to the bed."

Turning away, I laughed. I risked a sideways

glance at him, and my humor died at his stony expression. The hardness in his eyes was an unspoken challenge—one he wasn't going to back down from.

"You wouldn't." I corrected my words, "Couldn't..."

He raised one dark eyebrow as if to say 'try me'. But there was no way I was going to let him come out victorious. *So much for keeping a low profile.* My temper flared, and I saw red. All that mattered now was not letting him win.

"Bye." It was simply spoken, yet powerfully taunting. I let it roll off my tongue then turned again for the door.

He laughed. "Brave girl." His arms circled my waist, and he pulled me flat against his chest, forcing a breath out of me. "Yet completely foolish." He pushed his cheek to my temple before whispering in my in ear, "You do not want to get on my bad side. Not unless you want to be served for dinner."

My breath caught in my chest before I was able to exhale. Either I was feeling more confident than I should have or he was not a very good liar. If he thought he was going to scare me into compliance, he thought *wrong.* "Okay." I relaxed my body against his grip with a new plan in place.

His words caught. "Okay? Okay what?" He spoke slowly, his voice laced with suspicion.

"Okay, I'll lie down."

"Good. Yet, I was *so* looking forward to being creative with your punishment."

Ugh, he sounded truly disappointed. I squirmed again in the cage of his arms. His nose brushed my hair before he let go, and he nudged me with his body toward the bed. I tripped, but caught myself. Swinging around, I raised my fist, doing what I had yearned to do since I had first seen him without the scarf—wipe that smug smile off his face.

Although, technically, I got him square in the right eye.

My plan was to knock him out, step past him, and make it out the door, but the captain was still standing. All that resulted from the impact of my punch was that his face had turned as if he'd been slapped, not hit with four knobs of solid bone as hard as I could muster.

He turned back toward me with a slow deliberateness. My eyes widened as to what was to come. *Did he get taller?* When he finally faced me, I was met with a deadly gaze under lowered brows. I gripped my right hand in my left. It ached horribly. Things had not gone as planned at *all.*

Oh God, he was truly enraged now. I wasn't sure I blinked once as I waited with bated breath for what he would do next.

Finally, his brow cleared as if he decided something. "Sure, you're free to go out and mingle with my men. Why, you're practically a celebrity to them now, *prisoner.*"

"What?"

"Leave the cabin, *if you wish.*"

His self-confident command caused me to eye him with suspicion. What trick was he up to? Just seconds before, I was sure he'd throw me overboard as easily as my necklace.

"Go. I said you are free to leave."

My lips parted. I should leave. It was what I wanted, wasn't it? I'd won, hadn't I? Yet somehow, it didn't feel as if I had.

"Just remember, *prisoner.* No matter what plans or plots you come up with in that insignificant brain of yours, I—" He thrust a finger to his chest as his words increasingly dripped with more emotion. "—will be one step ahead of you. I *always* win."

Thoroughly insulted, I marched out. But not before I shot him a disgusted look. I slammed his damned door behind me as if that would show him. Finally, with a barrier between us, I exhaled a shaky breath and stepped into the light.

The sunshine beat down on me, and it took a moment for my eyes to adjust to the brightness. Men were scattered about, picking up debris and repairing parts of the ship. A trickle of prisoners emerged from the lower deck. I ran through the crowds, searching frantically among them for Lilou.

"Shaman Tamati!" I grabbed the sleeve of his robe as he filed by.

"Lux. What are you doing here? Did the captain let you out?"

"Kind of. He offered his cabin to me for saving his first mate's life—but never mind that. We need to plan a mutiny. I have new information, and I want you to reconsider—"

"I have." He folded his hands at the rope belt around his waist.

"You have?"

"Yes. I spoke with the other prisoners. They came from many other islands. They've heard your plan, and they will do what's necessary."

"That's great, but can I ask why?"

"Because of you."

"Because of me? Why? Never mind—let's go speak with them. I'm afraid we may not have much time to act. I might have done something to put myself on the captain's radar."

The shaman gave me a strange look.

"His attentions," I said, trying to explain the idiom.

"Yes, that you have." He tilted his head back, and I had a feeling he was about to make a decree. "Accept his offer. Stay in his cabin. Distract him. He seems to have a fondness for you... use it. I'll let you know when the time is right."

"What? No! I need to help you."

"You are."

"But—"

The shaman looked behind me, and his neck muscles popped out with urgency. "I have to go. It's best we keep contact to a minimum so as not to raise suspicion."

"Wait!"

Someone grasped my arm and I whipped around, readying to give the captain another black eye. How well could I throw a hook with my left hand? My right still ached like I rammed it into the trunk of a palm tree.

I gasped with relief. "Ahmed!" I threw my arms around his neck, glad to see him doing so well after what we had been though.

I had hugged a pirate, and I hadn't even given it a second thought. I would have to determine how I felt about that later. For now, he pulled back from our friendly embrace with a frown. "Lux, the captain's orders are that you aren't to leave his cabin." How did he know my name? I couldn't imagine his captain remembering it from when we first met. Besides, he only referred to me as 'prisoner' or, when he was better mannered, 'girl.' I remembered what the captain had said about torturing prisoners to get information about me.

"Where's Lilou? Is she all right?" I narrowed my eyes and frowned at Ahmed, who pulled me in the direction of the captain's cabin.

"Yes, she is fine. You need to go back to the cab—"

"There she is," a gruff voice interrupted as a crowd formed around us. There were bellows among them and a few shouts. "Let's throw her overboard," a man drawled through rotted teeth.

I turned to Ahmed. "What's going on?"

His eyes were closed and his head thrown back as if annoyed. "I didn't want you to have to see this."

My eyes scanned the dozens of pirates surrounding us. Their faces appeared even less friendly than before. Many of them unsheathed their weapons, the sharp edges of blades sparkling in the sunlight.

I backed into Ahmed. "Why does it look like they want to kill me?" *I'm 'good labor,' remember?* Besides, didn't saving Ahmed's life count for something? A nervous laugh escaped me.

"They think you're possessed. They don't believe what you did to save me was humanly possible." Ahmed's words were spoken so fast they could have been scripted. "I've had enough. I will get my captain."

"Ahmed, *don't* just leave me here with *them*." The volume of my words went up and down with emotion.

"Don't worry, you'll be safe," he called back, his words trailing off as he ducked under beefy, sweat-glistening arms.

I'd be safe? Was he *serious*?

Now that Ahmed was out of the way, I was fair game. The crowd moved forward, closing in. "Guys..." Another stupid, nervous laugh came out. "Let's discuss this like reasonable human beings." *Or not.* I winced as hands caught my arms, pulling me in all directions, but no sooner did my joints crack in protest, than a wave of silence fell over the crowd. "Great, I knew we could reason—"

One man was peeled off me. He went flying across the deck. His protests faded in the distance before cutting short with a rather painful-sounding thump. The pirates who remained were now pushing each other to get out of the way. I searched around, clueless as they scattered, only to turn back to find amused blue eyes studying me. He had all of his armor back on. *Oh, great.* So he took time to get dressed before he came to my aid? What, did he have a nice glass of coconut milk while he was at it?

"Have you learned your lesson?" The captain smirked. My jaw dropped open to speak, but before I could, he bent down and grabbed my thighs. The air left my chest as he threw me over his shoulder and stalked back to his cabin. The smell of leather filled my nostrils as I clutched the belt about his shoulders. Once inside his chamber, he effortlessly slammed the door shut with his foot and threw me on the bed. I scrambled to my knees.

I brushed wayward hair out of my face. "What the hell was that about?" I shouted, still feeling a little disoriented from the way he carried me. The *captain,* however, was unaffected.

"It pains me to say this, it really does, but *I told you so.*"

Ah, so he understood sarcasm after all. *Think...* The shaman said to use the captain's fondness for me against him. Fondness? *Ha!* He was as fond of me as I was of jellyfish. What could I do now? I dared a glance at the captain. He looked down on me. Smug, even. Maybe I could use that... As long as he didn't see me as a threat, he would eventually let his guard down. I just had to be the diplomatic, pacifist, mayor's daughter that I was. Not the vengeful Sirbiadian warrior I turned into when I was around him. Maybe that was what the shaman meant. He wanted me to play nice. I tossed my hair, ready to act civil. "Why does your gang want me killed?"

"My men are very superstitious. They think you are... Well, first of all, most of them can't swim, so that was a feat in itself."

Pirates who couldn't swim? It amused me, but I

grimly made note of it in case we could use it to our advantage at some point. *What, you think we'll just overpower them all and toss them in the water, Lux?*

I shook my head to keep my thoughts from wandering and got back to the issue at hand. "Well, thanks a lot. How could you let me go out there?"

He took a long step toward me, his voice shifting to a hiss. "*Let* you go out there? You are something, you know that? In case you have forgotten, you clocked me and then ran away!"

Oh, that little thing? I wish he'd forget that. That was *definitely* not something a mayor's daughter would have done. I narrowed my eyes at him. "You could have told me."

"You are kidding, right? I told you to lie down. I threatened you with force. You are the most stubborn, hardheaded—"

"And then you just leave me out there..."

His hands curled into tight fists at his sides, and I suppressed a shiver. "Leave you out there? You run away from me one minute and expect me to rescue you the next? I *should* have left you out there, and my crew would have saved me the trouble!"

"Yeah, well, maybe you should have. And don't you dare put your hands on me again."

He froze, the muscles in his jaw contracting as he clenched it. "If I didn't put my hands on you, how was I to rescue you?" he articulated in a maddeningly calm voice.

"Then you *shouldn't* have rescued me."

"Y-you... What? You are a pain in the ass, you know that?" He walked out the door and slammed it behind him. I ran toward it just as it shut and tried the handle. "Locked. Obviously..." The lock on the inside of the door had been removed. *How dare he do this to me?* As I took my frustrations out on the door handle,

I heard the click of his boots and a deep laugh as he walked away. I sneered at him through the door.

What was it about him that made me furious and intrigued at the same time? I had planned to play nice, to keep a low profile, but I couldn't help myself. He caused rage to roll through me like boiling water, and everything just spilled out of my mouth with no filter. It was like I purposely wanted to piss him off just so he could feel an ounce of the frustration I felt.

There was something about the captain that, despite my frosty demeanor, frightened me. It scared me more than being kidnapped, more than being punched by the brute, or the threat of being thrown overboard. No matter what, I had to do whatever it took to hide this fear. For if he saw it, I truly would be a prisoner.

I tried the door, again and again. The last time I tried, someone—the captain—yelled back, "It's not going to open on its own," and then let out a laugh that was deep and just a little sinister.

Pacing the room, I eyed the tray of food by the bed. I laughed to myself. Regardless of the fact I was starved, I was not going to eat. Yeah, like that would show him. When had I agreed to play this game of his, whatever it might be?

I took in the room to divert my thoughts from the delicious smell of breakfast. There was the bed I had woken up on, held in place by ropes. A desk was at one end of the room, with a closet behind it. On the other side, there was a mahogany table and the velvet chair he sat on before. It wasn't lavish like I would have expected, but rather simplistic and comfortable. I paused at a crest carved into the back of the chairs. Then it hit me. This was *his* cabin. I doubted he'd made the mistake of not removing his weapons before he locked me in there, but it was highly likely there had to be a hidden weapon. I raced over to the desk and frantically searched it. Pausing briefly at worn papers and pictures, I vowed to look at them later. *Or not.* I wouldn't be here much longer if I could help it.

I opened the last drawer and smiled. "Aha!" A pearl-handled dagger lay under a scrap of damask. I picked it up; it looked more like a decoration than a weapon. I pulled it from its leather sheath, revealing a sharp, curved steel blade. I slid it back in its sheath. I needed to get this to Shaman Tamati. I could use it to pick the lock on the door and escape. This time, no one would see me. I swallowed down a laugh as it bubbled up, thinking I wouldn't have to put on the act much longer...

Then what, Lux? You're just going to remain hidden and we'll all steal a dingy and sail away into the sunset? Shut up! Ignoring the doubtful, negative thoughts, I walked to the door. I crouched down and peered into the keyhole. A shadow passed by, and I shot backward. My heart sped up as a soft rapping sounded on the door. The lock clicked, and I scooted back as far as I could from the door, so as to not incriminate myself. The dagger was like a beacon in my hands. I searched wildly around for a place to hide it. With no time to put it out of sight, I tucked it in the back of my pants.

"Lux? May I enter?" Ahmed popped his head in as I adjusted my shirt to cover up any evidence.

I blew out a breath of relief. "Yes, come in." My cheeks burned as I cleared my throat. I hoped I didn't look as guilty as I felt.

He entered carrying another tray of food and a silk sack. Setting the tray on the table, he glanced at the uneaten breakfast with a frown.

"I hope the food is to your liking." He uncovered the tray, revealing mounds of fresh fruit and figs. The smell of warm bread and honey caught my nose, and my mouth watered.

I swallowed. "Thank you, Ahmed, but I can't."

He frowned. "Why not? You need to eat something."

I couldn't explain it to him; it would just sound silly. If I were honest with myself, the food probably wasn't poisoned. It wouldn't have made sense to kill me that way. Something told me if the captain wanted to take a person out, it would be by his own hands, watching as the life dimmed from their eyes. I shivered. "Have the rest of our—my people—been fed?" That was strange. I had said 'our' as if he were one of us. When had I started to think Ahmed as being on my side?

"I assure you, everyone is being well taken care of. I have seen to it myself that Lilou has been attended to. I put her and her sister in a private cabin."

"Her sister?" I turned, surprise and delight cracking my voice.

"Yes, her older sister is on board as well. She was in a different cell, but they were able to find each other after the storm."

A smile crept over my face as I turned around. I rubbed the curtains between my fingers, enjoying their softness as I stared hollowly out the window. I was relieved and a little distraught at the fact Lilou wouldn't need me anymore.

"See? You have nothing to worry about. Everyone is faring well. Please, just eat something."

I glanced at him in suspicion. "Why do you care so much?" I wasn't being rude; I genuinely wanted to know. Why had Ahmed, since the very beginning, been kind and looked out for my well-being? Not just physically, like getting me to eat, but emotionally, like when he gave me the courage to treat the injured crewman.

"Everyone is worthy of kindness." He slowly turned over a teacup as he spoke and poured steaming amber liquid into it.

I scoffed as I watched him. *Everyone is worthy of kindness.* I rolled my eyes, thinking of a few people who that *did not* apply to—the captain being one of them. And that didn't tell me what I wanted to know. There were the bad guys—the pirates—and the good guys—us. Ahmed didn't really fit into either of those categories. It left me uneasy. He didn't appear physically strong, but he had an air of secretive knowledge about him. Like he knew my deepest secret, but was wise enough to keep it to himself. If he fought an opponent, I imagined he would beat them with strategy and logic rather than force. No matter how hard I tried, I couldn't imagine him hurting another soul.

"Yes, but *how* are you kind?" I gestured with my hands, trying to articulate what I was thinking, while hoping I wasn't being insensitive.

He took a white linen napkin and wiped the neck of the teapot. "I have learned silence from the talkative, toleration from the intolerant, and kindness from the unkind; yet, strange, I am not grateful to any of those teachers."

"Yes, well, I'm sure we know the 'unkind' you're referring to." I mentally kicked myself for saying that, but it had just popped out. Ahmed had opened up to me with something so meaningful and intelligent, and here I was thinking about the damn captain again.

Ahmed stopped fiddling with the tray and stood. "People aren't always what they seem. Don't you think?" He laughed in a good-natured way as he walked to the door.

I scowled at his laughter before I realized I might have become too irritable on account of the captain.

What did he mean by that anyway? The door never opened. I glanced up to see Ahmed hesitating. Finally, he faced me.

"I want to thank you." He took a deep breath, and then the words that followed came out in a rush. "I owe my life to you. I know... I know my word may mean nothing to you now, but I am in your debt. You can count on me to return the favor. I don't want you to be afraid of the other crew... they don't really mean it. They don't *really* want you dead."

"Please just promise me you'll look out for Lilou— for all the prisoners."

He nodded once and started for the door again, but he swiftly turned back around. "I don't know why you did it. Why you would bother saving the life of someone like me, when you clearly find pirates so..." He made a juggling motion with his hands as he grappled with his choice of words. "Disagreeable?"

I smiled. "People aren't always what they seem."

His face shifted from confusion to amusement, and he laughed in that light, delightful way, but the moment quickly passed. "There are new clothes and a dress in the sack by the bed. The captain will be dining with you tonight and wants you to dress in clothes more... befitting." He wasted no time coming up with that word.

My mouth popped open, but Ahmed ducked out before he could get an earful. I shook my head in astonishment. Did I hear him correctly? The captain wanted to eat dinner with me and wanted me to dress up? This was probably his way of torture. Stubbornness washed away any hunger I might have felt. There was no way I would be eating, let alone eating with him. If that were the case, there'd be a knife at his throat before he could take his first bite.

Chapter Six

"The anger of an ignorant man is in his words, and the anger of a wise man is in his actions."
-Old Arabic Proverb

"I HOPE IT'S NOT TOO TIGHT," THE CAPTAIN SAID WITH A gravelly voice that contradicted his cheeky grin. He pulled the ropes around my waist and secured them to the chair. I sneered at him. "I told you, you would be having dinner with me one way or the other. Unfortunately for you, that meant having to tie you to a chair."

"The only way I would have dinner with you is if you forced me to. Obviously, you're desperate enough to do just that." I tossed my head and looked down my nose at him.

I hadn't put up much of a fight when he followed through on his threat to tie me to the chair. The dagger was still tucked into my pants, and I couldn't risk it getting exposed. He was clever and smarter than I originally gave him credit for. I needed to be precise in my actions and find the right time to either escape, or get the dagger in the hands of the right people.

Finishing the last knot, he walked over to his chair on the other side of the table. He eyed me up and down as he sat with perfect posture, shoulders back and neck exposed. "And do you like dressing like a boy... or do you just enjoy wearing pirate clothes?" He fidgeted with the leather around his wrist.

I choked on a lungful of air at the indignation. "You wish! I am not your crew. I am not your slave. You don't control me, and you can't tell me what to wear. I have warned you that if you continue to force me to stay in this disgusting cabin of yours, I will kill you." That was actually really convincing, considering I had seen—and smelled—Sokum to know I had it pretty good. I just couldn't help myself. I had no filter when it came to him.

His blue eyes turned stormy. I walked a *very* thin line between amusing him and pissing him off. "You should be thankful. I should put you in a cabin with Sokum, and then you would know the real definition of disgusting, *amira*."

Leaning forward as far as the ropes allowed, I bared my teeth. "Then we agree on something. I would rather be in the vilest cabin of this ship than having dinner with you."

"Your hatred intrigues me," he said in a disturbingly genuine way.

Exasperated, I tried to gesture with my arms, only to be reminded of the ropes. I yelled at him instead. "You're evil. You terrorize for the sheer joy of it. You take lives as if it's nothing. You kidnap people and take them who knows—"

He looked to the ceiling and blurted, "It's not as if I have a choice!"

I blinked at his surprising revelation. His lips were pressed in a line as if he already regretted saying it. I drew in my bottom lip. *Was this all part of his game?* Did he just *want* me to think that he had let his perfect stone wall slip to reveal something worthwhile? I carefully chose my next words. "What hold does Asmodeus have on you?"

His eyes burned into me with unspoken warning. "You've gone too far with your childish defiance this time, Lux."

The door creaked open, and we both leaned back as if something private had just been interrupted. Oblivious to the tension between the captain and me, a smiling Ahmed strolled in with a tray of covered food in his hands. He set the dishes before us and uncovered them, releasing steam along with mouthwatering aromas. My stomach grumbled at the smell of roasted, curried meat and saffron rice. I pressed my lips together.

Ahmed's smile fell as he looked down at me. His gaze lingered far too long on the ropes binding me to the chair, and I could have sworn he looked disappointed.

Impassive, Ahmed turned back toward where he set the tray. An instant later, he returned with more plates, this time revealing olives dripping in oil and the bright orange flesh of mangoes. I turned my head away. This wasn't helping my hunger strike. It had been a long time since I had fruit that wasn't native to Sirbiad or had the opportunity to have a meal with actual sustenance. I might regret not partaking in this indulgence one day, but I was too full of hatred for the pirate sitting in front of me to care.

My eyes flickered to the captain's only to find him watching me. He studied me under heavy eyelids and a lazy smile. *He enjoyed my torture.* The hunger subsided as I gained new motivation. *I would not give him the satisfaction.*

"Shurkran, Ahmed." *Thank you, Ahmed.* The captain said it while never taking his eyes off me.

"Shahia Tayebah." *Enjoy.* Even though it was in

another language, anyone who heard Ahmed's reply would know it lacked conviction. I was really starting to like the guy.

The captain's eyes fell to his plate as he shook out a folded, linen napkin and continued speaking to Ahmed in Arabic. "Did she eat at all today?" For all the boredom and indifference in his tone, he could be asking if the meat was salted rather than inquiring about another human being.

"No. I am worried about her. I, myself, found it difficult to regain my strength after what we went through, and she pulled us both to the ship. You have to make sure she is well. I owe her my life, Draven."

The captain's eyes shot toward me with alarm.

"What?" Two sets of eye were on me now, waiting for a response. "What are you saying? If you're going to talk in front of me, at least speak English!"

His smile returned at my ignorance. "Wouldn't you like to know?" He turned back to Ahmed and said in Arabic, "Be discreet, Ahmed. For a second, I thought she caught on to my name."

"She can't understand us." Ahmed filled a goblet in front of him with clear, sparkling water, never taking his eyes off the task.

"Honestly..." He shook his head and picked up the goblet. "What am I going to do... with her?" I thought I heard the last part correctly, but it was drowned out as he brought the glass to his lips and took a sip.

"What do you mean?" Ahmed filled the goblet in front of me as well.

I licked my lips imagining how cold and delicious the drink would be.

"She's the most trouble that has ever been on my ship. Sokum suggested just throwing her in the brig and being done with it, but I find her surprisingly refreshing. And you know bad things happen when I get bored..."

The blood drained from my face as I was frozen in place, forced to watch him thoughtfully study the wooden table. It was like watching the storm clouds roll in, but not being able to look away even though it was clear a hurricane was coming. At any minute, he could look up, see the expression on my face, and find out that I knew he was talking about me.

"There is something about her."

The captain scoffed. "I don't see what."

Ahmed picked up the tray briskly, and I forced down the impulse to make him stay so I could be privy to more of their conversation. "Your pride prevents you from seeing what, although I imagine even *you* aren't completely immune to her charms. There have been a great deal of island girls who have come aboard this ship for you, but none who have slept in your bed."

There was a time where my finger was caught between the stone hammer and plank on the boat I was building. There was even a time where I had stepped on a painful sea urchin, but nothing, and I meant nothing, made me want to cry out as Ahmed's revelation did.

Stealing a glance at Draven, I was grateful he was still looking away so he couldn't see the horror on my face. I studied his profile with the echo of Ahmed's words replaying in my mind. How could anyone want to be with *him?* Someone so cold and cruel? I shivered.

"Remind me why I put up with you." His words to Ahmed were harsh, but even as he said them, there was a fondness to his eyes. "And the only reason she is in my *bed* is because I don't trust her around the other prisoners. The last thing I need is for them to get any hope in their heads."

Ahmed paused at the door, tray in hand. "Don't

give her to him."

"Ha! I'm already returning that child you two are so fond of, and you know *exactly* why I can't return Lux no matter how much I want to. Once the prisoners are delivered, we'll finally have what we need."

"But you like her—"

"This conversation is over."

"At least admit she is the most courageous girl you have ever encountered."

"Unquestionably. Now goodbye, Ahmed."

"I understand, *Captain. Ma'salama.*" He bowed once and turned to me. "Goodbye."

My lips quivered as I tried to smile at him, but my mind—and heart—was on another part of their conversation. He was freeing Lilou and returning her to her family. He thought I was the most courageous girl he'd ever known. *Me.* The girl who couldn't lift a katana when she first started training. Who time and time again had deliberately freed animals/dinner because she was too scared to lower the axe.

I thrust my chest out, feeling taller and stronger than ever. "What were you two talking about?"

"Nothing that concerns you."

The coldness came back to his words. My face burned, but I wouldn't let him ruin my I-could-conquer-the-world confidence.

"We were talking about you, actually."

I lifted my gaze to meet his eyes, and my traitorous heart fluttered. "You were?" I asked softly, for lack of breath.

"I was telling Ahmed that I should put you on a skiff and send you off to sea, where you will most likely be found by other pirates—pirates who are far less gracious than I am."

My face was hotter than before, but I didn't care if I was as red as a lobster. He was a liar. He played my game as well as I did. *Almost.* I sunk my teeth into my lower lip, extremely close to revealing I could speak Arabic.

"Right," I finally said, grinding my teeth instead of punching something.

He stared at me for another moment, expecting me to say or do more. "Well, I am starving," he said. He then had the indecency to pop a juicy slice of mango in his mouth.

My mouth watered while my throat felt particularly dry.

"Hungry?"

"Never," I responded, more than a little embarrassed that my voice came out so hoarsely.

"Suit yourself." He then went about eating in the most irritating way. After a vicious slicing of things on his plate, he paused to take a surprisingly delicate bite. Eating slowly, he used his forks and knife as if he was dining with royalty. He drew out my torture by going as far as commenting on the taste.

I licked my lips. "How can I eat if my hands are tied?"

The knife in his hand paused. "So if I untie your hands, you will join me?"

"No."

His fork went down with a clank. He threw back a piece of silky, raven hair off his brow. "You are impossible," he uttered.

"Never said I wasn't."

"Are you always like this?"

"Always like what?" I blinked in innocence.

"*Difficult.* I wonder what kind of suitor you have who can handle that."

"A really good one," I blurted. The blood drained from my face, and my skin tingled. I hadn't meant to lie, especially not about something so trivial.

"I'm sure. He'd have to be a saint to put up with you. So what's the poor guy's name?" His mouth was set and his jaw was tight as he concentrated on running his fork through a fluffy pile of rice.

"Leif." I continued the lie, thinking of my best—and only—friend on Sirbiad. "He's perfect." *Flawed.* "Tall and attractive." *Lanky and average.* "Charming" *Shy.* "He's sweet, funny, and always there for me." At least the last part was true. "He's…"

"Enough!" Draven dropped his hands to the table, rattling the chinaware. "I don't want to hear about Prince Charming." He resumed eating, but stopped after one bite. "I'm getting extremely tired of being the only one eating. Are you going to join me or not?"

"Untie me."

"Will you eat if I untie you?" He accentuated every word.

"No."

He scoffed.

"I refuse to eat with someone like you, but if you untie me, I promise I will not try to escape for the duration of the meal." I had all night to do so.

His eyes roamed the length of my body, eying me with less emotion than the dinner menu, before looking away.

"Leif doesn't have to force me to join him for dinner."

I squeezed both armrests as he shot out of his chair and came toward me. Putting both hands on the back of the chair, he bent over to face me. "Where's Leif now?" In a quick movement, the ropes fell loosely against me. I threw them onto the floor and adjusted my outfit. As I pretended to smooth out my shirt, my hands went discreetly toward my back to make sure the dagger hadn't slipped.

Draven sat and motioned me to eat. I turned my

nose up.

After a while, he continued. "I don't see it."

My eyes snapped down to meet his. "See what?"

"I don't see why Leif would go through all the trouble of being with you. You're no different than the girls on any other island."

"Is that so?" I was choked with rage and irony, knowing that, according to him, I *was* different from any other girl. "And I assume you've had a lot of experience with that?" I couldn't help but ask. I shouldn't—*really* shouldn't—but I wanted to know. "How does your..." I struggled for the word. He was too young for a wife. Lover? I gagged. That brought some disturbing images to mind... I cleared my throat. "*Companion* feel about you capturing poor, innocent girls and tying them to chairs?"

A smile turned into laughter.

"I bet she is no saint. What—is she a pirate, too?"

A brilliant laugh escaped him. "Pirates or peasants. I hardly care what they are. So long as they are willing and interesting enough to tolerate for the moment."

I gasped. "Willing? I hardly think taking girls prisoner and seducing them is *willing*." My fists clenched, my fingernails digging into my palms. I hated him. I hated his arrogance, and I burned inside with frustration.

"No," he said, in a thoughtfully mocking tone. "It's a general rule of mine not to fraternize with prisoners who are so beneath me. The girls from the islands who come aboard this ship do so willingly. *Very* willingly."

He held his lopsided smile and I had murderous thoughts, but then it hit me. He mentioned again about other islands. It meant he had traveled what was left of the world. He had been everywhere and seen what countries, now islands, had survived. He would know what the US was like. Would know the truth.

"Tell me about the other islands." I softened my tone. "How many are there? How far have you traveled? Have you been to the north...?" My words flowed too fast.

"Whoa, slow down."

"Sorry. I—"

"What makes you think I will tell you all that? You have been nothing but trouble since you've been on board and you won't even share a proper meal with me."

Why was he so obsessed with eating together? It reminded me of my father. I thought it was just him, but now I was beginning to think it was a cultural thing. *Interesting.*

Draven's narrowed eyes shifted to the ceiling, probably calculating how to use this new advantage over me. Relishing in the fact I wanted something from him.

"I'm sorry, Draven, but I just need to know." Playing nice came easier than I imagined.

"Need to know what?"

"If there's hope—"

"Wait. *Draven?* Why did you call me Draven?"

Oops.

I let it slip. Hoping he hadn't seen that my eyes had widened and the muscles in my neck tightened, I swallowed down my surprise and tried to cover my mistake. "I overheard someone call you that. That is your name, isn't it?" I waved my hand with an air of casualness. Again, not a lie. I did overhear Ahmed calling him that. It was just in Arabic.

"Overheard someone? Who? None of my crew would call me by my given name."

"So it *is* your name... Good to know."

He straightened in his chair. "You are not to call me that. You'll address me as captain."

I chuckled that he was so distraught. Amused by how the balance of power changed so readily. "You're not *my* captain," I taunted with a wickedness I didn't know I had in me.

Those words sent him over the edge. He leapt up and came at me, but before he could reach me, I stood, taking the dagger from my back, its edge meeting his Adam's apple. A surprised breath escaped from us both. I was impressed I *had* actually learned something in training.

"Don't. Move," I instructed, coming up with a new plan on the spot. "I told you I would kill you, and now here's my weapon."

Draven sighed as his eyes traveled to the knife, *his* knife. He straightened, and his gaze darted to the side.

"If you try anything, I will slit your throat. Now you are going to listen to me very carefully. Is that clear?" Digging my teeth into my lower lip, I pressed the knife into his skin. I swallowed as bright red blood seeped around the steel blade.

His jaw muscles clenched before he spat out a 'yes' between gritted teeth.

"You are going to call Ahmed to the door and tell him to instruct your crew to turn the ship around, back to Sirbiad. Once we dock in Sirbiad, every one of the prisoners will be released. You'll live if everyone gets there safely. Do you understand?"

"And how do you plan on getting off the ship?" His eyes gazed calmly into mine.

My eyelashes fluttered. "What do you mean?"

"How will *you* get off the ship? For arguments sake, we'll pretend you make it holding me hostage

81

for the day's journey back to Sirbiad. But if you try to leave with me at knife point, my men will kill you the minute you step outside this cabin."

I blinked. I hadn't thought that far yet. So concerned was I with getting Lilou, Shaman Tamati, and the other prisoners back to Sirbiad, I didn't think before acting when the opportunity presented itself. Would I sacrifice myself as long my people got home safe? But if I did, what about my plans? *I'll never know what happened to my friends and family. I'll never know if I could have gone back home again...* "I will knock you unconscious and run." I shrugged.

Before I knew it, he darted away from the knife, grabbing my wrist and twisting it. My gasp was replaced with a growl of anger that he had caught me off guard. I fought to keep my grip.

"Drop the knife, Lux."

"Never," I gritted through my teeth. The ligaments in my wrist stretched under his grip to the point of a fracture. Despite the excruciating pain, I refused to let go. This would be my only chance. He kicked my feet out from under me and I fell to the floor, pulling him down with me. The knife fell out of my hand and slid across the room. I tried to stand in a rush to find it, but he grabbed one of my legs, pulling me back to the ground. Kicking him with my free foot until he let go, I scrambled across the floor toward the knife. He grabbed my foot again, pulling me backward. Getting up before I could, he lunged at the knife, retrieving it from under the chair.

Turning around, he pointed it at me with one hand. I threw my hands up in instinctual surrender.

"Hm..." he said, wiping away a ribbon of scarlet trickling from his lips.

I bent over, hand on my knees, trying to catch my breath. If I wasn't so weak—if only I had something to eat before, I was sure I could have taken him. *Dumb move, Lux.*

"And here I thought the Sirbiadians were supposed to be skilled fighters."

"I am!" All at once, I was proud of my training and ignorant of my shortcomings. "If I had a katana, you wouldn't stand a chance."

He smirked and walked to the door. "Ahmed," he called out.

What was he up to? I kept my eyes trained on him. He called again before Ahmed appeared hesitantly in the doorway.

"Yes? Captain?" Ahmed's eyes took in the state of the cabin before darting between us.

"Bring me two swords."

I didn't dare say a word or take my eyes off Draven.

Ahmed returned with another pirate, the burly, bald-headed one, who was holding two swords. Ahmed held out his hand in a serving gesture. Draven put the dagger in Ahmed's open palm and took the two swords from the other pirate. They were sheathed, the handles wrapped in black leather.

Draven came toward me with both swords. I used all my strength not to cower. One he held to his side, the other's point directed at my chest.

I flinched as Draven flipped the sword, catching the blade effortlessly in his hand, the handle now aimed at me.

Angling my body away from him, I furrowed my eyes.

He held the sword higher, offering it to me.

Tearing my eyes away from the sword, I met his gaze. His eyes were that perfect mixture of cruel and amused, and his mouth was still smirking.

This was it. This was my chance to prove myself. To utilize all my training.

I swallowed. He clearly doubted I could win this fight. I didn't know if I should be worried that he was so confident or pleased he'd just made a fatal mistake.

Before he changed his mind, I grabbed the sword, unsheathing it. Only the cover remained in Draven's hand. Both his eyebrows rose, as if he didn't think I would do it. Then his smile grew as he tossed the sheath across the room and drew his own sword.

"Leave," Draven ordered. The bald pirate exited immediately while Ahmed lingered behind. Ahmed's mouth popped open. "Now," Draven added in a quiet, dangerous voice.

He obeyed; the creak of the door shutting behind him was painfully slow. I warmed at Ahmed's concern, but what did it mean that someone who knew Draven better than anyone was worried about what he was about to do?

Doubt bubbled inside of me. I held up the sword. It was lighter than the katanas I trained with. My heart pounded, making it hard to remember everything I was taught.

First lesson: stay calm.

I took a deep breath to slow my beating heart. I needed to relax my muscles. I needed to be swift.

Second lesson: keep your feet apart.

This was a challenge for me as I always struggled with balance, but I moved my feet into position.

Third lesson: assess your opponent.

Draven stood waiting for me to make the first move. His confidence might be his downfall. He was also tall, so I could use his exposed legs to my advantage.

Finally: engage.

I wrapped both hands around the leather hilt and held the sword so it ran from my stomach to the top of my head. *Here goes...*

And then I swung.

Draven moved his sword faster than I imagined was possible. With a clash, mine was thwarted. "Nice form, but you're off balance."

I pushed my lips together, irritated. "I'll show you off balance," I muttered and attacked again.

He stepped to the side, escaping my blow. I thrust at him again and again, but Draven held his sword comfortably away from his body, keeping me on point.

"You tend to lean too much to your right."

Ignoring his comments, I aimed for his neck, but his sword came out in front of him to block my blow.

Our swords connected, and I was stuck.

"That's better, but you're still off balance."

I tried to disengage my sword without killing myself.

Draven chuckled before unlocking us, sending me reeling backward.

Glass rattled as I bumped into the table. Hot liquid splattered my back, and the sweet, minty smell of tea wafted in the air.

"You do well on the offense, but what about defense?" Draven came at me. I rolled to the side just in time, and his sword hit the table. I darted behind him, sword raised, but he turned. Our swords clashed again.

I backed up, the muscles in my arms aching at the exertion. I tried to remember lessons one and six so he wouldn't see I was becoming weak. To throw him off, I came at him aggressively again. We parried around the room until we ended up in the same position we started.

Draven came at me, and I dodged safely to the side. I blew the hair from my face, wishing I could wipe the sweat tickling the back of my neck. His sword swiped in front of me, and I pivoted my body, but the edge of his sword cut the collar of my tunic. The fabric fell down. Cool air touched my bare shoulder.

Enraged, I used my left hand to hold up my shirt while I stabbed.

Draven stepped out of the line of my attack and used his sword to push mine off to the side.

The hilt slipped through my sweaty hand. The sword flew through the air and landed with a clang somewhere on the other side of the room.

I gasped. *No!*

Draven tilted his head with a triumphant smile. Before he could move his sword, I threw myself toward the table. Picking up the gold serving tray, a plate of rice flying to the ground, I spun around, using it to shield myself. Draven's sword struck the platter, and I became trapped beneath his sword and the table. I tried to push him off, but his force met mine. Peering over the platter at him, I exhaled angry breaths from my nose. He stared down at me, his midnight hair loose over his amused eyes. "Resourceful."

He stepped back and I stumbled forward, the tray crashing to the ground. Before I could stand, his sword came down, stopping just before what would have been a beheading blow.

Letting out a sole laugh, he lifted his sword and turned away. I straightened, still trying to catch my breath as he retrieved my lost sword.

I scoffed at his back. "Don't act so full of yourself. I almost had you!"

He whipped around. "Ha. Even after all my advice, you were still leaning too far right. You let your emotions coach you rather than listen to instruction."

"I'm tired," I mumbled. But his words seeped inside of me, settling in a place that was already full of doubt.

"A true warrior doesn't let their stubbornness

prevent them from gaining the strength they need to fight."

I glared at him.

He moved his hands as if he were dusting his hands off. "Well, since that is settled, I have a ship to run. Good night, Lux."

He left. And for the first time, I actually cared that I failed a lesson.

Chapter Seven

THE MOON WAS HIGH ABOVE THE SEA WHEN AHMED came through the door again. I'd managed to stay awake; despite that, my stomach was eating itself. The food that was once so beautifully presented was now splattered across the cabin.

Ahmed walked to the dining table and started cleaning up. I watched with regret as he loaded the dishes onto a wooden tray. The growling echoed in my hollow stomach. I would have licked my lips if it weren't for my mouth being so dry that I couldn't swallow.

I watched Ahmed, waiting for him to speak. His eyes avoided me. *Good*, then he couldn't see how weak I had become.

"I'm not supposed to talk to you," he finally said.

"Do you always do what you're told?" I asked with harsh sarcasm.

He stopped loading the dishes. "Why didn't you eat something when you had the chance?"

"It's the principle of the thing. You wouldn't understand." I winced. No, Ahmed wasn't like the other pirates, and that wasn't fair.

He let out a resigned breath. "Lucky then that I brought another tray for you."

My jaw slackened as Ahmed left the room and returned instantly with a new tray.

He set it down, winked at me, and then left.

I went over to the food. Grabbing a glass of thick, yellow juice, I gulped it down before I talked myself out of it. I dunked tiny fried fish in hummus, eating bones and all. The food wasn't warm, but that was irrelevant as I washed it down with the sweet, syrupy mango drink. Food I'd been deprived of for five years. Even in the US, this would be considered a delicacy. I remembered the last time I had a meal with such substance. Before The Floods, I took everything for granted. Now, I had nothing to take for granted.

Nausea bubbled in my stomach as the memories hit me. Who knew that our 'family vacation' would be the sole reason we survived? Burnt out with politics, my father picked the most remote, primitive place he could find to 'unplug'. That place was Sirbiad, A pristine tropical island in the South Pacific. If we went to Hawaii as I wanted to, I wouldn't be standing here right now. My parents were quick to move on and call themselves Sirbiadians. My dad was nothing but honored when the Sirbiadians chose him as mayor. But I protested it even though all the while, I'd slowly been forgetting my old life. Whether I liked it or not, I was getting used to this new world. Soon, it would be all I knew. *I had to do something before it was too late.* I never gave up hope that my other family and friends had survived. They could be out there, living and surviving just like us. Just waiting for someone to come and find them. I told myself if there was the smallest chance that was true—that I could somehow resume my old life—I would take it. I would *have* to take it. And I did...

I rolled my head back as the memories faded, leaving me tingling and feeling like I had the morning after Leif gave me a homemade concoction.

Knocking jarred me from my thoughts, and I inhaled my last bites of food. I flew to the chair and flopped into it a second before the door opened. It was just Ahmed. He glanced at the food and then back at me with a grin. I pursed my lips and rolled my eyes up to study the ceiling, wishing I had one more sip of the mango juice. I was tempted to lick the sea salt off my fingers.

"He's not a bad guy, you know."

"Who?" I cocked my head, not sure if I heard him right.

"Draven."

Oh, I heard him right. "You have got to be joking. This cabin isn't in a state of disrepair because he wanted to settle our dispute with a game of cards!"

"I assure you, we go back a long ways. The only reason I'm here is because of him. But how do you know who I am referring to?" He paused, collecting the dishes from the table to study me thoughtfully.

My mouth snapped shut. When Ahmed had said Draven wasn't a bad guy, he had said it in Arabic, and I'd answered him.

He picked up the tray with a wink. "As I said before, people are not always what they seem." His voice faded as he took his time and all the care in the world to quietly shut the door behind him.

Sheesh! I tucked my hair behind my ears with frustration. Ahmed knew the exact moment to enter a room, the precise amount of liquid to pour into a teacup, and my deepest secret. He was wiser, *way* wiser than he looked. Yet, despite his suspicions of me and mine of him, I liked him. There was something honest and warm about his eyes that, under any other circumstances, would beckon my friendship.

Since my thoughts were on friendship, I pondered the relationship between Ahmed and Draven. Ahmed's loyalty seemed to go beyond that of a first mate, and he had said the only reason he was on the ship was because of Draven. Did that mean they were friends? It was hard to imagine any two people more opposite being friends, but as Ahmed had also said, people weren't always what they seemed. I sank into the velvety back of the chair. Belly full and mind exhausted, my eyelids slid closed.

⌒⌒⌒⌒⌒

"You snore in your sleep."

I had never been a morning person, but waking to Draven's annoying voice at an ungodly hour made it even more unwelcoming. Still half asleep, I used the armrests to push myself vertical. I winced at the ache in my neck from sleeping in the comfortable, but unforgiving, winged-back chair all night. My hand reached around the floor to locate the chair's pillow that had fallen there. I caught the silk pillowcase between my fingers.

Then I chucked it at him.

"Shut up." My voice came out husky from sleep.

Draven dodged the pillow, never taking his eyes off me. As if he didn't have a concern in the world, he shrugged. "At least it's not a dagger." He ran his fingers through clean, slightly damp locks. His black hair fell to his shoulders, curling out slightly at the ends. His clothes were new, without a wrinkle or crease to be found. The smell of fresh soap came off him. *God, I thought pirates didn't bathe for weeks.* I frowned. Why had Draven's hygienic practices irritated me so much?

I pulled my own wild, unbrushed hair back and wiped under my eyes, suddenly feeling self-conscious. "And I don't snore in my sleep," I murmured. "I suppose a toothbrush is out of the question?"

"As always, I'm one step ahead of you." He tossed a twig onto my lap.

"What am I supposed to do with this?"

He just laughed. *The arrogant—*

"It's called *miswak*. It's better than a toothbrush."

I narrowed my eyes and let my gaze travel from his face to the tips of his boots. Draven was playing me yet again. I just knew it.

He laughed again. *I swear I will—*

"It's been used for centuries. I promise it will clean your teeth, and it has a lot of health benefits."

Is that why yours are perfect? I mentally scolded myself for having such a thought.

"Also, there is a tub in the closet. Ahmed will bring you soap and water so you may bathe." He raised his eyebrows. "And a brush—your hair is hideous."

"It is *not* hideous!" I quickly combed my fingers through it. "It's... beachy."

"*Beach-y?*" He laughed. "What do you know of that?"

"I know more than you think." I walked toward the window to look anywhere but at Draven. As I watched the ripple of the water, the ocean's therapeutic properties kicked in. "The open sea air has a way of bringing back memories."

I turned to find Draven occupying my chair.

He muttered something under his breath before rubbing his brow as if to ward off a headache. "Couldn't you have slept on the bed? At least the sheets can be washed. Now my favorite chair smells all girly."

"You just said I needed a bath."

"You know you still smell good."

"Yeah right. Like what?" I lowered my gaze and tucked a strand of hair behind my ear.

"Like lavender, *amira*."

I froze at his accurate description. I had been joking. I didn't expect him to actually respond. Although any kind of beauty products were scarce on Sirbiad, I would spend time finding flowers to crush and wash my hair with. My favorite was also the most abundant—lavender.

My face tingled. The only reason he knew what I smelled like was because of how close we had been yesterday. When he carried me to his cabin, when he tied me up, when we fought...

It had to stop.

My face burned, and I knew I had to change the subject. "Whatever." My words came out with a rushed breath and didn't sound as indifferent as I was trying for.

"If you insist on dressing in my clothes, can I at least get you a clean pair?"

"*Your* clothes? That's surprising because the way you dress, I wouldn't think you owned anything but leather and armor. Besides, why would I want to dress in your rags?"

"*Rags?*" He glared. In two strides, he was before me. "That *shirt* you're wearing is made from the finest silk."

I remembered he was volatile and that I really shouldn't taunt him. *Too late.*

"Oh, really? And who'd you steal it from?" If I had stuck out my tongue just then, I would have succeeded in acting ten years younger.

"*Steal* it?" While childish, my comments had their desired effect. And though it was a little like poking at a caged shark, I couldn't help the satisfaction I felt from ticking him off. To know he was every bit as angry, frustrated, and put out as I was made any retaliation worth it.

He took a step toward me. "It was my... Never mind! You are completely irritating." He said the last part slowly, the syllables breaking on his tongue.

I turned my face away. "Well, it doesn't matter how you got it, I don't want to dress in anything that belongs to you."

Two slender fingers caressed the line of my jaw. I sucked in a breath. Somehow, the delicate touch was more unnerving than if it'd been rough and punishing.

Wow, it's hot in here. Clearing my throat, I resisted the urge to fan myself and cursed his bloody cabin for lack of air circulation. I glanced over to see if any windows were open.

"Then why are you still wearing my clothes, sweetheart?" His eyes were warmer, mirroring the blue-green of a Caribbean sea. My gaze shamelessly drifted further down to his parted lips.

It had to stop...

A tingling spread through my body from the tip of my nose to my bare feet. The warmth and tingling actually felt sort of nice.

Oh no. The room wasn't hot—*I* was.

And now I was practically panting.

I abruptly pulled away from him. What was next, drooling?

It had to stop...

He is my enemy. He is my enemy. He is my enemy, I chanted, which, thankfully, worked. "I can't change while you're in here." I shot him a look of disgust completely contrary to what I was feeling thirty seconds ago.

"I just came to make a deal with you. Then I will be out of your way."

"A deal? I thought you didn't 'do' deals?"

He let out a single, short laugh. "I've been doing a lot of things lately that I don't normally do."

My heart fluttered. What did he mean by that?

"Anyway, it has come to my attention that I have

information you want." He stopped pacing and laced his fingers together.

And how did he come to that conclusion? I rolled my eyes.

My eyes fell back on him to find him watching me. His eyes widened and his chin jutted out in silent warning. "Do you want the answers to your questions about the islands and Asmodeus?"

"What's the catch?"

"No catch, *amira*."

"Quit calling me that!" Princess? *Please.* I started to roll my eyes again, but then froze mid-roll and looked sideways at him to see if he caught it. The knowing smirk he wore said he did. This time, I couldn't help sticking my tongue out at him. "If it is a deal, what do you want in return?"

"Nothing at all."

"Nothing at all," I repeated, in a tone that said I'm-not-buying-it-for-a-minute.

He paced again. Paused. Regally held out his arm. "You just have to have dinner with me. *Willingly*." Turning, he walked to the door with unnatural confidence.

Interesting. He wanted to keep me in his cabin so I was away from the other prisoners, and Shaman Tamati wanted me in here to keep him away from them. "Fine," I said quickly before he left. I couldn't resist asking, "But why?"

He hesitated in the doorway with a pleased smirk on his face. "Just would love to see what it's like for poor Leif while he is trying to court you."

"Court me? What—?" I protested to a closed door. Grunting, I dropped down on the bed. Why on earth was I smiling? Something was changing inside me, and I didn't like it.

It had to stop, I told myself again.

The only reason I agreed was to get information

from him while 'distracting' him as Shaman Tamati had said. Yes, he was attractive. Okay, he was more than attractive—he was *stunning*. My smile fell, and I straightened my back. At least I could hate him so intensely, yet be objective about his striking good looks. Other than that, there was no good in him. He was just as evil as Asmodeus. Well, not *just* as evil. He did have one, two, okay, maybe three, redeeming qualities. I shook my head to clear those thoughts. The point was, he was a pirate and was on the verge of driving me *insane*.

Courting, he'd said. There would be no *courting.* Passive-aggressive fighting, as well as yelling and fighting. Yes, lots of fighting, but courting? No—there would be none of that. Courtship. *Ha!* I'd never been courted in my life. Being the mayor's daughter, I was effectively off-limits.

I had to admit the thought of growing old on the island disturbed me. Marrying someone from Sirbiad, having my own hut on Sirbiad, raising children on Sirbiad... The thought was repulsing. I had never thought about my future in this way. Which was exactly why I was on the beach the night I was kidnapped... to change my future.

I felt guilty I had looked down on their lifestyle before. Many Sirbiadian families had that life and were quite happy. Leif would have that life. It hadn't gone unnoticed that many of the girls were starting to give Leif attention. I'd joked with him about it, and he, of course, humbly brushed it off. I smiled, remembering Leif's laugh.

I took a deep breath, freeing my imagination and letting it wander further. Imagining what it would be like to be attracted to one of the boys from our island. Not just anyone from our island, but *Leif.* The shudder that shook my frame stopped those thoughts.

This time, I felt guiltier than before. Leif was my best friend, and there was no doubt that was all he would ever be. A new anguish seared my heart. As the hope that I would ever return to my old life diminished, the realization that I might very well end up alone blossomed.

But then I imagined that scenario again, with someone else. The crashing of the waves against the shore seemed real in my head, and the full moon gave off a romantic glow on the water. This time, it was tanned hands cupping my face, and he smelled of ocean, not incense. I actually welcomed his warm, velvety lips when they connected with mine. I hadn't had nearly enough when my mysterious suitor pulled back and looked hungrily at me, with a familiar set of blue eyes—

Craack. Oops. I had snapped the *miswak* in half. *There goes my toothbrush.* But more regrettable and worrisome was that Draven could ignite feelings in me that weren't hatred.

Chapter Eight

*"You give but little when you give of your possessions.
It is when you give of yourself that you truly give."*
-Khalil Gibran, *The Prophet*

I SIGHED LAZILY, MESMERIZED BY THE STEAM COMING off my skin. The corner of my lip curled. *This feels so good.* I probably looked like I was finding sweet relief in a bucket of cool water after my behind was started on fire. Which, coincidentally, actually happened to someone on Sirbiad. The thought still made my insides quiver when I remembered how hard Leif and I had laughed after that.

Minutes before, Ahmed brought out the tub, along with buckets and buckets of scorching hot water to fill it. The copper tub was large and beautifully crafted. Before he left, he set a thick, ivory-colored towel on a stool next to the tub as well as a comb and two little vials. *Ohhh.* I grabbed the bottles, the glass clinking together. Uncorking the first vial, I saw it held an oily, gold liquid. *This must be for after. How nice.* I set it aside and uncorked the second vial, which held a gel-like bubbly substance. The strong smell of jasmine flowers brought memories of souvenirs from the East.

Dumping the entire thing all over me, I washed every bit of salt off me. I pinched my nose and submerged my head to wash my hair. My hair, which usually hung well past my shoulder blades, had tangled so badly it had shortened by inches. I brushed while it was underwater, just to get the tangles out. By the time it was smooth to my satisfaction, my skin was wrinkly and the water had become tepid. *What was I doing?* I almost forgot where I was. How could I enjoy this luxury when I had to think about getting everyone back to Sirbiad? I still had to make it back to shore to meet the fisherman, and I was running out of time. If I wasn't stuck in this stupid cabin... Wait. I was in *his* cabin. I would search it top to bottom. There had to be something here that could help me.

I stood, water rolling down my oily skin. Grabbing the plush towel, I wrapped it around my body while I considered my wardrobe choices. There were Draven's oversized clothes in the closet, my sundress that suddenly looked even more dirty and worn than it had while on Sirbiad, and then there were the clothes Draven had picked out for me. I sorted through them. A pair of satin slippers, black leggings, and a beautiful *abaya*. The gown was purple satin and floor length, with long, sheer, flared sleeves. The sleeves and low collar were adorned with crystals. It was beautiful and regal—something I would have chosen for myself. *Stop—you're a prisoner. Get off the ship. Get back to Sirbiad. Meet the fisherman. Go home.* With a regretful last glance, I grabbed the slippers and leggings and borrowed another tunic from Draven's closet.

One landless map, five books—three in Arabic, two in English—one locked chest, and one curious family portrait...

99

I scoured the entire room for hours, taking inventory. There were no more hidden weapons.

I checked.

Thoroughly.

A thin film of sweat had resulted from my efforts, and I blew a strand of hair off my face. I walked to one of the small port windows, pushing it open. The fresh air was cooler. Greedily taking a few salty breaths, I studied a crest carved into the wood. I had seen this symbol in several places during my search—two swords crossing under an open-palmed hand. It seemed familiar somehow. There was Arabic writing underneath it. *Al-Sabriye*. Was that his last name? Draven Sabriye. It had a nice ring to it.

I shook my head. Strolling back over to his desk, I let my mind go back to the books I discovered. Picking up an old copy of *One Thousand and One Nights,* my lips curved with satisfaction. I flopped on the bed, and flipped open to my favorite story and spent the next hour escaping the dangers of reality for the fictional dangers of the Maghreb. But even then, I couldn't escape Draven, whose similarities with the powerful and evil sorcerer, who I seemed to despise less than the previous times I'd read it, were undeniable. I should be rooting for Aladdin, not feeling pity for and trying to justify the actions of the villain. Just as Aladdin found himself trapped in the cave, the lock at the door clicked.

Irritated at being interrupted while so thoroughly into the story, I ignored the visitor—and my manners—so I could finish the chapter.

Curiosity got the best of me. I lifted my head to see if the visitor was a *friend* or *foe* before turning to the next page of my story. Unfortunately for me, the dark and brooding figure towering over me was very much a *foe*. Therefore, Aladdin would have to be stuck in the cave a little longer. I snapped the book shut.

"What are you doing?" the looming figure asked. "Did you steal my book?" The scowl was gone, replaced with a teasing curiosity I had so seldom seen.

"I didn't *steal* it. Pirates steal. I *borrowed* it." The words were impatiently ripped from me.

He tilted his head and raised an eyebrow. "What's the difference?"

"The difference is stealing means taking."

"Did you not take the book from my desk?" Another step. Almost predatory.

I cleared my throat and sat up in the bed, feeling imposed upon. "Well, yes. But stealing means you take without asking."

"I must have missed when you asked to borrow my book." He stepped even closer; he appeared concentrated, absorbed, and not at all cruel. His smirk was gone, replaced with a warm smile that showed his teeth. His playfulness was somehow harder to deal with than our fighting.

I cocked my head, frustration building. He knew what stealing was. Why did he need me to explain? "You know what I mean. Borrowing means you will return what you take."

"Well, give it back then."

He reached for the book slowly, giving me time to grab it and hold it behind my back. "No."

The wolfish flash of teeth. "Really? So, you *won't* return it? According to your definition, that is considered stealing." He placed both palms flat on the bed, and I backed up farther with the book.

I lifted my chin with determination despite the smile threatening my face, tugging the corners of my mouth. My teeth struggled to break free. I couldn't help but enjoy his teasing. "I'm not done reading."

He reached for it again by kneeling on the bed.

My hand shot it in the air safely above me.

"Stop." A bubbly laugh spilled out, contradicting my words. Suddenly, he smiled, and it was the first time I had seen him smile in such a genuine, carefree way. A *real* smile. One that stole your breath. One that made you smile back. One that was as bright as a freshly sharpened katana. *Why can't he be like this more often?*

"Like what more often?" he said as he grabbed the book out of my hand. I was caught off guard that I had said those last words out loud, so I didn't have time to keep the book out of his grasp.

He backed off the bed. Now that he had his prize, satisfaction was so irritatingly written on his face.

"You should stop scowling all the time." I jumped up, but he anticipated my move. "Give me the book back." I tried for a threatening tone, but he just laughed.

"Come and get it," he taunted, the challenge gleaming in his eyes.

I shrugged one shoulder casually to show him I wasn't worried about losing. "I could take you now that I've rested. You've seen how I punch." I gave him my most wicked smile. My very own *'try me'* smile.

The creak of the wooden door interrupted his laughter.

We both turned in a flash, as if we were caught doing something illicit. In the brief moments prior, I had forgotten the role I was supposed to be playing. Being amicable, yes. But laughter and teasing should have no part in it.

A young boy strolled in, wearing robes similar to the other pirates, but worn out and frayed.

He carried the tray usually held by Ahmed.

"What do you think you are doing?" he barked at the boy. The spell was broken, and old Draven, and his scowl, had returned.

"Ah... Ahmed asked me to bring this," he stammered.

"That is obvious, but you think you can enter *my* cabin without permission?"

"I'm... I'm sorry, Captain. It must've slipped my mind to knock." The boy's eyes were as big and round as the portholes.

"Save your excuses." Draven made his way over to the door and called out two pirates' names.

I gave the boy a sympathetic look as Draven returned with two crewmen I recognized, the bald headed one and the older man who was there looking on uncomfortably when I patched up Kamran. "Now that the cells are empty, they're looking for company. Put him in one!" The men grabbed the boy, whose wide eyes matched mine. "And no food or water until he can remember how to knock."

"You can't be serious!" I ran over to the door.

"Yes, I am. This is my ship, and this is how I run it."

I stood in front of the door, breathless from rage. "I won't let you punish him for trying to bring me something to eat."

"I didn't ask a captured slave for her opinion." His voice was dangerously low and tightly controlled.

My throat tightened to the point it felt like a boa constrictor had wrapped itself around my neck. All at once, the previous fifteen minutes were forgotten, and I remembered the position I was in. "If you insist on punishing someone, then let that person be me." Dropping my lashes quickly, I refused to let him see the sting of his words. I turned to the crewmen. "Let the boy go. I will take his place."

Draven met me at the door. "You will not!"

"I will, if it means he won't get punished."

He scowled at me like usual, and I threw daggers

back at him with my eyes. We stared at each other so hard it could've left a bruise.

No one moved. Not the boy. Not the crew.

Draven whipped his head away with a scoff. "Let the boy go. I've decided imprisonment is too generous a punishment. Let him scrub the head for a month. Now, get back to your duties and not a word of this or you'll be dead before sunrise."

"Yes, Captain," the crew replied in unison. The bald headed man was the first to leave but before the old man could, he gave that nod again. *And was the corner of his mouth turned up?* I couldn't tell. He was gone. Draven followed them out.

He paused at the door. "You'll be the ruin of me." There was a faint tremor in his voice as though some emotion had touched him.

I hardened my heart by erecting barriers of anger. "You've already done a pretty good job of that yourself."

He slammed the door.

I no longer felt like reading the book Draven had forgotten on the bed. I should leave this room, *his* room, and tell Shaman Tamati he could forget it. My feelings were out of control, not because of how furious I was, but because I was so... so... *never mind.* Draven Sabriye would not get the best of me.

When we were alone before, it was like he was a different person, and I was dangerously close to no longer pretending. But that was because I'd forgotten he was cruel and just how dangerous he could be. He was going to punish a boy over a simple mistake! I couldn't imagine what would have happened to him if I hadn't stepped in. But then, that was the other thing. I *had* stepped in, and he listened to me. He risked losing the respect and authority of his crew just to please me. What did that mean? *Why would he do that for me, a captured slave as he put it?* My stomach fluttered at the thought of what that could mean. *Stop.* I had to think of him for what he was: a pirate, a pawn of Asmodeus, my enemy.

After a few hours, I was worse than before. While I sat in a comfortable cabin, the prisoners were doing the real work. I could plan a fight, but not *this*, whatever it was. They would have to find a new pawn. My skin prickled at the sudden lack of air in the enclosed cabin. *No more.* Running for the door, I irrationally turned the handle, even though it wouldn't budge. Trying the lock on the door, one, two... a million times, I kicked it as if that would magically open it. "Ahmed," I called through the door. After a few moments, there was the click of the lock. He peeked his head in and scanned the room before entering.

"You were calling for me?"

"Yes. Yes, I was." I crossed my arms.

"Do you wish to see my captain?"

I narrowed my gaze at his traitorous words. "Never."

He cocked his head to the side, giving me a shaky smile. "What is it that you need then?"

"I *need* to get out of here. I need sun. I need air. I need to move."

He regarded me for a moment before his lips twitched. "I can't let you do that. I've been ordered."

I let out an exaggerated sigh at his loyalty. "Look. As I recall, I saved your life. You spoke of returning the favor. Well, time to pay up." I rubbed my thumb to my index finger, palm up.

His brown eyes were round with sympathy. Just when I thought he was going to give in, he turned his gaze to his feet. "I'm sorry, I can't."

So it's come to this, has it? "I was afraid you'd say

that. In that case, I'm leaving anyway. So if you'd kindly step aside..."

He blocked my path. "Lux, please."

"Ahmed," I yelped, surprised he'd physically tried to stop me.

"What the hell is going on?" The door was wide open, Draven filling the doorway.

"*Salam,* Captain." Ahmed darted a glance at me and continued to speak in Arabic. "Lux requested to go out on deck. She needs the fresh air."

"No."

"You can't keep her cooped up in here."

"And why not? Am I the only one who remembers that she is a prisoner? Besides, last time she tried that, I had to come to her rescue."

"The crew did as you asked and scared her, but they don't want to lie anymore, especially since she saved my life."

What? He tricked me! Grinding my teeth together, it took all my restraint not to blurt out murderous threats.

"Suddenly, they have morals?"

"Yes, why not?"

He rubbed his lips with his finger, absorbed in thought. "Fine. I guess I'll have to figure out something else, but in the meantime, make sure she doesn't figure it out. I don't want her leaving the cabin. Understood?"

My insides turned to stone, and the restraint was painful as I chose my next words. "Hello?" I interjected, hoping my timing wasn't too precise. "I'm still here."

"Yes, Lux, we know. *Everybody* knows."

The rock melted back into lava. "What's that supposed to mean?" I put my hands on my hips, ready to challenge his criticism.

"It means you are loud, destructive, don't know your place in life, and have a general disrespect for authority."

I gasped. "I do not!" Then lowered my tone, because I didn't want to prove his point. "You know nothing about me."

He smirked and stalked into the room. "Let me guess. You're privileged, your father is probably some sort of influential man on your island from the way you carry yourself, but you still lack the self-confidence to actually lead. Your misplaced superiority is probably from the fact that you are delusional about your lot in life. *And* you're impulsive and have anger issues."

"Oh really?" I ground my teeth together, fighting the urge to do something like slap him, but then again, that would prove he was right about me being impulsive and having anger issues. *Damn it.*

"And what about you? You're the one who thinks he is better than everyone else, but all I can see is a pathetic, lonely *thief!*"

Ahmed tiptoed away. "I, ah, need to go check on the rice pudding I left on the fire."

"No," Draven and I yelled in unison.

"I'm tired of arguing with you. I'm going outside one way or the other." My glance drifted to the open window.

"I knew you weren't smart, but I didn't know you were suicidal."

I glared at him. "So now you're calling me dumb? Well, add it to your list of insults. Just move out of my way."

"I'll be glad to." Draven appeared unconcerned. "Go ahead and walk out there." He waved his hand with indifference. "My crew thinks you have been possessed. They have been waiting for me to step aside so they can get you off the ship. I heard them say something about how eating a person would be the only way to get rid of a *jinni*. Isn't that right, Ahmed?"

Ahmed continued looking at his shoes.

I smiled. Draven was trying to call my bluff. He knew I had heard the tales of pirate cannibalism. He thought I would be afraid. What he didn't know was that I spoke Arabic.

"I come from a small island. I'm used to men and their tempers, and I can handle your crew just fine. I think I'll take my chances." I stepped past him, resisting the urge to flip my hair in his face.

"Lux..." he called behind me.

The warmth of the sun and the salty breeze hit my skin at the same moment. It made it worth turning my back on the wrathful captain.

I walked over to the rail, remembering the last time I was here, when Lilou and Ahmed went overboard. Blinking the images of violent sea creatures out of my mind, I concentrated on the roaring blue-white waters below.

Someone's arms wrapped tightly around my waist and my heart stopped, but the arms were small. I turned with a smile.

"Lilou." I pressed my cheek to the top of her head while returning her hug.

"I knew you would save me; you'll save all of us."

I laughed. "I've missed you too."

Her lips pouted. "Why are you staying in that big room? A woman said that's where the captain sleeps and he was locking you in there. Everyone is let out of the cages now. Why can't you sleep in our room? It's really nice."

I tucked a strand of wayward hair behind my ear. "I—"

"Come on, Lilou. We should get back to the cabin

for lunch." An older replica of Lilou gripped her hand.

"This is my big sister, Kileigh."

"Nice to meet you. I'm Lux." I smiled at Kileigh, but she pulled me into a hug, squeezing even tighter than Lilou. *Can't. Breathe.*

"I just want to thank you," she said, finally letting go.

"You don't have to do that. Really." My heart warmed as Lilou innocently tossed crumbs of bread over the side of the ship. I turned back to Kileigh. "She's helped me more than she'll ever know."

"I wouldn't have been able to live with myself if something happened to her." She exhaled a shaky breath. "I didn't know she was on board until after the storm. It was my fault she was taken in the first place. I had been out by the water late at night; she had just come to look for me. She would have never been taken if I would have just stayed home."

Lilou clapped the last of the crumbs off her hands and turned her attention back to us. "Did you hear? We get to go home. We all get to go home."

I forced a smile, not having the heart to correct her of the fact that not *everyone* would be going home.

"Let's leave Lux alone now, Lilou." She pulled her sister away, but she turned back to me one last time. "Shaman Tamati wanted me to give you a message." Her lowered voice hinted a secret. Was it time already? My heart sped up, and I turned my ear toward her. "He said whatever you are doing is working. The captain's been unfocused, and they were able to secure some weapons. Keep it up. They will be ready to mobilize shortly."

Holding onto my breath, I nodded.

"And Lux? It all worked out though, don't you think? Maybe it was destiny. Thank you again."

I said goodbye to them, turning my thoughts away

from destiny and back toward the horizon. I sighed. If it was destiny, it was ironic. Ironic that Draven seemed to know me better than anyone. He saw me for what I was. My parents, the people on my island—they all saw me as the ideal daughter, the ideal citizen, always helping others. But Draven was right; I was selfish and that was why I was at the shore that night—to run away. I was paying for that now, *the damned irony.* I'd gotten just what I was looking for. The open seas, *freedom.* Just not the way I'd planned. And not with the ending I had in mind either.

I squeezed my hands into fists, running the pads of my fingers over the calluses, scars, and splinters that resulted from building the stupid boat.

The smell of clover and smoke crept into my nose. Noticing someone on my left, I turned. A man in baggy clothes with sun-drenched skin was leaning over the railing, inhaling from a small rolled paper.

"Those will kill you, you know." I was still in a bad mood.

He didn't seem as startled by my presence as I was by his. "So I've heard. Besides, you know it's not real tobacco."

I sighed.

"I'm just surprised I haven't turned to stone yet."

My temper eased, and I fought a laugh. "It's still early, and why aren't you trying to kill me like the rest of the crew?"

"They're all idiots."

"Tell me something I don't know. And led by the idiotist idiot of them all." *Is idiotist idiot even a word?* Right. Draven was touchy about titles. We would have to call him *Captain* Idiot.

"The captain is no idiot."

"Oh, really?" I turned, seeing him for the first time.

He was much older than I originally assumed. His

skin was leathery and his hair, nearly white, was tied back. A tattoo was etched on the nape of his neck. It was a single hand above two crossed swords. Where the palm should be, there was an eye. I'd seen the very same one before, but this time, it was in a flag.

"What *does* that tattoo mean?"

He was looking at me now, as if for the first time as well. "Why do you ask?"

It was the same symbol I had seen replicated in several places in Draven's cabin. I half expected it to be a family crest or symbol from his old life. I didn't expect it to be answered with another question. "I've seen the same one in Dra—your captain's cabin, so I just want to know if it means anything."

He flicked some burning ash overboard. "It means something all right. *The captain*, huh?"

"I like the evasive thing you got going on; it really works for you."

"Aye. I'm just a seadog, but I've been told mystery is part of my charm. Besides, some things are better left untold." He laughed, his eyes gentle. "You don't come from the same place as the rest of the people you came aboard with."

"No. No, I do not." I pushed my lips together. *Way to point that out, buddy.* "I was *trying* to go back home when I was kidnapped."

"And where's that?"

"The United States."

"Yer a long way from home then."

"Got that. But I'll get there. I found a way before, and I'll find a way again."

"What if you couldn't go home? Would you move on then?"

I stepped back. Who was this guy? "Why would I need to move on? I didn't belong on the island. My history, my culture, it's not the same."

"The world *you* knew wasn't always that way."

"What do you mean?"

"People in your land didn't just appear there. They came from different places. They made a new home, and in the process, made a new culture because of it."

"Why are you telling me this?" I was fascinated by his history lesson, but I didn't see how any of it had to do with me moving on.

He slapped the railing with his palm. "Ye can claim a new land, too. Ya don't have to go back to something just because you think that's where ya ought to be or where you'd fit in. Ye say you're American, but I see something else in ya. Ye remind me of the story. Different cultures, different languages, which came together. Savvy?"

Was he talking about my father? He had always insisted I took after my mother. Even though he taught me Arabic, we lived like any other Americans. We even took my mother's maiden name, Aiello, and my father always went by Ray instead of Rayan.

I had never thought much about my heritage. My father said my grandparents had died at a young age, but what of his cousins and uncles?

I never thought about it like that. I was half my father and had a right to be as Middle Eastern as he was American. Could I belong to another world? And even if I could, what would I choose? I let out a shaky breath.

"Ye wanna know something damn funny that Sokum did today?"

"What's that?" I smiled, relieved he'd changed the subject.

I laughed as he told me about Sokum's mishap and then talked for a while more. He told me about sailing and we chuckled together at stories of mishaps at sea. A handful of the crew emerged from below deck or stopped their chores to join us. They seemed different in the light, so normal as we listened together to an old seaman's tales. My soul felt lighter. The warm, salty breeze allowed feeling carefree much easier. It was why I didn't stop myself when I knew I was slipping into the unfamiliar territory like I had with Ahmed. Instead, I made chairs from the stack of crates, and they begged me for information about the island life. Of what it was like to be settled down. Little did they know I longed for the very life they lived. Everyone, it seemed, wanted what they didn't have. *The water is always bluer on the other side.* Well, that wasn't how the saying went, but it worked anyway. It was these realizations that made me uncomfortable and want to go back to the distraction of laughing at their jokes.

I raised my hand in the air to protest. "No more about Sirbiad. I want to hear the story about Sokum getting all tangled in the rigging again." An unfamiliar ache formed in my gut from laughing. It wasn't at all terrible but rather freeing. It had been a while since I had laughed that much.

"Get back to work. The ship doesn't sail on its own." Draven dispersed the group quicker than I could beg them not to go. My laughter died, but the after affects remained. I wasn't about to let Draven ruin my good mood.

The old man nodded once at Draven and turned to leave. He paused. "Lux?"

"Yes?" I lifted my head, smiling.

"Think about what I told you about your people. And remember, all stories have a meaning; you just have to figure out the riddle."

My eyebrows furrowed but before I could ask questions, he was out of sight and only Draven remained. I faced him, already bored with what insults he would say to me now. My lips parted. Droplets of sea had sprayed his cheek and his hair was loose again. I stared at it, wondering what it would be like to run my fingers through it. He tossed it back, looking almost uncomfortable. I tore my gaze away, my face in flames.

He cleared his throat. "I let you outside for a moment and you have my whole crew at your feet."

I snorted. "You're just jealous."

"Of course I am. Now go back to the cabin. We have dinner plans, *remember?*"

His revelation left me speechless and unable to argue with him or at the very least come up with a witty response. I walked away, his words replaying in my head. I had only been joking, and he admitted he was jealous. Turning back to him, I spoke the truth. "You are *so* confusing."

Chapter Nine

"The essence of all experiences in love is that we don't love when we choose to, and we don't choose to when we love."
-Abbad Mahmoud Al-Akkad

"LAST CHANCE TO BACK OUT..." I TAUNTED HIM.

"Never." Draven used my words, his cultured tone clipped.

"So, let's get this over with." I purposely sat at his end of the dining table. What was he going to do about it?

He tilted his head.

Maybe he *was* going to do something about it. My face fell, my cheeks felt droopy. But then he just shook his head in wonder, shrugged off his coat, and sat at the other end.

Not the reaction I expected, but... "Why did you want to have dinner with me?"

"Like I said, I wanted to see just how Leif does it." He gave me a wicked smile.

"Seriously?" I crossed my arms.

He sighed, but he didn't answer.

Add it to the list of things I would never know the truth about—

"I don't know; I just thought it would be nice."

Whoa. His response wasn't cruelly spoken. It was sincere and completely unlike him. *Shaman Tamati said that the captain had been unfocused. Could that be because of... me?*

My heart skipped a beat. No, that wouldn't do at all. I had a plan, and that plan was to get off this ship and help my people. It didn't include falling for the enemy. I knew enough to know he saw me as a challenge. And something told me he didn't like to lose. Besides, he was cocky and conniving and confusing. *Well, not at this very moment.*

I was already softening up to the crew, which wasn't going to make it easy when we took the ship. *Oh, no.* What if I softened up to him, too?

My throat tightened and started to feel like I swallowed a sea urchin whole. I needed to stop that from happening at all costs. I needed to hate him. You couldn't warm up to someone when you're fighting with them all the time...

A knock sounded at the other end of the room. I didn't need to turn to know Ahmed had come with the food.

"I'm strangely disappointed." I was proud of the air of boredom I added to my scripted words.

"Really? How so?"

"Dinner in your cabin again? How unoriginal."

"Didn't know I had to impress you—"

"You don't," I corrected him. "But Leif would have."

His jaw clenched. "I'm sick of talking about Leif."

Ahmed served the food without a word. The plates were set a little harsher than necessary. He spun out of the room before he could hear my thank you. *What'd I do?* I frowned. I wasn't as pleased as I hoped at the tension between us.

"So, tell me what you know." I got right to the point.

Draven took a bite and chewed slowly. Sensually. Suddenly, I was thirsty.

I took a sip of water, cleared my throat, and asked him again.

"Tell me about you first. There will be time for that later."

"Me? Why?" I blinked rapidly as if that would help me understand.

"Tell me about your life on your island. What do you like to do?"

Again, what were his motives? Did he just want to know how boring my life was so he could brag about his life at sea? I rubbed my forehead, too worn out to try to figure out his game, so I chose to be honest. He could do what he wanted with the information after that.

"Well, there's not much to tell. Sirbiad is probably just as boring and miserable as any other place in this godforsaken world."

"It's your home."

"It's not my home," I quickly amended. "It's my island, it's where I live, and I care about it, but it will never be my home."

"Still holding onto things past?"

His smoldering gaze made more words spill from my mouth. "A home has a bed. I sleep in a hammock." His eyes darted to his own bed, and then back at me.

I shifted in my chair. "But hammocks are comfortable," I squeaked out, then swiped my tongue over my teeth and focused on my plate.

"Tell me more," he encouraged. I blew out a frustrated breath. *Don't answer him.* But when I looked into his eyes, they were bright with genuine curiosity.

I described to him what our house looked like. He asked me if we had an education system, and I told him about the small library my mother started and the books we collected. The same books I read over and over and over again. I told him about my best friend who was humorously afraid of water and since he didn't want me talking about Leif again, I left his name out. Finally, I told him about the shore where our people were stolen from. Where *he* stole me from.

"So your father is the mayor of your island?"

"Yes..." I dragged the word out in several syllables and clenched my fists. But I wasn't annoyed as I usually was when someone brought that up. *My parents.* My stomach twisted, feeling violently ill like the one time I was so hungry I ate spoiled fish. I never planned on missing them this much. Who cared if my father was mayor? I was sick of it! Tired of his position putting me in the spotlight my entire life.

He laughed as he lifted the cup to his mouth to take a drink. "Something tells me that doesn't make you happy."

"No, it's not that..." I hesitated, torn by conflicting emotions. "It's just that being the mayor's daughter isn't me. It's not about who I am. Even if I wanted to be that person, I don't think I could." But it was who my father was. My father had always been a leader, with his job as a politician in the US and now with Sirbiad. He was a natural. He enjoyed it. Why should that bother me? Wow, had I really been looking at it the wrong way all this time? *How does Draven do that?* My eyes shot up to meet his.

His stare drilled into me.

"I don't know why we keep talking about this. This dinner was about you giving me answers."

"Our deal was that you would eat with me; I see none of that happening on your end."

"Fine." I picked up my fork and took the smallest bite of saffron rice as dramatically as I could. "Happy?"

"No." He set down his cup.

Wood scraped wood in a sharp, pitched sound. Draven placed his linen napkin next to his plate and stood. He was leaving? *Good.* Agreeing to this dinner was a stupid idea, anyway. He picked up his coat and walked over to the window.

Wait a second—I should be the one who gets to walk away. "Where are you going?" Heat filled me. I pushed my chair back, screeching it against the floorboards, and threw my napkin on the table. I stomped over to him. He studied the moon-glistened water with more attention than seemed warranted.

I blinked away traitorous thoughts and searched around, trying to find something else—*anything else*—to focus my attention on. My eyes stilled on a sparkle of light out the window. "The sea is beautiful at night," I said to myself, stepping next to him to peer out the window.

His penetrating gaze shifted to me before looking back outside, but he took a step closer and I could feel his armor against my back. "There's an old story about how the night came from the sea," he purred into my ear. I froze. He was so close to me it was almost... intimate.

The wind blew through the opening, and the scent of leather and sea spray intoxicated me. The fresh scent of Draven. I inhaled deeply, the smell turning my insides upside-down. I turned my head to glance at him over my shoulder. "I love stories," I told him in a whisper.

Draven's eyes narrowed at the ocean, as if he was silently debating with himself. I studied his profile in the moonlight, wondering why he looked different to me. When my eyes rested on his full lips, they parted and he spoke again. "An ancient Brazilian legend said there used to be only daylight on earth. The sun never set and the earth never saw the darkness of night."

He peered down at me, searching my expression, and then exhaled. "Lemanja, the Goddess of the Sea, had a daughter. Together, they lived peacefully in the deep, dark depths of the sea. Lemanja loved the darkness and loved the water. But her daughter didn't know if she felt the same way. She didn't know if she liked the dark shadows. In turn, she didn't know if she could be the goddess' daughter."

"So what did she do?" I hungered for more.

"One day, she went ashore and she fell in love with a man. They got married and lived in happiness above the sea—"

"That's it? Happily Ever After?" I liked this story.

"No. Not quite. Soon, Lemanja's daughter thought the sunlight was too bright for her. Although she loved the mortal, she became homesick. She wished for the dark world under the sea. Lemanja granted her daughter's wish and sent her a cool, dark blanket that covered the world. She called it night. And now on earth, we have day and we have night." The smile he finished with told me there were memories attached to the legend.

How charming he was when he let his guard down. Like I was the only one in the world who had seen him like this. An irrational protectiveness came over me. I really wanted to be the *only* one who got to see him like this.

I turned back to the ocean. "That's a beautiful story." The world seemed to slow down, and my chest ached. I wanted to know more about the daughter's story. I wanted to know if her family was okay with her never returning to the sea. Didn't they miss her? And how did she know she was making the right decision? Didn't her sea people need her?

"You're beautiful," Draven said suddenly.

I spun to face him. "What?" I asked breathlessly.

How could he say such a thing?

His azure eyes were warm and lidded with desire. "I said you are beautiful, Lux. You are the most beautiful girl I have ever seen." A delicate touch on my cheek sent an exhilarating shiver through my body as he swept back a piece of hair that had blown loose from the breeze.

His gaze searched mine before settling on my lips. My breathing increased.

He wanted to kiss me.

But that didn't make any sense. Why would he want to do that?

The millions of questions soaring through my mind didn't matter. My body warmed like I was wading in the ocean when a sun-warmed wave poured over me. My forehead creased. *Oh, what is that feeling?* It wasn't a bad feeling. Just a new one. A shifting in my chest that sent my nerve endings tingling.

He wanted to kiss me, and I was going to let him.

He would probably do something bad if I didn't... Well, that was the excuse I gave myself anyway, and one I would tell if anyone ever found out. I closed my eyes and leaned in.

What are you doing, Lux? My eyelashes fluttered, my sense fighting to return.

"Do you want me to kiss you?" His gaze was still on my lips, and his thumb swept across the line of my jaw to cup my chin. *Yes.* God yes, I wanted him to.

Don't let him see it—don't let him see it. Don't let him see how he affects you. "N-no." It was hard to say the word when my body was screaming *"Yes." Shut up.* "No." There. That sounded more confident.

His smile returned, revealing a perfect set of white teeth and a purring laugh that could win any resistant girl over. "Yes, you do."

His arrogance astounded me, and the passion

turned to anger. "No, I don't." It was then I remembered when he said he was just bored.

The feelings had washed away.

The spell had broken.

What was I thinking? Roughly, I thrust away from him.

"Why can't you just admit what you want?" He stalked me, and I backed into the wall.

"Because I don't want anything from *you.*" I placed my palms flat against the wood behind me.

"Then *prove* it," he murmured. "If you are so certain you feel nothing for me, then what's one kiss if it's without desire?"

He inched forward, his mouth brushing slowly against mine. It was a chaste, achingly incomplete kiss. When my lips parted in response, a noise came deep from his throat. I whipped my head away, angry with myself for responding to him.

Out of my peripherals, Draven's eyes opened and his breathing leveled. "Are you always this cold?" he snarled.

"I told you no." His comment didn't wound me; my skin had become as thick as his leather armor.

"I didn't see you putting up much of a fight when I tried to kiss you."

My mind was spinning. He was right. I had punched him in the eye and tried to kill him once—at least only once so far. I had been trained to cause crippling pain by using any of the eighteen pressure points. I could have done a lot worse than just turn away. The fact that he was right didn't anger me as much as the fact it meant my resolve was slipping.

He was staring at me again.

My hand reached for my necklace, only to remember it was no longer there.

And it was all his fault.

Draven's eyes flickered when they followed my hand to my chest. The anger returned me to the comfortable place of hating him, and I twisted my head away so I wouldn't have to look at him.

"Is this what you want? Is this why you hate me so much?" He fished something out of an inner pocket. A shimmering gold chain dangled from his hand.

Heart failure.

My necklace!

He grabbed my wrist and pushed the chain into my palm.

I finally could breathe again.

"How? I saw you drop it in the ocean."

Draven smirked. "Did you now? Is that really what you saw?" He picked up a spoon from the table and held it out the porthole, just like he held my necklace over the water. He dropped the spoon and walked back over to me. "Haven't you ever heard of pirate magic?" he said as the spoon appeared back in his hands. It was nothing but a slight of the hand. He had played me once again.

I clasped my necklace tightly in my hand. "Y-you..." My brain wasn't functioning, and my body couldn't decide whether to be happy to have my necklace back or angry that he had tricked me.

I settled on angry.

"How could you do that to me?" I pressed a hand to my heated face. "Never mind. I know exactly how you could do that. It's nothing to you. It's just a part of who you are. You... you... pirate! You thought you could just give me back *my* necklace and all would be forgiven? I *hate* you!"

"Because of that damn necklace? You were going to let one of my men die because of your stubbornness. It was that or his life."

I was not! And I didn't have a choice. I had just

been kidnapped, and I needed to use what I could to survive. "Just get out!"

"This is my cabin. You are sleeping in *my* bed, remember?" He grabbed my wrist. I tried to pull away, and his hand tightened.

"Bastard." I yanked my arm out of his grasp.

"I never said I wasn't. You should know that now." His laugh was just evil enough to prove it.

I clasped my arms over my chest as if to shield myself. "Yes, thank you again for reminding me. For a second, I actually thought of you as a real person. Now move so I can leave this room and not have to sleep in *your* bed!"

His features twisted.

Frozen in place, I waited for him to step out of the way.

"No." The word was barely audible as he stared at the floor.

"No what?" I dreaded hearing the answer, but then I felt a shift in energy and no longer feared for myself.

Draven turned away and I thought he would leave without saying a word, but he paused mid-stride. With his head still turned, he ran a hand through his hair and closed his eyes. "You may stay here. I'll leave."

I let out the breath I was holding.

His eyes flashed open, devoid of anger. I found it more chilling than when he snarled at me. He walked to the door, and I thought he uttered an apology behind him as he disappeared. But I couldn't be certain. He had never apologized for anything, and I wasn't sure why he would start now. The creak of wood and click of metal as the door closed sounded final.

My shoulders sagged. Remembering the necklace in my hand, I opened my palm and studied it. It had been in his pocket this entire time. I put it back on, slowly securing the clasp in the back. I touched it

where it rested over my heart. Cold against my skin.
It didn't make me feel whole again like I thought it
would.

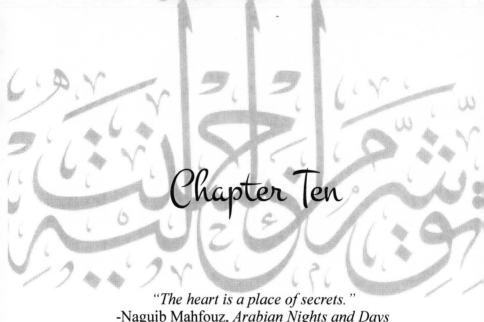

Chapter Ten

"The heart is a place of secrets."
-Naguib Mahfouz, *Arabian Nights and Days*

THE FIRST RAYS OF SUNRISE CAME THROUGH THE PORT window, and I awoke, restless and skin tingling. The humidity made it impossible to sleep. I threw my feet over the bed and stomped over to the window, hoping for a cool sea breeze. The wind was calm and warm with a smell like wet stones. Rain was coming.

I looked at the position of the sun and then back to the door. Why hadn't Ahmed come in yet? With a frown, I used the last of my water to wash away the heat and then flopped back on the bed.

There was *nothing* to do.

I chewed on my lip angrily at the thought of being completely dependent on another person for the simplest of needs. Releasing my lip in mercy, I stared at the beams on the ceiling. It was *too* quiet in his cabin. The creak of wood as the ship rolled made it seem even more so. I needed something, but I didn't know what. Food, sleep, something to read. Maybe all three.

The decks were probably bustling with crew preparing for the rain. Which probably meant Ahmed wouldn't be coming for a while or when he did, he

126

couldn't stay. *Wonderful.* I would be alone all day. *Alone.*

Wasn't that what I always wanted on Sirbiad? Peace and quiet. Privacy. No training or tutoring. Exactly what I was experiencing?

A familiar knock rapped on the door, and all my previous thoughts were forgotten.

I shot up with a smile. "Come in." The door popped open, and my eyes darted down to adjust my clothes that were ruffled from bed. "Ahmed! I'm so happy to see you; I wanted to tell you—"

My smile died as Draven walked in. He fumbled with the tray Ahmed usually carried. Ahmed *had* made his duties look so effortless. I continued sitting on the corner of the bed, watching him. Liquid spilled from the goblets as he set the tray on the table. I brought a hand to my mouth to smother a giggle. It was so unnatural I wanted to stop him.

He turned, and I half expected his glare. "How lucky Ahmed is to be in your favor. If I didn't know him better..." He let his words drift off.

"What are you doing?" I asked two questions in one—what was *he* doing bringing me breakfast and what was he *doing* bringing me breakfast.

He only answered one of them. "I thought we could eat together. Ahmed was all too eager to switch duties with me." There was a ghost of a smile on his lips. Draven walked toward me, stopping right in front of where I sat on his bed. I didn't like looking up at him, so I stood and tilted my chin up. *See, you can kiss me senseless and I'm still not intimidated by you.*

He smirked. "Lux..."

The way he said my name quickened my heart. It wasn't a warning, or a reprimand, but a surrender. I needed to think of something to change this conversation. Fast.

"I just wanted to apologize for last night."

Draven *apologizing?* That was unlike him. How was I supposed to hate him if he expressed such regret?

As if thinking my silence was a signal for him to elaborate, he continued. "I shouldn't have been so rough with you."

"It's not like I can't take care of myself," I interrupted.

"I know, but you didn't want me to kiss you,"

Hm. That seemed more like a question than a statement. I sank my teeth into my lower lip. There was a big difference between what I wanted to do and what I thought I was supposed to do.

"But I just wanted you. I wanted you *so* badly." He ran a hand through his hair as he got out the words.

I let my eyes wander around the room, how was I supposed to keep my guard up when he tried to behave so tenderly?

Draven let his arm drop and took a step closer. My eyes snapped back to him, and my lips parted in a gasp. He brushed the hair from my temple before holding my face in his palms. His hands were rough, yet warm, and I couldn't help but relish the feeling of someone touching me. He let out a tortured sigh as my face instinctively turned to nuzzle his palm. His thumb caressed my lips, and I found myself, wishing it were his mouth.

"Draven, I can't," I said, surprised by my spoken thought.

He turned his head away as if I slapped him. "Why not?" He spoke in an odd, yet gentle tone.

Like he had to ask. "Because you're the bad guy and I'm *not* supposed to have feelings for you."

At my rushed words, he closed the distance between us. Our lips met as he gave me a punishing kiss.

One hand went to the back of my head while the other went to my waist, pulling me against him. The metal and leather of his armor dug into my soft skin and didn't feel terrible at all. Shocked at the warmth that spread through me, I slid my hands down to his chest and pushed him back, breaking the kiss as rudely as he took it. I hardened my heart, knowing that every act of compassion toward me was countered by cruelty toward someone else.

In turn, he leaned back to me, giving me a surprisingly gentle kiss on each corner of my mouth before settling his lips on mine again. My lips parted to feel his tongue, but, instead, he took my bottom lip between his teeth, tugging gently.

When he let me go, something like loss flashed in his eyes. I couldn't form one coherent thought, let alone a word.

⟡

I couldn't believe Draven kissed me. *No.* It was all just part of his game. He was probably enjoying my torture and confusion. Here I was, supposed to be distracting him, yet he was the one distracting me. It wasn't enough to keep me away from the other prisoners; he was trying to make me fall for him so I would be under his control. Well, there was no way I would let that happen. *No way.*

After Draven left me alone in the cabin, with nothing to do, I went to bed early that night. A fitful sleep awaited me. I tossed and turned, my limbs feeling like they were crawling with fire ants. Finally, with an irritated exhale, I sat up in bed. The oil lamps had long ago been extinguished, and I squinted in the darkness. The moon was high, indicating that it was, in fact, the middle of the night. I walked toward the window.

I cursed the moon, determining it was my cause of restlessness. It had waned further, and there was hardly a sliver of crescent left. Time that I couldn't afford to lose was ticking by, and I had no idea how much of our journey we had left. I felt so far away from everything. My journey to the US was reduced to merely a dream and nothing more. The vast open sea was a relief to the overly familiar scenery of Sirbiad. I felt free, yet trapped at the same time.

I ignored the nagging inside of me and attempted to navigate the dark to find the glass and pitcher of water Ahmed left earlier.

I let out a yelp when I tripped over the leg of Draven's chair.

And then the leg moved.

I shot off the ground, the blood draining from my face. The chair was breathing. *Oh my God, someone is in the room.* Maybe one of the crew? Sokum? I scrambled the papers on top of Draven's desk, searching for something to defend myself with. *Calm down, Lux. If he were going to harm you, he would have already done so.* He was watching me sleep, then. What kind of sick—

"Would you cease that annoying clatter? I'm trying to get some rest."

I gasped, instantly wide awake. *Draven.*

"What are you doing in here?" I whispered, my tone harsh and accusing.

"In *here*? It's *my* cabin."

I squinted through the darkness. "You've been sleeping in here?"

He scoffed with disdain. "Where do you expect me to sleep—in a hammock with the crew? I'm the captain."

I considered my options. All of which sounded exhausting at this time of night. "Just... just stay on your side of the room. And don't get any ideas." I made my way back to the bed, bumping into the chest on the way. *Smooth, real smooth.* I gritted my teeth as I gripped my shin and hopped on one foot the remaining distance.

His laughter cut through the room. It was deep, rich, and warm, and it could make a blind woman swoon. "My *side*? Oh, Lux. You're so disillusioned."

I crawled back under the sheets, pulling them to my chin in modesty despite the darkness. "Whatever. Just go back to sleep."

"I can't now that you've woken me in such a manner. *You* go back to sleep."

"I'm not going back to sleep. I got up for a reason."

"Fine."

"Fine."

A pregnant silence filled the air.

"Draven?"

"Hmm?"

I turned on my side, propping myself up on my elbow to face him despite only seeing a silhouette. It was easier that way for what I was about to ask. "Tell me another story. Like the one about Lemanja." I didn't want to fight, and I hoped he could hear that in my voice.

His shadow straightened. "If I do, will you sleep?"

"Sure." *Not.* I didn't bother hiding the lie in my voice.

He sighed. "You're insatiable."

"Tell me what your home was like. You were from the Middle East, correct?"

He paused. "What do you think happened to the world, Lux?"

"I was told everything that wasn't burned to ash is now underwater except for a few islands in the South Pacific. But honestly, who knows if *everywhere* was

131

destroyed," I said cynically, thinking about the US.

"That's why you want to know about the other islands so badly..."

I fell silent, debating whether I should ask him and risk him shutting down again. "So, where did you live?"

I heard him adjust his position in the chair. "In a huge, white building. All of my family lived there. My father and his brothers and sisters and all the children. It was designed by my grandfather, who helped build it with his own hands. He wanted our family to be kept together, and he wanted to build a... home that would be the pinnacle of our family throughout generations."

"That sounds wonderful." My own family was small and our extended family was distant.

"Everyone had their own wing of the house. The main areas were made with the finest marble, stucco ceilings, and the walls were adorned with tiles in turquoise, teals, and sapphires. As was the fountain and dipping pool in the courtyard. The rooftop terrace was my favorite though. I spent hours there as a boy gazing up at the constellations and planets."

I thought about where my father had lived when he was born, before he came to the US as a young boy. Why hadn't I ever asked him about that part of his life before? Maybe it was because I never thought of it as being a part of his life. I pictured Draven's house and what I knew about the Middle East. I could picture myself there. "I bet it was beautiful." I yawned and laid my head back on the feathered pillow. Outside the window, rain slowly fell from the sky.

"It is. Except for the infuriating monkey that also lives there." He laughed at his own musings. "My grandmother owns a small monkey. She calls it a pet; I call it a pest."

I giggled. "Why? It didn't get along with anyone?"

"No, Muuse got along with everyone, but he *loathed* me."

"He hated you? How dare he?" I gasped in mock indignation.

"You laugh, but I can assure you, he is a real nuisance!"

"I bet he was an adorable little thing." My voice was suddenly husky from sleep. "Tell me more." I let my eyes drift closed as I listened to his soothing, soft voice mixed with the gentle pitter-patter of rain against the ship.

"I can only assume this rivalry started years ago when I refused to give him a piece of my fruit. Ever since, the blasted creature has hated me. I just refuse to spoil him like everyone else does."

A bemused smile curved my lips.

"Lux?"

My eyelids were too heavy to try to open them. "Mm-hmm?"

"Goodnight, *amira*." His whisper drifted into my unconsciousness. That night, I dreamt of a beautiful mosaic-tiled fountain, a cute monkey who stole bananas, and a welcoming family.

Chapter Eleven

RAIN POURED UPON THE SHIP AND EVERYONE EXCEPT the crew was to remain off deck. The cabin was locked, and I made no attempts to get out. Thinking about the waves and slippery wood followed by what had happened with Lilou and Ahmed, I reluctantly obliged. I hoped Shaman Tamati knew what he was doing. During the day, I saw no one except for Ahmed as he brought me things in passing. At night, however, I would wake up to find Draven resting in the chair. Draven was absent during the day. He claimed it was especially important for him to monitor the direction of the ship so we weren't set back any more days then we already were. He said the crew at the helm were brainless and couldn't be trusted to keep us on course. He could only allow a few hours of rest each night. This particularly disturbed me as he spent those few hours talking with me until I fell asleep. Every night, in the pitch blackness of his cabin, we talked. While Draven told me stories, I gathered as much information as I could. Draven explained to me, with all the patience he could gather, the mechanics of the ship and of his—and my father's—homeland.

The moon was hidden by rain clouds. If it weren't for me meticulously keeping track of the days, I could have thought I spent months on the ship. Had Shaman Tamati changed his mind? Did something happen? When would he give me the signal so we could make our move? I needed to know how much more I would have to hold out. I didn't want time to go on because I didn't want to get to know Draven better. Each day, he was becoming less cruel and his touches were more frequent, and more lingering. Something had changed. It didn't happen all at once. The change must have been gradual but now, when I thought about what we were planning behind his back, I was worried. I wanted to prove myself wrong. Wanted Draven to be incapable of this tenderness. Wanted to believe he really was the enemy. Wanted to believe it didn't feel like betrayal.

On the sixth day, I woke to clear skies. Trying the cabin door, I found it unlocked and walked freely into the sunshine. A creeping feeling of surprise and dread came over me. Draven trusted me? What did it mean? I almost preferred his anger. At least I knew what he was feeling.

Outside, I willed myself not to look for him and searched elsewhere for a distraction. The main deck was once again filled with people. I was glad to see I recognized some of the crew and happily picked up where we left off days ago. I had eaten every meal alone in the cabin. The food alone was something new, and having time, and privacy, was something different altogether. After being inside for days, I wouldn't go back to the cabin even if they dragged me there with fishing hooks.

By midday, I was in a better mood after talking with Lilou, glad when she asked me to have lunch with her. I got in line with everyone else, and Lilou and I found a nice little corner to have a 'picnic' as she called it. Without the Sirbiad sand to cushion us, it would be nice to have something soft to lie out and sit on. A certain purple velvet cape I had found in Draven's closet would've been perfect. Whom it belonged to was another mystery as it was clearly female. *Careful, Lux. You're becoming too intrigued by him.*

I had the taste of warm bread in my mouth and was considering "borrowing" something of Draven's again when a voice called out, reverberating like an echo. It wasn't so much the words that were yelled, but the complete silence it caused around us that had captured my attention.

Another ship was approaching. I thought back to what Draven had said about other pirates. Ones *far less gracious* than he.

I took a few more bites before leaving Lilou and her sister. The need to walk around and see what I could eavesdrop on filled me. I needed to let the others know. We were not going to be caught unprepared again.

Draven and Ahmed stood several feet in front of me, talking in hushed tones. As I approached them, Draven turned with an irritated scowl.

Someone woke up on the wrong side of the chair.

"Lux, glad to see you're going back to *my* cabin." His possessive tone sent chills across my flesh.

"Actually, I *wasn't*," I said with a defiant *what-are-you-going-to-do-about-it* smile.

He let out an exasperated sigh, turning without a word toward the upper deck. I tilted my head to the side as I pondered what could put him in a bad enough mood to not argue with me. He paused at the stairs to give Ahmed a quick command before ascending. "Keep an eye on her."

Ahmed and I exchanged a knowing look. I pressed my lips together as my cheeks burned under his scrutiny.

"The sunlight suits you."

"I think it brings up everyone's spirits. Well, maybe not *every*one's." I shot a glance at Draven on the upper deck. "Can I help you with anything?" I rocked on my feet, eying the cloths in his hands.

"Trying to get information out of me again?" His gentle laugh rippled through the air. My cheeks flushed, and I bit my lip. I had no idea I could be so easily read.

"I can assure you my intentions were unselfish, but since I'm helping you prepare for someone to come aboard, you could tell me why. And perhaps for *whom*."

"I'm afraid to say no."

"I always knew you were smarter than you let on."

"It's helpful to know I don't act as smart I should."

My eyes widened until they ached. "I didn't mean... It was a—"

Ahmed let out a boyish laugh. "I was jesting! My English isn't completely hopeless. I know a joke when I hear one."

I let out a breath of relief. "Ahmed!" I nudged his shoulder with my own and fought against the grin pulling at the corners of my mouth as we walked toward the crew's quarters. When we were alone in the galley, I nudged him again. "So spill," I commanded.

"I should say 'it's really nothing to be concerned about', but you wouldn't take that, would you?"

"Not when it means I get to know why Draven's scowling more than usual. Where are we going?" A desire to investigate shot through me as we ventured into an area of the ship I had never seen before.

"This is where I stay while I'm here."

Hm. Where did he stay when he was *not* here?

I nodded and took a quick look around. His room

was characteristically more colorful than Draven's. Middle Eastern influences splattered the room with lobster reds and bright oranges. A painting of a narrow street running through a town with ancient buildings and minarets hung on the far wall above a chest. Sepia portraits of stiff, unsmiling people in Islamic garb lined the top of the chest. I had no portraits of my own. My fingers itched to hold them and know their histories.

Ahmed set the sheets on the small, round table. He removed a beaded pillow from the varying mound atop the bed, and I rushed to help him set them in a neat pile on the floor.

"Who are we getting this room prepared for, Ahmed?" I asked while I worked on removing the sheets.

"Treymore."

"Treymore," I repeated, trying the foreign name out. "Is he a pirate, too?"

"Yes, he is definitely a pirate in the traditional sense of the word." Ahmed's lips curled inward, and he shook his head.

"Does he work for Asmodeus?" Then another question occurred to me. "Why does Draven not seem happy about seeing him?"

He angled his body away from me and raised a chocolate-colored eyebrow. I threw my hands up. "Last question, I swear."

"He took something of Draven's long ago."

In seeing my eyes widen in interest, Ahmed added, "Please don't make me tell you anymore. When it comes to you, I have been walking a very thin line. Having to come up with possible reasons how you knew my captain's full name was less than honest."

I blushed and decided to leave the subject alone.

He brushed back his brown hair with one hand.

"When the time comes, I'm going to have a lot of questions I expect answered."

"Of course," I added quietly while helping Ahmed put on the new, less colorful sheets.

We worked in silence as I helped move Ahmed's things to a downgraded room. The new cabin was bone bare, smaller, and had no windows. I felt a pang of guilt at the luxuries I had in Draven's cabin.

When we finished, I put my hands on my hips, feeling ashamed Ahmed had to give up his room to someone he didn't even like. "Is there anything else I can help you with?"

He laughed lightly, and it was a relief he didn't seem bothered by it. Actually, he never seemed bothered by anything. "No, I'm sure you wouldn't want to help me prepare his bath later."

Boom! The bump that hit the hull sent me stumbling and nearly knocked me off my feet. Ahmed raced out the door and I followed, ready to see just exactly who the new visitor was.

A smaller, modern sailboat bobbed next to us. Pirates climbed on board, a few of the stronger ones jumping across with authority. The new pirates dressed differently; their clothing was more colorful, in shades that brought to mind leaves falling in autumn. They were flowing, unlike the dark, armor-like clothes Draven's crew wore.

Once the new pirates came aboard and were satisfied, a walkway was set across the ships. The man we had all been preparing for took his first booted step onto the plank.

Could you dislike someone just from the way they walked? Yes. Yes, you could. He walked with an air of entitlement that he just couldn't pull off, not like Draven did. Every step was forced and more sinister than the last. When he was finally helped down, his red robe adjusted and his long hair combed back, I searched for Draven. He was notably absent from greeting the new visitor. I walked a few steps toward his cabin, to see if I could find him on the upper deck.

As I stopped in front of his cabin, he came down the stairs, at a pace all his own. Draven stared straight ahead. He held his hands together at his buckle, and his confident shoulders were lowered and loose. It was vastly different from the tense state he was in earlier. The new visitor walked toward us and stopped a few feet from him. Draven had failed to notice me. I felt uneasy coming between the two pirate lords, so I stepped away until I backed into the wooden door of the cabin.

"Draven." The man's goatee curled with his smile. "Look how much you've grown since the last time I saw you."

I wanted to rub my ears at the sound of his voice, which faltered at every word and failed at sounding ceremonial.

Draven's jaw had clenched before he managed, "Treymore." He smiled politely, but it wasn't genuine.

"Ah, well, I see you are not in the mood for formalities. No matter, I will take a rest until dinner. Hopefully by then, you will be less... cranky." He waved his hand about the air.

Treymore took a step toward Draven's cabin. I panicked and searched for an escape, but I found nowhere to go.

Draven intercepted him with nonchalance. "Your cabin is this way." He held out a hand to steer him toward Ahmed, who waited patiently to receive him.

Treymore looked appalled. "I'm a guest. Certainly you don't expect me to stay in one of the crew's cabins."

"The cabin is Ahmed's, who kindly relinquished

it for you, as I have other another guest staying in my chambers." Irritation harshened Draven's tone as he spoke the last words through clenched teeth.

"Really?" He straightened. His eyebrows furrowed and then his lips released, "Who?" He turned on his heel as he searched the crowd around us. Like an arrow meeting its target, his eyes, as black as his goatee, landed on me. His expression was calculating as he narrowed his gaze. "And who might this be? I'm disappointed Draven has failed to introduce us." He held out a thin hand in a feminine manner.

"I'm—"

Draven quickly cut me off. "Nobody. Now—" He took a hold of Treymore's shoulder. "Your cabin is *this* way."

Nobody! I was *nobody*? I took out my frustration by biting the inside of my bottom lip.

Treymore craned his head back. "But wait, I had yet the opportunity to ask if she'd like to join us for our meal."

"I'd love to," I replied.

"No," Draven said at the very same time.

I narrowed my eyes and tossed my hair over my shoulder.

Treymore clapped his hands together and let out a high laugh; clearly, he enjoyed taking part in something Draven didn't like. He stepped out of Draven's grasp toward me.

"Wonderful. It's settled then. We'll all dine together." As if he had a thought, he peered around the deck. "I don't know where we will eat though. This ship is so small. I suppose we will have to bring out some tables here." He waved his hand imperiously.

Draven glared at me. I swallowed hard, lifted my chin, and boldly met his gaze.

Treymore clasped his hands together. "Now,

where's my cabin?" He said it as if he was waiting the entire time.

Draven reluctantly turned on his heel and was gone.

Several sets of eyes bored into me, one of them Ahmed's.

Feeling him still behind me, I fidgeted with the knob to the cabin.

I strolled inside, then spun around to find Ahmed had followed me in. "What?" I asked as innocently as I could manage.

"I know what you are thinking."

"What's that?" I swallowed, but it was more like a gulp.

He crossed his arms. "You are thinking this new person presents opportunity. You are thinking this new person might be able to help you escape. If all else, you are thinking this new person will give you information that you could use."

My jaw dropped open at his accusation, but then snapped shut. He was right. That was exactly what I was thinking. *Kind of.*

"Actually, there was something I didn't like about Treymore from the second I saw him. So if I went to him for help, I would only be jumping from the frying pan to the fire. To be honest, yes, I am curious why Draven hates him so much, how they know each other, and why Treymore has a ship, but that is all. Does he work for Asmodeus, too?"

"Lux..." He said my name with a sigh. "Some secrets are not mine to tell. And although I consider you my friend..." His eyes were pleading. "If I tell you these things, I feel like I am betraying Draven, and betraying Draven I cannot."

My eyes widened. His loyalties really ran deep. I moistened my lips.

"I will be honest with you, Ahmed, as you have been nothing but open with me. I'm not sure when or even how, but at some point, I failed to see you as an enemy, but that applies to you and you alone. Draven, *especially* Draven, is a different story. I won't use you to get my information, but know that I *will* get it."

He shook his head, a slow, surprising smile coming across his face. "This is exactly why I think Draven has met his match."

"Don't say that!" I rushed over to shush him.

"I meant it in the most innocent way possible."

I cleared my throat, feeling incredibly foolish. "Of course you did." And I didn't know why that had bothered me so much. "Come get me when it's time for dinner?"

"If you wish..." Ahmed made his way to the door, the ghost of a smile still on his face.

<hr />

The sun had set long ago, and there was still no sign of Ahmed. A knot in my belly told me he would *never* be coming to fetch me. I stopped pacing and went to the door, relieved to find it unlocked so I wouldn't have to break it down, possibly with Draven's favorite chair. Popping my head out the door, I was immediately greeted by chattering voices and the glow of firelight. *Oh, that's it.* I pushed the door open. With a forced calm, I walked out to the deck.

"Oh goody! She made it. Draven, I thought you said she'd fallen ill?"

There was a makeshift table set for three in the middle of the deck. Ahmed poured water into Treymore's glass as he watched me approach the table. I shot him a wrathful look, but his eyes were apologetic. Of course it wasn't his fault.

I turned to Draven.

"Well, it looks like I've recovered." I took my seat at the table.

Treymore's eyes probed between us. "Wonderful."

Draven never took his eyes off me.

"Now, where were we?" Treymore tapped a slender finger to his lips, "Ah, yes. Amina, on the other hand, misses you dearly, so you know she says hello."

Amina? My heart suspended in my chest. Of course, he was a pirate *and* a liar!

I stole a glance at Draven. My breath caught in my lungs to find he still watched me. My eyes fell to my lap as I squirmed in my seat, wondering how much I'd given away in my expressions.

Ahmed first set a plate in front of me, followed by one in front of Treymore and Draven. The preparation was less intimate, and far more formal. It was unlike the other dinners I had shared with Draven, where we had many shared dishes arrayed on the table. I hated that I preferred eating that way.

Treymore picked up one of his forks and ate a bite with distaste. "Oh, these poor people. What do you feed them?"

"Ha!" I couldn't control my burst of laughter, bringing my hand up to stifle my giggles. I just couldn't help myself. Even if Treymore said it as an insult, there was no comparison between this food and what we had on Sirbiad.

Treymore's eyes widened in astonishment, and he gave me a sidelong glance as if I'd gone mad.

Draven gave me an irresistibly devastating smile that sent my pulse racing. The glow of his grin warmed me from across the table, infusing my body with heat at his approval. Something inside me, suspiciously like jealousy, wondered if he gave Amina that same smile.

I cleared my throat. "Sorry," I mumbled.

Treymore quickly shut his open mouth. "Some salt may improve it, hm?" He snapped his fingers at Ahmed, who pretended to ignore him.

Way to go, Ahmed!

I squirmed for the hundredth time under Draven's unwavering dark stare. He sat there, not speaking a word, just watching me. I had never felt so thoroughly *looked* at.

"Well, Draven," Treymore continued, a little agitated. "You should be pleased to know everything is managed better than before. My—"

"What do you want?" Draven had finally spoken. And in Arabic.

Treymore sat there with his mouth slightly open before he replied in the same language. "What do you care? I do what I please or have you forgotten?"

There were others who survived who could speak Arabic? How many more? Draven and Treymore were far more than acquaintances. Maybe they came from the same country. *Interesting.*

"No, I haven't forgotten, *Uncle*. Every day is a constant reminder of what you have taken from me."

Uncle?

Ahmed interrupted both the conversation and my thoughts. He matched their Arabic, "Captain, if you will, why don't you discuss this elsewhere?"

He glanced over his shoulder. "Why does it matter? No one can understand us."

Ahmed didn't reply, and I felt childishly giddy I would be able to hear more.

"The past is the past. Let's get to the present, shall we?" Treymore's eyes flicked to mine. "I see you're in no mood to negotiate, but I was just headed to Asmodeus. I'm willing to take the carrots the rest of the way for you."

Carrots? No, not carrots—he must have meant

people or slaves. Oh, what did that word translate to?

I was looking too thoughtful and turned to Ahmed. His arm bent at his side and his finger curled to slyly tell me to come with him.

Draven laughed, the sound hoarse and bitter, directing my attention back to the table. "This is *my* shipment, and I will deliver it. I'm sorry to say if that's why you've come, you are going to sail away *very* disappointed."

Ahmed cleared his throat in warning, and I was torn. He didn't want me to hear their conversation, and I suspected he knew something about me more than he let on. Would he expose me if I ignored him? With a huff, I set my napkin on the table, my chair noisily scooting back. "If you'll excuse me..." I interrupted their arguing in a language I wasn't supposed to understand.

"No, deary, I think you should stay." Treymore's previous playful, smug tone turned dangerous as cold fingers coiled around my wrist, stopping me midstride. Anger bubbled up, and my gaze narrowed at his unwelcomed hand touching me. *That's it—*

"Don't touch her." My thoughts were scattered into a million pieces as I flung my head toward my surprising protector. Draven's chair crashed to the floor behind him. He stood with his legs braced apart.

Treymore's previous lighthearted tone returned, but his fingers dug into my arm. He spoke in Arabic, his words contrasting his tone. "Your interest in her intrigues me." Despite wanting to do a swift, yet disarming chop to Treymore's throat so he would release me, I stayed put. Curiosity froze me to the spot until I unraveled a little more of their conversation. I had to find out why Draven hated Treymore and what he took from him.

"Take your crew and sail away before I do something I should have done a long time ago," Draven said in a chilling calm, his eyes threatening.

"I wouldn't, unless you want to *do* something you'll regret. Then you'll really lose everything." Treymore's hold tightened. I fought his shackle around my wrist, ready to show him that he severely underestimated who he was trying to use as a pawn. "Oh, Draven, don't look so sad. You've always said I wanted to take everything you had. Well, in this case..." He tried to hold up my hand, but I finally pulled free. "I think I will." Treymore's menacing eyes followed me as I dashed away and stood next to Ahmed.

"You should leave *now*." Ahmed spoke in English, louder than necessary.

At his words, some of the crew stopped working and took a step closer to the table. *I wouldn't mess with this bunch if I were you, Treymore. Sokum can throw a mean punch.*

Draven stared at Treymore, a murderous glint in his eyes. His hardened face matched the metal and leather of his armor and promised he was capable of the violence he'd been accused of.

"No." Draven stopped Ahmed. "No one is leaving." A feral smile spread across his face as he pulled a saber from his belt. "At least not alive." His eyes were dark and powerful. I froze and was unable to look away from him. The side of him that fought for what he wanted captivated me. The side that fought for me. Something inside me came to life, and my heart sped up. Adrenaline coursed through me and I no longer felt like running. I wanted to fight. Was this what it was supposed to feel like in training?

"You foolish boy!" Spittle flew from Treymore's mouth as he snarled. "You'll never get what you want if I'm dead. You think that will earn their respect? You think they'll just accept you—after you ran away? Ha!

They see you as nothing but a coward! They *blame* you."

Draven's eyes glowed with a savage inner fire. "Sokum, take Lux to my cabin."

"What?" I protested.

"'Ello again, love."

"Don't you dare, Sokum. I'm not going any—" *Oomph.* The air rushed out of me as Sokum picked me up.

"Sorry, Cap'n's orders." The wink he gave me said he wasn't sorry in the least. He opened the door with one hand, dumped me inside, and slammed the door shut. I ran to it, my hands slapping the wood.

"Sokum!"

The iron locks clicked in place. I pounded harder. "Sokum! Ahmed!"

The crew roared, followed by the subsequent clashing of steel. I retreated from the door as if I'd been burned. *Boom!* The ship shook, followed by the bloodcurdling sounds of men roaring. *Oh my God, what if Draven doesn't make it?*

He was right; I would much rather be at his mercy than Treymore's. The thought of what would happen to the other prisoners locked safely below deck caused unease to gnaw at my insides.

Draven's chair caught my attention. I ran to it and picked it up. *Damn, it's heavier than I thought.* I dragged the thing toward the door, used my body to lift it, and swung it at the door. It bounced back. Neither the door nor the chair suffered any damage.

The sounds of fighting rang in my ears. I picked up the chair again, higher than before, and threw it. The chair cracked, but the door was solid. Grabbing the splintered leg, I broke it off. I was helpless, beating the door with the leg. I sank to the floor, Draven's chair in pieces around me. My chest was racked with frustration as I waited.

The cries diminished to intermittent grunts and the clashing of steel. I looked out the window at the moon, and for the first time, I wasn't gauging the phase to determine how much time I had left. I was remembering the legend Draven told me about how night came from the sea. *Oh, Draven.* He didn't deserve this.

Did he?

When the lock clicked, I instinctively spun around, arming myself with the closest thing I could find—an oil lamp. My heart beat wildly in my chest as I waited to see who would come through the door.

"Lady Lux?" A young cabin boy burst in, holding a small sack. *The surgeon's supply bag.* "It's Draven." His free hand repeatedly touched his soot and crimson-smeared face.

"Yes?" I suppressed a sob. "What happened?"

"He's... he's hurt."

I covered my mouth with my hand. Not dead. *Thank God.* "Bring him!" I dashed over to take the bag from his hand.

"I'm fine." Draven strode in, looking disheveled, but all in one piece. My smile at him walking on his own faded as my gaze roamed over dark, damp locks, to a bloody and crestfallen face. His usually lively eyes sparkled with weariness.

"Leave. The ship fared worse than I," he commanded the cabin boy. With a quick nod, he disappeared and Draven shut—and locked—the door behind him.

"What happened? Are you all right?" I risked asking.

Draven walked to the washbowl on his mahogany dresser and rinsed his hands. "I said I'm fine."

I shook my head at his stubbornness. I guessed it wasn't the best time to ask about Ahmed and the others.

He leaned over to wash his face and let out a hiss. His body stiffened, and he bent over slowly this time.

"You're hurt." I made my way over to him, my eyes running over his armor.

He ran water through his hair with his fingers, straightened, and grabbed a towel.

"It's nothing that won't heal on its own." His voice was muffled as he patted the towel against his face.

"Let me see." I grabbed his shoulder to turn him when he bit back a moan. "Your shoulder," I exclaimed, shocked at the blood now on my hands. My eyes went back to his armor, to where blood seeped from between his shoulder plates. "It's obviously a lot worse than it looks. Let me help." Since he was so unappreciative about it, it would serve him right to let him deal with it himself, but somehow, I didn't want to see him suffer. I was too tired to play these games; I was going to tend that wound whether he liked it or not.

With a dismissive gesture, he walked away before the crunching of wood stopped him. "What is—?" He took a long look at what he stepped on.

Uh-oh.

"What in the devil happened to my chair?"

"I warned you not to lock me in here."

His jaw clenched and he said nothing, just walked toward his desk. He fell into another chair, laying his head back. Even though he had closed his eyes, I could see him wince. Looking at his ruined chair, I felt terrible. I'd never been more ashamed of my impulsiveness. *I should have used another chair...* I walked over and crouched beside him.

"Go ahead and ask. I know you want to. Ahmed fared well. There are no fatalities, not on our side, at least. Treymore sailed away with his tail between his legs. Can't say the same for some of his men though."

He spoke with his eyes still closed.

I blew out a breath of relief and set the sack of healing supplies next to me. "Now, sit up. I'm taking a look at your wound whether you like it or not."

He seemed so young, resting in the chair with his arms dangling over the armrests. He looked good when he wasn't glaring daggers at everyone and everything. It took all of my courage to consider him a patient for what I was about to do next.

"Come on." I reached up and tried to remove his outercoat.

His eyes flashed open and then softened. "If I let you play nurse, will you stop prodding me and let me rest?"

"Yes."

"Fine." He sat up in the chair and removed his wrist coverings, tossing them to the floor.

I fiddled with his breastplate and shoulder thingy before he let out an exasperated breath and took over.

I gasped at the sight of the gash. "I knew it was worse than you let on."

"It's fine," he said through gritted teeth. "Barely a scrape."

"Sit up." I tapped his knee as I stood. "You may need stitches," I said over my shoulder as I walked to the chest and returned with the copper water bowl, a vial of alcohol, and fresh linens. Sitting on the ottoman, I placed the bowl on the side table. I grabbed a cloth, poured the antiseptic over it, and then tried to dab the gash through the tear in his tunic. "Take off your shirt."

He smirked. "So eager to get me undressed, Lux? If I knew all it took was a flesh wound, I would've had it done sooner."

I let my face go blank. "I'm only looking at your body as a patient's and nothing more. C'mon."

151

He pulled his shirt over his head, stopping abruptly when he winced in pain. After a moment, he resumed more carefully and tossed the bloody shirt in the direction of the discarded armor.

The sweetly intoxicating musk of his body was overwhelming. An unwanted, delightful shiver ran through me. I carefully studied the wounded shoulder, pushing aside the little thoughts that kept daring me to look at his sculpted chest.

The gash needed stitching. I opened the sack and pulled out strips of gauze, along with a needle and thread. After nine stitches, I dabbed the cloth against the wound. Draven winced and cursed under his breath.

"Does that hurt?" I asked innocently, adding a little more pressure to my dabbing. The hiss of his breath was all the answer I needed. "Good. Next time, you'll think twice before having Sokum manhandle me and lock me in this cabin."

"Taking your revenge on me, Lux? And here I thought you were just a kind-hearted soul who likes to play nursemaid," he teased even as he grunted in pain as I pressed a little harder than necessary.

"Quit squirming. Who knew pirates could be such babies?" I wiped the last of the blood from the surrounding skin and tossed the washcloth back in the bowl. "There. I've finished cleaning it; although I would feel better if I could bandage it."

"I think I've been at your mercy long enough," he said, though he made no move to turn away from me. I put my elbows over my knees and studied his blood stuck in the creases of my fingernails. We sat in silence while I worked up the courage to say something.

"Who is Treymore? Does he kidnap people too?"

"No, he hardly leaves land unless it's for pleasure; but, apparently, he took up salvaging as well, thinking there would actually be something valuable in the US."

"The US?" I perked up.

He gave me a sidelong glance. "What is your obsession with the United States?"

My head fell. "It's not an obsession. It's my home."

"You're from the US? How did you survive?"

"Why do you say it like that? Why are you so surprised?"

"That question in itself just shows that you couldn't be from there, because if you were, you would know that it's uninhabitable. *No one survived.*"

I shook my head in denial, but my blood turned cold. "That can't be true. There must be something left."

"You wanted to know about the other islands, well, I am telling you. There is nothing left."

"You're lying," I stated, half in anticipation of the truth, half in dread.

"I am telling you the truth, for God's sake. You can ask anyone. Ask Ahmed since you trust him so much. Most of it is underwater."

"Stop it!"

"Why would I lie to you?"

"It's another game you are playing to toy with me."

"I wouldn't do that. When are you going to stop thinking of me as a monster?"

"When you stop being one!" Screams of frustration built at the back at my throat. It couldn't be true. He was lying. I just knew it. He was getting back at me for my defiance.

"You truly are from the United States, aren't you? But how? How did you survive when no one else—"He held up his hand as if he was going to touch me, but he clenched his fist instead. "I'm... I'm so sorry, Lux. I didn't know."

"I don't believe you," I yelled. It couldn't be true.

I had held on for all these years and finally I had, or almost had, the means to return. If I accepted what he said—what everyone had said—then that would mean... just thinking it shattered me.

My gaze clouded with tears. *Stop it.* I did not cry. Crying would mean they were all dead. My world was lost forever. I gulped hard, hot tears spilling down my cheeks.

He leaned toward me. "I'm so sorry, Lux."

I tingled as he said my name and drank in the comfort of his nearness. All it took was for me to inch forward in invitation before he pulled me roughly, almost violently, to him. I buried my face against his neck and didn't, for the first time in five years, hold back my tears. He whispered a soothing prayer in Arabic into my hair that was hard to understand over my sobs. I delved my hands in his thick hair and allowed my heart to break into a million pieces.

Chapter Twelve

I AWOKE THE NEXT MORNING, TUCKED IN DRAVEN'S BED, the smell of him on the sheets now familiar and comforting. I didn't know when I had cried myself to sleep, only that I had, and it was in the hollow between Draven's naked shoulder and neck, where my head had rested perfectly, that I had done so. He said nothing, except for the occasional words of comfort, while I cried for my family, my friends, my home. His hands on my back were almost unbearable in their tenderness.

I stared at the wooden ceiling, feeling empty. Now that I didn't have hope, I had nothing. My eyes were finally open, seeing for the first time just how naïve and optimistic I used to be, despite objections from my parents, from the villagers, even from Leif on occasion. How was it that Draven was able to unravel it all? All it took was for him to tell me it was so, and, suddenly, everything made sense.

I scanned the room to find I was alone. What did I expect? That he would stay with me the entire night? Even when he slept in the chair, he was usually gone before I woke. Nothing had changed between us. It was just a rare moment in which, out of desperation, I took comfort from the most unlikely person. My head rolled to the other side. On the pillow next to me, I found a note. I propped myself up on one elbow, grabbing the slip of paper with my other hand.

There are other lands that did survive, and I look forward to telling you all about them at dinner tonight. You're free to roam the ship as you please. ~Draven

A rapping sounded at the door, but no one entered. The noise sounded again. I sat up.

My name was whispered from the other side of the door. I tiptoed over and pressed my ear against the wood.

"Lux?" It was Shaman Tamati.

I fidgeted with the handle.

"Don't open the door. I must be quick. I've came to tell you we will make our move tonight. We need you to—"

"Tonight?" Rocks filled my stomach.

"Yes, after the battle yesterday, we were able to gather all the weapons we needed. We have to take them out *now.*"

"So, we'll have to hurt them?" I chewed on my thumbnail, thinking of Ahmed, Sokum, and... Draven.

"If we have to."

No. I needed more time. There was more to Draven then just a heartless captain who kidnapped for monetary gain. No one would have to get hurt. "What if there was another way?"

"Pardon?"

"What if I could convince the captain to return us, without any casualties on either side?"

"What *if?* We can't risk it. Do you understand how difficult it was to acquire the weapons and hide them with pirates coming and going and watching our every move? They will discover our weapons; I can assure you of that. It's not a matter of *if* but *when*. We must act quickly!"

"I need one more day!" I said hastily, desperately.

The other side of the door fell silent.

"Just one more day. Please. After that... After that, I will do whatever it takes." I rubbed my hands together and swallowed.

"You have tonight only. After that..."

"That's fine. Thank you." The breath I exhaled felt like relief.

"I pray you know what you're doing."

I didn't need to reply. The swish of robes and tapping of feet told me he had left.

Nothing has changed, Lux? Right. I just risked everything on a whim. I would speak to Draven tonight. Find out the truth about why he had to kidnap us, and if my feelings were right, we could figure out a way to get around it. If not...

In my hand, I was still holding onto Draven's note. I released it, and it floated like a feather to the ground. *I* had changed since last night. I was comforted as I grieved for everything I had lost. It would take longer to erase the pain. I had spent too long holding on to know anything else. Turning, I buried myself back in the bed. Pulling the covers over my head, I slept the rest of the day.

With the setting sun, time felt as if it was slowing down. My insides quivered. Pacing didn't ease my restless legs. I would take it with me to my grave, but the fact was I had spent longer than usual that day bathing and combing my hair. I worked to braid my hair so it stayed on top of my head and rubbed in the fragrant oil I found in the chest.

Draven gave me a sidelong glance of utter disbelief when he came into the cabin and I was waiting for him at the table dressed in the purple *abaya* he had given me.

"So, let's get this over with." I tried for indifference.

His face hardened, and I hated to see the disappointment there. "Fine. There's only one reason why you'd have dinner with me and that's to get information, right?"

I shouldn't feel guilty.

"We're not eating here," he added as he offered me his hand. "Follow me."

I stared at his hand, wanting to take it, but stood instead. "Where are we going?"

"You'll see." His hand clasped over mine, and he whisked me outside. He pulled me behind him out onto the deserted deck.

The sky dripped with stars. Since I no longer had a reason to meet the fisherman, it was bittersweet to see the phase of the moon and not have a sense of panic fill me. Timber creaked beneath my feet as Draven brought me toward a table set up in the middle of the deck. Candles flicked light across the display of food waiting for us.

It was a much nicer arrangement than what Treymore had. The thoughtfulness and planning behind it caused me to lose my appetite. I wished that he hadn't pulled out the chair for me, but he had. And at that moment, everything pieced together: I kind of *liked* Draven.

How did I let that happen?

How *did* I let that happen?

How did *I* let that happen?

How did I *let* that happen?

How did I let *that* happen?

And finally, how the hell did I let that *happen*?

All good questions. None that I had the answer to. Just potently sweet thoughts of last night.

Ugh. How had we gotten to this point? When had

I stopped hating him? The ice between us had slowly melted, and I wasn't sure how I felt about that.

"So," I immediately started as he sat across from me. He glanced up, giving me an alluring one-sided smile. The moonlight illuminated his features, and I lost my train of thought.

"The cook may have gone a bit overboard tonight."

I tucked a strand of hair behind my ear before he piled food on my plate. The offerings smelled fresh, rich, and aromatic. If food could sooth souls, this would have done the trick.

"Hummus. A few sticks of kofta." He gave me a big serving of each dish he named. "Manakeesh." He set a slice of round bread sprinkled with cheese and herbs on my plate.

"Pizza?" I commented in a dry tone.

"Manakeesh," he repeated firmly with a smile. "You have to try this; it's my favorite dish." The final scoop filled the last remaining space on my gold-rimmed plate.

He watched me as I sank my teeth into a curried potato. "Mmm," The flavor burst into my mouth, followed by the heat of the spices. Even though I had to take a sip of water to cool the fire on my tongue, it was surprisingly good. I smiled around a bite. "What?" I asked after realizing he still stared.

"Nothing." He blinked and stared down at his own plate. That was it? *Nothing.* No insults, no comments? Just nothing?

"Yeah, you're sure acting different today." *And yesterday, when you held me all night while I cried.* I shook my head.

"No, I'm not." His voice rose in defensiveness.

"Whatever you say." The breeze ruffled his dark hair, and I was reminded of how it felt to run my hands through it. I took another sip of water.

"So, you had questions for me..."

I put my fork down, finishing a bite. I had almost forgotten about the only reason I agreed to have dinner with him.

"Tell me more about you."

"About me?" An arched eyebrow indicated his humorous surprise.

"Tell me about your family."

His expression clouded. Did I hit a sensitive area? I should have been pleased, but suddenly, I felt sad for him. How could I not show him the same sympathy he showed me last night? I wanted to bury my face in my hands from frustration.

He was a pirate.

He did not feel sympathy.

Last night was... Last night was a fluke.

"What about them?" His voice was low, almost a growl, as he avoided my eyes.

"Where are they?"

"They're dead. Look—are you going to keep talking or are you going to eat?"

I pushed my lips together. I *had* been eating until a second ago, but I wasn't about to correct him. I picked at my plate more before finally meeting his eyes. "I'm sorry, Draven." I had wanted to ask how they died, but I assumed it wouldn't go well. He didn't respond. If I had thought the ice had melted, I was mistaken.

Staring out at the ocean, I listened to the sound of water slapping against the hull as I took another bite.

"My family was murdered." His voice cut through the silent, salt-drenched air like a dagger.

I swallowed and my lips parted open to gasp.

"Don't. Don't you dare pity me."

I leaned forward, putting both arms on the table and shaking my head. "I wasn't..." *I was.*

"It's been four years." He pushed his plate back

and mimicked me by leaning forward.

"Four years? They were murdered *after*? How?"

"There was a revolution. After the Floods, it was chaos. We were one of the few surviving countries. People were scared. They started a revolution. My family was caught in the crossfire... My father, and my mother... and my baby sister."

"Why... how did you...?"

"How did I survive? Why am I alive and not them? I ask myself that same question every day. I should have died with my family, but when I saw the mob coming, I ran away. I left my family... my baby sister. To save myself. I was selfish. A coward. I'm a monster, Lux. The hate I've seen in your eyes is the same hate I see reflected in the mirror every single day."

I don't hate you. I closed my eyes. His words hit too close to home. My throat tightened as I tried to shut out the images of an innocent family and a young boy who made a mistake. Everything was so much clearer now.

"Why—" I cleared my throat. "Why do you work for Asmodeus then?"

"Asmodeus is... He's not what you think."

"What is he then?"

"He helped restore order to my country after the revolution. I had a ship. He needed someone to do his dirty work. I'd say it worked out nicely."

"But you don't want to live like this."

"How do *you* know what I want?" he said flippantly.

I lowered my gaze to my plate, my cheeks burning.

"Forgive me... for my harshness," Draven spoke.

My head snapped up.

"I don't know why I am telling you all this." He shook his head.

"Maybe because I'm the right person to tell."

His eyes widened at my comment, and I didn't know what came over me to say that. But he softened and continued talking anyway. "I owe him. It started out that I only owed him a year of service. Then it became three more."

I leaned further over the table. "Why do you have to work for him? You have a ship, just leave."

He inclined his dark head in a deep gesture. "You don't understand. This is my last year of service. When my contract ends, Asmodeus will get my land returned from my uncle, and I'll be able to go home again."

"Your uncle? You mean Treymore?"

"How do you know this?" His eyes narrowed at me suspiciously, and my heart stopped. "So you know about Amina and Treymore. Is there anything Ahmed hasn't told you?" His eyes softened as he erroneously deduced where I got my information from.

I played along, hoping he would reveal more if he figured I already knew. "Ahmed wouldn't tell me anything, much to my disappointment. It was obvious enough. But how does your uncle know your girlfriend?"

"Who?" He seemed distracted.

"How does Treymore know Amina?" I tried keeping my head held up high as I asked.

His eyebrows furrowed at my question, but after studying my expression, the laughter was back in his eyes, "Are you jealous, *amira*?"

"Jealous," I scoffed, realizing with the force of a hurricane that his accusation was entirely true.

He threw his head back and roared with laughter. "Amina is my aunt. There would be no way I am related by blood to Treymore. He is my aunt's husband."

Something suspiciously like relief washed

through me. Amina was his aunt. Of course! My shoulders relaxed.

"So if Treymore is your uncle, why would you be concerned with getting your land back from him?"

"It is rightfully mine!"

"Who were your parents?"

"So many questions for someone who shouldn't know the answer."

I stared at him with no emotion, not buying into his temper tantrums anymore, and hoping it would prompt him to continue, but he didn't pick back up the conversation. "Well, why not just let go. And start over? I'm sure your parents would have wanted that."

"Let go? You are so naïve. I have a duty. There will be no happy ending for me."

I set my fork down with a sigh.

"I'm sorry," he said softly, closing his eyes and pressing his lips together. "You just don't know anything about me."

"Apparently, I know you better than you think, *Draven*. I can see right past this act." I waved my hand angrily at him. "For someone who talks a lot about other people's lives, you're a hypocrite. The way you carry yourself and the languages you speak are a damn big giveaway. The past haunts you, and you pay for that every day—I get that now. You put up a wall with everyone who gets close to you. You're younger than you'll ever allude to, and you carry on the ruthless demeanor so people will fear and respect you. The truth is you are capable of being good. You don't want to be the person—this pirate you've become." The emotions built up, and my chest heaved with each breath.

His jaw twitched under his skin. "Since we are talking about other people's images, let's talk about yours, shall we?"

"Go right ahead," I spoke, confident that I had nothing to hide.

"Let's start off with the simple fact that you're aboard my ship. You wouldn't be here in the first place if you hadn't been by the water late at night. So I ask you, *Lux*, what were you doing, hm?"

I stared at him, open-mouthed. *Damn him.* How did he ask just the right questions?

"Maybe I should just ask what were you doing with Leif?"

I rolled my eyes, knowing where he was going with that. "You have no idea what you're talking about." Was that jealousy in his voice? *Good.* I should let him think what he wants, but I was just tired of all the lies and deception. Tired of fighting. "You know what—?"

"Captain?" I hadn't noticed when or how long Ahmed was standing there.

"What do you want, Ahmed?" Draven answered, but his eyes were still burning into me.

"My apologies for interrupting, Captain, but the crew heard arguing and they're concerned."

"Tell them I am fine, Ahmed."

Ahmed cleared his throat and dipped his chin down. "They're—they're not worried about *you*, Captain."

Draven's head shot toward Ahmed, and quickly turned to Arabic. "What are you saying?"

Ahmed's eyes darted to me briefly before matching his Arabic. "The men just want to know if she is okay and that you won't hurt her?"

"They want to know that *I* won't hurt *her*?" His expression bordered on mockery, and he gave a scornful laugh.

"Yes, Captain."

"What is happening to this ship? What is happening to *me*?"

"You're in—"

"Don't even think about finishing that sentence."

"I've watched you moping around all day because this is your last night with her." Ahmed gestured firmly with his hands.

Draven turned his head toward me, as if to make sure I didn't hear. My gaze darted between them with a blank stare. Inside, I was panicking. Our last night? I told the shaman to give me one more day; I didn't consider it would be our last. I should say something; I should get up and go warn the others. But somehow, I was more concerned with wanting to hear what Draven had to say.

My heart pounded as I checked my emotions, not having the courage to walk away. Or maybe I just desired too much to know what was truly in Draven's heart.

"Don't give her to Asmodeus tomorrow," Ahmed continued.

"Does it look like I am insane?"

"Maybe. But you know what they say about those in—"

"Stop. She hates me. She sees me as the ruthless monster everyone thinks I am." He turned in his chair to face him. "You've been all too forgiving when it comes to her. Did you forget she tried to kill me?"

"Exactly."

"Exactly? Exactly, what?"

"Nothing." Ahmed turned to walk away, a secret smile on his lips.

"She has a boyfriend." Draven's voice stopped him.

"People aren't always what they seem."

"You're always speaking in riddles! Just say what's on your mind, man."

"You should heed your own advice." Ahmed

laughed then disappeared into the dark.

Draven turned back to his plate without a single glance at me.

Just look at me. Give me one look that tells me it's real.

He ate absentmindedly, glancing up at me every once in a while before turning his head away. It was obvious he was wrestling with something in his mind, but I fought a battle of personal restraint of my own as unfamiliar feelings of longing flowed through me. I couldn't speak, still overwhelmed by their conversation. I now understood what they said about eavesdroppers.

Listen long enough, you'll end up hearing something you don't like.

I went over their conversation, making sure I had each word right. Draven made it clear that he had some sort of feelings for me. But he was still bringing me to Asmodeus. Would I stay if given the choice? Of course not! What was I just going to join his crew, sail around the globe, seeing with my own eyes how the world had changed, going on countless new adventures?

Wow, that actually sounds pretty amazing. I swallowed and wiped my brow. And I didn't belong on Sirbiad. I knew that even if I never got the possibility of going back to the US in my head. Maybe I knew the truth all along, but held onto hope so I wouldn't have to admit I was lost. Apparently, I might never have belonged in the US either.

But what about my parents?

Would I just leave everything behind?

Wasn't that what I was going to do anyway? And if I could feel an ounce of what I felt last night in his arms, wouldn't it be worth it?

This was stupid. It was foolish. Yet, it didn't feel

completely wrong. I was astonished at the sense of fulfillment I felt last night. But none of that mattered. He said he was bringing us to Asmodeus. If he truly felt anything for me, then he would fight for me. He wouldn't give me up. If he was true in his intentions and I wasn't just some challenge to him, he wouldn't have to wrestle with it in his head. I was ashamed of the feelings I admitted to. My melted heart quickly picked up, and the passion turned cold. I would tell the shaman we had to go through the plan tonight.

I stood, clenching my teeth, fists, anything. "I have to go."

He caught my arm as I stormed away. "What? No. I promise I'll be better company."

"I don't care. I'm done. Now, let me go, Draven."

"Why?"

"I realized that any information you give me isn't going to change anything."

"Why don't you just tell me the truth for once?" His raised voice hinted at exasperation.

"Why don't *you?* I don't know why you wanted to have this stupid dinner with me in the first place. If it is to help you ease your conscience after you send me off to Asmodeus tomorrow, well, sorry to inform you, but I don't even think you have a conscience at all."

He froze. "How did you know we would arrive tomorrow?" The venom dripping from his voice could have frozen into icicles.

"Your crew told me earlier," I hastily replied. I was a terrible liar. *Walk away before he notices!* "Forget it. I'm out of here."

He followed me inside his cabin, catching the door as I tried to slam it closed behind me.

"Ilaa ayna tazhab?" *Where are you going?*

"Tarek leh wahada!" *Leave me alone!"*

I turned on my heel and clapped my hand around

167

my mouth. *Crap.*

"You speak Arabic?" He said through clenched teeth.

My face burned. "I don't *not* know Arabic—"

I was silenced by his dark, angry expression. "Stop playing games." He clenched his fists tightly at his sides.

"Yes," I admitted. "But you tricked me."

"*I* tricked *you*?" He laughed as if he'd gone mad. "*You* tricked me! All those conversations I had in front of you with Ahmed, you could—"

"Yes." I dropped my head.

"How is that possible? How do you even know Arabic?"

"My father was a US Diplomat and traveled a lot. My parents speak several languages and taught me most of them." I shrugged one shoulder. It wasn't a time to add that my father was born there, too.

"You are something else." He shook his head and drew his lips in thoughtfully. "All this time..." He shook his head again, let out a resigned breath, and the corner of his mouth turned up. "Well played, Lux. Well played." He said it like I held his respect. I narrowed my eyes at him in suspicion.

He came toward me, and I took a step back. Stopping three inches from my face, he peered down at me with an intense stare. "You know what else I left out about you?"

"What?" My face hardened, waiting for the insult. All the while, my traitorous heart fluttered wildly at the smell of sweet ocean and leather coming from his proximity.

"That you're bold, compassionate, intelligent, and I think I'm in love with you, Lux." His hands shot out, grabbing my face between his hands, just holding me as he looked down at me with unleashed tenderness and passion. Slowly and seductively, his gaze slid downward and settled on my lips. I didn't have time to protest before his lips crashed into mine. He didn't take it slow this time; he was as eager and erratic as a summer storm.

Forget right and wrong. I melted into him.

His lips moved hungrily against mine, forcing my mouth open as our tongues met. The taste of his mouth and lightly salty skin sent me shivering. He pulled me tighter in his arms, lifting me higher against his chest so he could deepen our kiss. I felt a sense of belonging, and I no longer cared what was right or wrong.

I wrapped my legs around him, my dress hiking up in the process. He groaned when his hands gripped the bare flesh of my thighs. Moving, he then bent down, still holding me tightly as books and papers from his desk crashed to the floor with a swipe of his arm. He set me down on the edge, and his hands were free to touch me. His caresses were urgent and exploratory. He broke our kiss, pulling back to study my face. I could scarcely breathe at the sight of him losing control, his lips bruised from our kissing, his black hair deliciously disheveled. In desperation, I slid an arm around his neck to pull him to me again. He resisted for a moment.

"Lux." My name was smothered on my lips as he kissed me. *Really* kissed me. And this time, I wouldn't hesitate to kiss him back. Because as *wrong* as it may be, it felt entirely *right.*

Chapter Thirteen

"Love sees sharply, hatred sees even more sharp, but jealousy sees the sharpest for its love and hate at the same time."
-Arab proverb

I HAD SLEPT THE ENTIRE NIGHT TANGLED IN DRAVEN'S arms and legs, so when I woke up, I was cold. A lonely cold.

But that didn't stop me from being foolishly happy. My mind burned with the memory of last night. *Draven gently eased me down onto his bed, his eyes raked my body with a hunger so long denied. His elegant, strong hands unlaced the top of my tunic. When his hands slipped under, and I felt his fiery hot palm on my bare skin, I sucked in a breath and looked up at him with unguarded fear. His eyebrows furrowed as he caught my gaze, and then cleared with understanding. "Oh Lux," he said in relief, his glorious dark hair spilling onto my bare stomach where he rested his forehead. When he looked back up at me, his expression was fierce, protective. "We can wait, Lux. I'll always wait for you..."*

I savored the feeling of satisfaction he left me with. Never feeling as complete and hopeful as I did just sleeping in his arms. "Draven?" I softly called out.

170

When I didn't see him in the cabin, I got dressed. I couldn't stay in his shirt all day even though I could now admit I liked wearing it. It smelled deliciously like him. I wistfully took one last inhale—the deep kind that ended with an audible sigh. My sundress was clean and hung over a chair, so I slipped that on.

I wondered what Draven had planned; breakfast outside came to mind, and I smiled. Anything to do with sunshine would be heaven. I felt like singing my joy, but I didn't really remember any songs. Sirbiadians weren't very musical and only chanted at gatherings. I laughed at myself, but didn't really mean it. Lux from two days ago would make fun of Lux from today. How soft I had become.

Or was it just because I was happy?

Whatever it was, I could thank Draven for it. I thought back to a riddle "love and hate can both lead to sorrow and happiness." Those damn riddles. I would have to think about it another time.

Right now, I had to find Draven.

I went to the door, but couldn't open it. I turned the knob again, pulling it back and forth only to hear the lock catching.

That's strange.

My heart beat loudly. No, there had to be a reasonable explanation.

I tried the handle again.

The door pushed in, but not by my doing. I fell back as the young boy who opened it came in and shut the door behind him.

It was the same young boy who had interrupted Draven and had almost paid severely for it. *But also, the same one he took mercy on.*

"Hi," I said pleasantly. "I remember you. How are you doing?"

The boy walked past, ignoring me.

My eyebrows furrowed. *Maybe he hadn't heard me?* "Where's Draven?" Without a word, he set a tray down on the table. Why was the tray set for one? Worse, why hadn't Ahmed brought it in for me?

"Hello?" Why wouldn't the boy answer me? Panic wrapped around me like a blanket. "Where's Ahmed?"

"I'm not supposed to say anything, just make sure you have food and received your old clothes. Ahmed will be coming soon. We should be docking shortly," he said with his back to me.

"What?" Docking shortly? We were still going to Asmodeus? Things had changed last night between Draven and me. We wouldn't still be going there. He must be mistaken. After everything last night... B-but... he said he loved me. *No, he said he* thinks *he's in love with me. Oh God.*

"I need to talk to the captain." My voice shook. "Please."

The boy diverted his gaze and tried to shuffle to the door. I blocked his path.

"Please, just tell me what's going on."

His lips twitched into a frown. "You've been nothin' but nice to us all, and I will never forget what you've done for me..."

"Please, just tell me." I felt bad for pushing him. He was just a boy after all, conflicted between loyalty and honesty, but I had to know what to expect. I couldn't go in blind.

"I wasn't supposed to speak a word to you. Not one word. But—" He breathed. "We are headed northeast to The Island. I was helping the prisoners scrub the deck when I overhead the captain say to the first mate to keep the prisoners locked up until we got to The Island. He was worried you would try something again."

Again? What? No, Draven couldn't have said that.

Not after last night.

"I need to talk to him." I turned around and threw open the door before the boy could do anything about it.

"No, wait! I wasn't supposed to..." The boy ran after me.

I threw a "sorry" over my shoulder as I stormed onto the deck. I didn't have time to change or throw on slippers for that matter, and my bare feet beat loudly against the wood.

"Draven," I yelled. Crewmen stopped their work to stare at me. I searched around for him, my eyes drifting to the upper deck. The morning air was foggy, and I could scarcely see twenty feet in front of me. "Draven," I shouted again, vulnerable, but I didn't care. I was past caring and playing games. The slow, chauvinistic beat of boots sounded on the upper deck.

My heart stopped beating. *Calm down. You knew you'd have to face him.*

The footsteps grew louder as he descended the stairs, and then abruptly stopped. I allowed myself to glance at him briefly. When our gazes locked, he was quick to resume his descent. I continued watching him with the best-controlled expression I could manage. He caught an unsuspecting Ahmed by the arm. "What is *she* doing here?" he spoke in a harsh whisper.

I turned on the crowd, rolling my eyes as if to say, *can you believe this guy?* Now I was just pissed. "Ah, if I remember correctly, *you* took me from my island and brought me here," I announced loudly with all the spite and sarcasm I could manage.

He winced. In anger? *Good.* Irritation? *Even better.* Frustration? *Perfect.*

Ignoring me, he directed his attention back to Ahmed. "What is she doing out of the cabin? I told you—"

173

Tired of being spoken about as if I weren't there, I stormed over to him. I crossed my arms over my chest, and he finally turned his attention on me.

His full armor was back on, and he appeared exactly like he had the first time I had met him. I shook my head. We had come so far since then. "So it's true. You tried to lock me in the cabin. You are still bringing me to Asmodeus? I am still your *'prisoner'* after everything that's happened between us?"

His body shook with his scoff. "Nothing happened between us except that we passed the time at sea."

I clenched my fists at my sides, longing to slap him. The air pent up in my chest burned as I exhaled. I didn't believe it. What he had told me last night was real; it was genuine.

"Why are you doing this?" The edges of my heart burned. Tears blurred my vision, and I blinked them away, willing myself not to cry. *I don't cry, remember?* No, not necessarily true. I *used to* not cry. Until *he* opened the floodgates.

My face must have revealed my every emotion and all the pain I experienced, because he laughed mockingly before his face became cold and his tone slightly angry. "You thought you could change me? I'm not something broken that you can fix! I am a monster, remember? What did you expect?"

"You're not a monster. And you're not broken. I was the one who was broken—"

"Enough!"

"—and it was you who fixed *me*."

He came at me, like a pouncing tiger. His gaze raked the length of me in superiority. "You are *still* broken."

My breathing came out ragged, and I pushed my quivering lips together. "And what about my people? Is that their fate as well?"

"Everyone is going to Asmodeus' island. There are no exceptions."

No! I had to warn Shaman Tamati. We had to act *now.* I wildly searched the deck. The cold sharpness of dread oozed into my stomach when I noticed there were no prisoners on deck anymore, only pirates. *Oh my God.*

"You look unwell, Lux." Draven's tone was amused, not concerned.

"Shaman Tamati," I panicked, screaming his name, hoping, wishing, praying that they would come out of the rafters charging and I hadn't just made the biggest mistake of my life.

"I wouldn't bother. We discovered the prisoner's weapons last night."

Because of me. I asked Shaman Tamati to trust me. They waited when they could have fought. *For me.* Now they won't get the chance to go home. Because of *me.*

"You know, I considered maybe you weren't involved. It is why I kept you locked in the cabin after all. I kept telling myself it was impossible. I didn't believe that you could have been so convincing in your performance. But we... 'questioned' your fake holy man and he told us how you orchestrated the whole thing. Well, done Lux. You really went above and beyond to keep me busy last night." He swiveled quickly, turning his back on me.

"What? You think it was an all act? Draven—"

He paused with his foot on the bottom step and turned back, venom dripping in his voice. "You. Will. Call. Me. Captain. Now, I suggest you prepare yourself for port because you will be going even if I have to tie you to the prow of the ship and make you the figurehead!"

"No, I won't." I shook my head and backed up until

I hit the capstan. "Y-you said you loved me."

He smirked, the devil himself, and walked back down the stairs toward me. "And you believed me? I'm a pirate. We lie, we steal, and we *kill*."

I tried to cling to the memory of last night as I would to a life preserver on a stormy sea, but I could feel his words start to seep in, to taint that memory and cast doubt. Smothering a sob, I screamed. "You're a coward!" I turned around to shield my vulnerabilities, the fact that I was brought to tears over something I'd always guarded.

Draven came up behind me. Angry breaths beat down on my bare shoulder, and I recoiled. He spun me around.

"What did you say?"

"I said you are a coward. You're a coward for believing that I could fake my emotions like that. You're a coward for not fighting for us, and you're a coward for hiding your true feelings behind this mask of indifference!"

He took a step toward me, but I was unable to back up further. I was trapped. His enraged expression filled me with fear for the first time in a while. His knuckles were bare white fists at his sides. I turned away, unable to look at him. He kicked a wooden box, and it broke against the side of the ship. "You think you know me? You think I don't make good on my threats? Well, I'll prove to you just how ruthless I can be, *amira*."

He grabbed both of my arms, and Ahmed stepped forward to stop him. "Draven, stop. You'll regret this. We can find another way to—"

"You will address me as captain, Ahmed. Now tend to the wheel. That is an order!" Ahmed paused before walking away, leaving a strong air of disappointment behind him.

"Let me go, Draven. You have completely lost it."

His grip tightened. "If I have lost it, it is because you drove me there."

"I can't *make* you do anything."

I let out a scream as he threw me over his shoulders and turned toward the cabin. He kicked the door open.

I thought he would drop me and leave, but he carried me to the bed.

He gently set my head on the pillow. My eager heart sped up. He rested my arms above my head, and then slid his hand into mine. My lips parted in defeat, and I tried to control my breathing as he inched his face near mine. The warmth of his breath touched my cheek. What was he doing? My heart soared with hope.

His other hand lingered by my face, and he brushed my lips with his thumb. I squeezed my eyes shut at the longing for him to kiss me, to hold me. His hand pulled away and slid up to my hands. I felt a tightening around my wrists.

My eyes shot open to find him with a wicked, crooked smile.

"I'm not taking any chances this time," he said plainly, tightening the rope around my other hand. By the time he secured the ropes to the bed, I had stopped breathing. There was no air left in my lungs. I forgot how to inhale. Everything on my body tingled—my legs, my cheeks, my nose. A tear painted down my cheek. I turned my head as far as I could in the other direction.

"Cat got your tongue now, huh?"

I didn't answer him. Just strained my neck as far as I could in the other direction. Tears blurred my vision, and they slid closed as Draven finished tying the knots on my wrists.

"Did you really think you could change me, Lux?"

Silence.

"Did you think I couldn't pretend just as well as you were?"

I let out a muffled whimper as the rope on my left hand was pulled tightly. He finished and stood, but didn't leave my side.

"What? No smartass remark?"

My eyelids were heavy, wet, and warm, and I never wanted to open them again.

"Answer me! I've spent four years as Asmodeus slave. You know what I'd lose if I broke my contract? And for what? So you could go back to an island you hate? You snaked your way into my heart just so I would return you."

I was numb—angry, hurt, *empty*—the same feelings that filled me when I thought he threw my necklace overboard. I felt like my heart had been ripped out then, but this was a million times worse.

I didn't open my eyes. *He thought it was an act, to what, save myself?* It was so meaningless to him that he couldn't even tell it was real?

I couldn't even look at him... Everything was his fault! I wanted to hate him... Well, it looked like I got my wish...

Leaning over, he hovered inches from my turned head. "Who's the pirate now?"

My eyelids twitched at his proximity, but I held my lips together, tighter than if I sewed them together myself.

He let out a growl of frustration and stormed to the door. The door opened, but he hesitated. He mumbled something, and I wasn't sure if he was talking to me or himself. What difference did it make anymore? With a resolved breath, he left the cabin, the door slamming loudly behind him.

A quivering breath escaped my mouth when he left.

I fought the tears.

Feeling paralyzed, I didn't know what to think anymore. I'd ruined everything. I sacrificed the lives of my people, and for what? For a feeling I had? How foolish could I be? Draven had always planned on bringing us to Asmodeus. He said himself that he wouldn't give up what he spent years working for. He wanted to go home again and he wasn't going to let anything—or anyone—get in the way. I could understand this more than anyone. Like me, he had been holding onto a dream for years.

He couldn't move on, and I couldn't *make* him move on like he had done to me.

If it were possible, would I have given up my boat, my chance at returning to the US, to be with Draven?

Yes.

But to Draven, I wasn't worth it.

The doubt crept in like a poison through my veins. I was wrong about him. It *was* all an act, and I gave up everything because I believed it.

I had more than a few choice words for Draven, and a string of profanities came through my mind. *Ah, there you are, anger. I could always count on you.* Anger was safe. It wasn't vulnerable; it allowed me to think clearly.

I wanted to drag my hands down my face, but they were knotted tightly above me. *Oh, God.* What a mess this had become.

I needed a new plan.

I could still get my people home.

I just needed to find Asmodeus.

Chapter Fourteen

I STAYED AWAKE. IT COULD HAVE BEEN MINUTES OR hours later that the entire cabin shook. We must have reached our destination. I took a deep breath, not knowing what was worse—that I was going to meet the most hated man in the world or that Draven was sending me to him.

Restless, I listened intently to the bustling of activity outside my door. My arms had stopped hurting hours ago. Now they were numb from being tied over my head. Would I be able to use them after being drained of blood for so long? The walls seemed to be closing in, and I found it hard to breathe. It reminded me of when my lungs filled with water while trying to save Ahmed: I was suffocating.

The boat was drained of noises and people. *Don't think it, don't think, don't think it.* It was useless. I had already allowed myself the false hope that maybe Draven changed his mind. As soon as my heart swelled at the thought, the door burst open, slamming against the wall. I lifted my head and dizziness washed over me, followed by regret I had moved at all.

A man I had never seen before came over to the bed. He was not wearing the armor like Draven's crew, nor the flowing robes like Treymore's, or the tunics like Sirbiadian's. It was a more severe style, colorless and uniformed. He was right next to me before I noticed the dagger in his hand. It lifted to my head. I gasped and squeezed my eyes shut. The ropes loosened against my wrists, and I opened my eyes. The man's leathered skin wrinkled even more as he laughed at me.

My arms came back to rest at my sides, and it was just as I expected. They were useless. As the blood flowed back, the pain was indescribable. *Oh God.* I sucked in a breath through clenched teeth. It would have hurt less if he had cut them off.

"Come." The man's voice was as scruffy as his salt-and-pepper beard.

I didn't move, physically incapable of pushing myself up with my arms, so he hoisted me to my feet. Well, at least those were working.

"Wait," I requested, lifting my arms, which were like octopus tentacles, toward my neck. Pins and needles spread through my arms as I fumbled with the clasp of my necklace. I set it on the small table next to the bed. I didn't need it anymore. Maybe it would help him get home someday.

The pain in my arms slowly receded as we made our way across the deck. It was deserted with the exception of a few unlucky boys cleaning the floors and carrying crates back onto the ship. Draven was probably collecting his 'payment' right about now. I glanced back at the upper deck anyway.

I stopped mid-stride and a smile tugged at the corner of my lips in naïve hope.

Draven.

He stood with his hands clasped in front of him. His expression stony and cold as ice. He had to have been staring right at me, but it was as if he didn't see *me.*

Because he doesn't. He just sees a slave being taken from his ship. The pain at the back of my throat returned. Nothing had changed. It was as if it were the first day I met him all over again. I belonged to Asmodeus. There was nothing he could do, he had said. I tried to remember all the rage he had made me feel that day. I wanted to remember how much I hated him. He was my enemy. I licked my trembling lips and kept walking. *Goodbye, Draven.*

～～～

We stepped onto the dock, and I couldn't help but gape at the sight before me. It wasn't just an island— it was a city. My eyes stretched to the limit as I tried to see everything at once. A smell I hadn't experienced in years brought back memories I had long ago buried. *Smoke.* But not the kind from a wood fire. *Exhaust.*

A brick building lined the perimeter of the city and seemed to be built right into the cliffs on my left. My stomach dropped as if I jumped off said cliffs. Who knew the world could be held in one man's hands? If someone were able to predict *if* and *when* the floods would happen, they would be able to dominate the world. It was rumored that Asmodeus was that someone. He was a scientist working for our government. Instead of warning our country, he used that information to prepare himself—to control what would be left of the world.

He had let entire nations drown—my home and my people, *gone.* Now he was jeopardizing the only thing I had left—Sirbiad. My blood ran cold and my chest hollow. I may have lost everything, but Sirbiadians still had their island. I wasn't about to let him destroy their life too. I had to get them home.

As we walked along the dock, I shook my head in disgust and awe at the buildings scattered throughout the city. They were real buildings made of brick, glass, and steel, not just structures made from clay and thatch like on Sirbiad.

We walked through the perimeter under arches and toward the main building that seemed to connect with the others. I paused to stare at a mansion at the other end of the lawn. My muscles tightened. There was no doubt to who lived there, and what the mansion signified as an eerie replica of the White House. *Gee, he couldn't have been a tad more original?* The guy had some major power issues.

The man grunted at my dawdling then pulled me inside behind him. Smooth, white marble chilled my bare feet to the core despite seeming to shimmer warmly when the fluorescent lights overhead caught the sparkles. I rolled my head back to stare at the electric lights. Wood scraped metal and I spun around to see real doors opening, the kind with levers and places for key cards. There were more people inside coming and going through doors. Some wore the plain, outdated clothes like the man beside me, and even more were dressed in the militaristic jumpsuits I had seen on the men who had visited Sirbiad.

No one seemed interested in a burly man walking with a scarcely dressed girl.

The hallway opened into a courtyard below, and it was only then I realized we were on the second level. I fled to the railing and peered down onto a huge lobby. Five or six tunnels led out on every side. The prisoners from Draven's ship—my people—huddled in front of a row of Jumpsuits, who we called the people who worked for Asmodeus and wore the military-style clothing.

I scanned the group with panic, putting a hand over my heart when I didn't see Lilou or her sister among them. My heart tore apart in confusion. What if Draven had really kept his word and was going to send her home? What did it mean then that he didn't do the same for me? I couldn't think of it; I had the rest of my people to save, and I wouldn't be leaving without them anyway.

At the same moment I spotted Shaman Tamati, he lifted his head and met my gaze. There was an unspoken accusation in his eyes. He thought I betrayed them all. *No.* I shook my head, but he coldly turned away.

I gripped the railing, my knuckles going white as the clean Jumpsuits picked through the weary crowd and sent them one by one through different tunnels. *Great.* It would be harder now that they were separated.

I looked at the men and women in charge, wondering which one could be Asmodeus. Most of them were young and uniformed. I doubted Asmodeus was among them.

What was my plan now?

This place was far more advanced than I expected, and it was clear we couldn't sneak off in the night and sail away like on Sirbiad. There was only one person who had the power to send us home—Asmodeus himself. He knew my father. The Maritime Codes stated that the islands were allowed to appoint representatives, or Mayors. Every month, Asmodeus' men came to Sirbiad for inspections and the report from my father. Anything interesting that was found had to be reported as well as a log of new visitors and their purpose. If they were satisfied with the report, they would leave another crate of food.

My father never met Asmodeus in person, but frequently corresponded with him. If I could just talk with him, surely he would see reason why it would be beneficial to return the Mayor's daughter and a few "key members" of our society. I knew diplomacy better than anyone. I could convince him while wanting to kill him.

Negotiate with the person who is behind the kidnappings and the destruction of your homeland? I rubbed my temples. That wasn't too far off from what my father used to do in the US. Besides, it was the only plan I had and our best shot.

"Hello."

Turning with a jump, I found an unfamiliar face in front of me. I looked around for the man who brought me off the ship.

"He left," the person in front of me confirmed. Wonderful, I was deserted. How would I get down to the tunnels now? With hesitant eyes, I studied the person in front of me, and then gasped. His accent. And he looked so familiar...

"Are you American?" I gripped his arm.

His forehead puckered and his firm mouth curled as if on the edge of laughter. "Yes?"

"Oh, thank God!" I practically whimpered as I pulled him into a hug. He tensed in my arms. "Sorry." I cleared my throat and took a step back.

"No harm done." He smoothed back his hair with a smile. He was young, but mature, his youth well hidden. *Like Draven*, a cynical voice interrupted. I shook it from my mind and regarded the person in front of me once again. He was a good foot taller than I was, with perfect blondish-brown hair and a strong, fresh scent. His smooth face was ingenuously appealing and his body was beautifully proportioned. He stood as if he prided himself on good grooming. To me, he was unnaturally attractive. His features were so perfect, so symmetrical, that any more delicacy would have made him too beautiful for a man.

He reminded me so much of a boy that was in

my sixth year of class at the academy. *Oh, what was his name?* I couldn't remember. This couldn't be him, could it? He looked older than I was, but I instantly connected to him as if we were long-lost friends.

"I thought no one had survived. Are there more of you?" My spirits rose wildly with a hope I so badly needed.

He narrowed his eyes at me. Did I say something wrong?

"I'm sorry—I didn't mean—I was just told no one survived the disasters. How did you make it to Asmodeus' island?"

He seemed taken aback.

"How did you survive? Did you come here with your family?" I was really screwing this up...

But his expression cleared with understanding. "Ah." He smiled and I exhaled, glad I didn't offend the first American I met in five years. "When you asked, I thought you meant originally. I came here before the Floods."

My spirits were dashed as quickly as they rose. So he worked for Asmodeus. And there were no other survivors. Of course. Asmodeus had this island all planned. He and his soldiers could have come here safely before the disasters began. Asmodeus probably offered them their lives in exchange for working for him.

I surveyed him and was again reminded of the boy in my class. He reminded me so much of home. I couldn't judge him. He could have arrived here with his parents; it didn't mean he believed in what Asmodeus had done.

"How did *you* get here?"

I sighed. "I was living in Sirbiad when I was kidnapped and brought here against my will by pirates."

"Kidnapped?" He leaned back, appalled, and

placed a fist across his heart. *See, he couldn't have been a part of what Asmodeus was doing.*

"Yes. They said they worked for Asmodeus. As the daughter of the Mayor of Sirbiad, I insist on speaking with him immediately about our treatment." I channeled my inner politician and hoped my voice came across as firm.

His eyebrows shot up. "The mayor's daughter? *No.* I'm sorry for what you've been through. This isn't how things work on the island. People are here because they want to be. They work and, in exchange, are well provided for. The ship that brought you gets a finder's fee for every new citizen they bring. Obviously, they've taken the easy way out and stooped to kidnappings." He shook his head in disapproval. "You can be assured that they will be punished for their unlawfulness."

I thought about Ahmed... "We really just need to return to Sirbiad." My hair shook loose from my braids and came spilling forward.

"Of course, you shouldn't expect it any other way. As I said before, people are here because they *want* to be here. Kidnapping is not necessary. Asmodeus is away on business at the moment, but I'm positive he'll return shortly, and then we can get this whole situation worked out. You'll be back in Sirbiad in no time."

I closed my eyes and exhaled. I guessed waiting for Asmodeus was my best option.

But that meant Draven had lied to me. He *did* have a choice. He didn't have to kidnap people while working for Asmodeus, but if that were true, why were they still treated like prisoners?

"What's going on down there?" I leaned over the steel railing.

"Oh, that? When new citizens arrive, it's the first

step in their new existence. They're assigned roles—the jobs they will carry out here. I will notify the guards immediately of the situation and assign them guest rooms in the meantime. They won't be required to work, but don't be surprised if some would rather stay here after all."

I doubted it. Why would anyone want to work for Asmodeus? Did they know what he had done? I could never forgive him, but that didn't mean others couldn't or had simply forgotten. He still committed genocide. He sent my people and many others to their extinction. Though how many others, I wasn't sure anymore.

"Again, please accept my apologies for this mis-understanding. This is not the welcome a mayor's daughter should receive. Why don't I show you where you'll be staying?"

"What, I don't get the honors of being sorted like cattle?" I snapped. *That was mean.* I shouldn't take my anger out on someone who was only trying to help.

"No, the cattle are kept in the pasture behind the building," he teased, and my spirits lifted.

"You have animals here?" A smile tugged at my open mouth.

His infectious grin set the tone. "Come." He held out his hand, but I walked past him, ignoring it.

"Thanks. I'm sorry, but I never got your name?"

"My name?"

I nodded. The situation didn't exactly make it easy for proper introductions.

"It's Wilson, actually."

"Will," I repeated, trying to make that stick in my head. He seemed to know what was going on around here and was my only connection to Asmodeus and going home. Even though we were from the same country, I wasn't entirely sure yet if we were on the same side. He did come here with Asmodeus, after all.

"I'm Lux."

He laughed. "Your name means light. It matches your beauty."

Changing the subject... "Um, so, where are we going?"

He nodded at people as we made our way across the quad.

"To where you'll be staying."

"In the White House?" I asked as he led me through the columns.

"It's not the White House anymore." There was darkness in his voice.

He was right; it wasn't the White House anymore. Inside was completely different. Although, I had never been to the White House myself, obsidian walls and dark burgundy carpets was not how I pictured where our president lived.

Will spoke to another Jumpsuit seated at a security desk just past the grand doors. The man's eyes widened at me before he quickly glanced away. He nodded to Will.

As Will returned to my side, I couldn't help but ask, "What did you tell them? The whole 'the slave is with me' bit?"

"I didn't have to." His charming smile was gone, mirroring the tight lips and clenched jaws of soldiers. "They would never question me."

I crinkled my brow. "So what—are you an officer or something?" I asked as we climbed a staircase.

"Exactly."

Weird, I thought, but said instead, "This place is so disturbing." We were on the second level now, in a hallway with two doors.

"I think you'll come to like it, Lux." He stopped at one of them. "This is where you'll be staying." He

189

unlocked the door and pushed the decorative brass lever down, swinging it open.

I wouldn't be *liking* anything about this island. Besides, it would only be temporary. If only I could find Asmodeus... "Does Asmodeus stay here, too?"

"He hardly sleeps." There was a dark humor in his voice, and I shivered.

"Of course not." I wouldn't be able to sleep at night either if I had done what he had.

"Why don't you get settled in and rest?"

"Shouldn't I be with the rest of my people?"

"Are you worried about them? I have already alerted the proper people of the mix-up when we were downstairs. They will be well taken care for their stay here."

I chewed on my lip. "You didn't happen to see a young girl and her sister go through the tunnels, did you?"

"A child? No, why do you ask?"

"No reason." If Lilou and Kileigh weren't on the island... did that mean Draven kept his promise? Why would he do that?

"Trust me. Your people are in their rooms being sent meals as we speak. Let me show you around the island so I can prove to you it's not a bad as you're making it out to be."

The way he said it as a statement not a question made me want to refuse. I didn't like to be bossed around anymore than the next girl kidnapped by pirates and brought to the most hated man in the world, but I wanted to see with my own eyes how this place operated and see my people.

I started down the hall, back the way we came.

"Where are you going?" he asked again in that voice of amusement and intrigue.

I squinted at him like the answer was obvious.

"The tour?" I reminded him.

"I was waiting for your answer."

I raised my eyebrows. "You never asked me a question."

His mouth popped open in protest, but it snapped shut. and instead split into a devious smile. He laughed throatily as he walked toward me. "Touché."

I continued toward the stairs when I felt a pull on my arm. I turned in panic to see Will had slipped his arm in mine, our fingers now entwined.

"What the hell are you doing?" I pulled my hand free.

"Holding your hand."

"You can't just hold my hand!"

"Why not? I thought I didn't have to ask you any questions. I wanted to hold your hand, so instead of waiting for an answer, I just did it."

My smile flattened at the game he was playing. Whether or not it was done in good humor or more seriously, if he was testing me, it wasn't a game I wanted to play. The strangeness of his touch reminded me of how naturally Draven's felt. My stomach rolled at the thought of Draven. I wish I hadn't cared for him. If I didn't have feelings for him, it wouldn't hurt so much. It was infuriating and painful all at once. I longed to be the person I used to be before him. Longed to be naïve and feisty and defiant. Even if I was selfish and ignorant... I just longed for anything but a broken heart.

Pre-Draven Lux would have no problems holding a boy's hand. I wanted to do it. Just to prove I hadn't changed.

My fist opened, my fingers spreading in a fan. I lifted my arm....

But I couldn't.

I turned and continued walking, hoping Will

would ignore what just happened.

When we entered the main area on the first floor, he took us directly outside and I was glad for it. I couldn't care less about the extravagant mansion; I wanted to know where my people were and where the tunnels led. As we walked across the foyer, everyone seemed to stop working and glance at us. Was I doing something wrong? I lowered my gaze and adjusted my outfit.

"Am I allowed to just roam the island freely?"

"Of course. Like I said, you're a guest here. This isn't a prison."

I just nodded. I'd heard too much about Asmodeus to be reassured. We continued walking across the quad in silence. Why was I so suspicious of the first guy to be nice to me? He was American. He understood me, and we shared the same loss. God knew if I'd ever be the same again after Draven in this lifetime. I stopped walking. A surge of frustration shot through me. "Damn him!"

Will stopped and studied me under lowered brows.

"What?" I tapped the fingers of my hands against my thigh.

He shook his head. "What I wouldn't give to know what you're thinking right now."

I tightened my lips and pulled him to a walk. "You know what they say, 'All truly great thoughts are conceived by walking.'"

"Nietzsche." Again in the voice of surprise and intrigue. Suddenly, that tone made me feel unique, like I was the smartest girl in the world.

"You know him?" I was curious how much information Asmodeus made available to his soldiers. While we had no formal school on our island, my father and mother took their time to teach me things

considered invaluable by many of the more traditional Sirbiadian's.

"Of course. My surprise was that you were familiar with his work."

"I guess I'm just full of surprises." *Sheesh,* did I
have a bad attitude today.

"Yes, you are," he said, his eyes widening in realization. "So tell me about Sirbiad."

"Sirbiad? Wait, how do you know where I come
from?"

"You told me when we first met." He spoke with
cool authority like it was the easiest question in the
world.

"Oh, right." I covered my face with a hand. Of
course, how oblivious and paranoid was I?

I took a deep breath and for the rest of our walk,
I told him about my family and our island. It wasn't
until we stopped to enter the first building that I considered I might have said too much. I felt comfortable
with him, knowing he was from the US. He was the
only one who could truly understand my loss.

Our conversation came naturally and easily—
normal. It helped that I was surrounded by things eerily reminiscent of the US. The institutional buildings,
the perfectly manicured grass, architecture, building
materials, even the military-like Jumpsuits were re-
minders of what I missed. Even though it meant the
buildings blocked the view of the beach, the machines
tainted the smell of fresh ocean air, and the hard grass
covered beautiful white sand.

The island was smaller than I originally imagined,
but most of it was manmade. Anyone who had forewarning of the floods could build such a place. Not
anyone—Asmodeus.

Will showed me the tunnels and explained how
each of them worked. I was relieved to know that the

system was more humane than I originally suspected. Will said the tunnels just indicated what job they
would do on the island and sent them to their correct
posts for training.

We were on our way back to the White House
when we passed a door that looked different from the
other metal ones. This was made entirely of wood.

"What's behind this door?"

He slid in front of it. "Some areas are restricted.
No one is allowed past them."

My curiosity instantly piqued. "If it's so restricted,
why isn't it guarded?" Why was it a simple wooden
door? It didn't even have locks on it.

"It doesn't need to be. If someone is disloyal
enough to break the rules, then they deserve the unknowns that lurk there."

My interest must have been written all over my
face because he pulled me well away from it.

"Let's watch a movie tonight."

Again, I noticed how he hadn't asked and had to
laugh. "A *movie*?"

"I thought you were from the US. Don't you remember moving pictures?"

I smiled in pure joy.

Encouraged by my laughter, he continued. "We
can have dinner first, and then make our way to the
outdoor viewing area. Just tell me what you want to
eat, and it's yours. Anything you can dream up. Fruits,
meats, breads, desserts."

"Hm," I answered, a feeling like cold steel slipping
through my gut. I wanted more than anything to feel
normal, but I just... couldn't. Couldn't stop thinking
about Draven. Couldn't forget how he made me feel.

But I shouldn't refuse. I was a stranger in this
place. It wasn't like I had anywhere else I could go
until I found Asmodeus and was sent home, and I still
needed Will in order to get access to him.

Chapter Fifteen

THE BRISK WALK TO MY ROOM WAS IN SILENCE—ON MY end at least. I was too busy thinking about how advanced the island was. They had gardens, livestock, and stores of supplies with everything ranging from antibiotics to chocolate. Now I knew where the pirates got their food.

Will left me in my room to rest. I told myself the only reason I was going with him tonight was because of his connection to Asmodeus, but I so badly wanted to find comfort and familiarity in my new friendship.

The room had a real bathroom, with real plumbing, and much to my excitement, a garden tub I was reluctant to leave. I didn't need to carry any water in, I just turned a porcelain knob and the water flowed to the exact temperature I wanted it, which was scorching hot. An hour later, I forced myself out.

I emerged from the bathroom, wrapped only in a plush burgundy towel. The sight of an unfamiliar set of clothes on the bed sent my pulse racing. I rushed over to find a new dress. It was in the same style as my old one with a scooped neck, empire waist, and slightly puffed capped sleeves, but in a stunning canary yellow. And the big difference: it was brand new.

A chill ran through me.

Someone had entered my room.

The lack of privacy in this place unsettled me in ways I never felt while sharing a cabin with a pirate. I gathered up the new clothes and matching sandals against my damp body and hurried into the bathroom to get dressed.

After I managed to work through the tangles in my hair, I pulled back the velvet curtains and my eyes widened. It was already sundown. My heart cemented harder than the bricks on the buildings. I put a hand over my mouth as I watched the darkening sky and the waxing crescent moon. The moon would always serve as a reminder of what I'd lost. I'd spent too long looking at it and imagining home.

Blowing out a breath, I released the curtain, letting it fall closed. Exiting the bathroom, I felt clean but emotionally and physically drained.

The bedroom was bigger than our entire tent back on Sirbiad. A canopy bed took up one side of the room, while a living area with a fireplace and chaise were on the other. The décor didn't match the rest of the house; it was a great deal lighter, with elegant creams and golds. It was open and airy and yet the walls were closing in on me. I paced the room. A quick and painful memory of the time I spent in Draven's cabin flashed through my mind.

I stormed out the door to find Asmodeus on my own.

"Oh!" My hand flew to my chest. Will was waiting for me outside the door, leaning casually against the wall

"You look... lovely. I hope you like your new dress."

I shrugged in indifference. "Thank you. It was either this or my dress that smells like I spent the past week on pirate ship."

He let out a sole chuckle. "I'll send someone up

to have it cleaned, but what I wouldn't give to know what would impress you."

I opened my mouth, but had nothing to say. "You look... nice." In truth, he looked more than nice. His hair was slicked back to perfection. Despite the light, fresh scent that clung to him, his eyes were still a dangerous brown. I gave his khaki shorts and casual, short-sleeved cotton shirt an appraising look. "Are you the only one who doesn't have to wear the ridiculous jumpsuits?"

"No, not the only one." He took one step toward me, and my breath froze. He cast an approving glance at my tanned thighs before capturing my eyes with his. Something intense flared through his entrancement. The brown almost seemed to swirl with the color of honey, and I found myself unable to look away.

I broke our gaze, instantly able to think again. When I took a step back, he laughed, directing his gaze to my outfit.

I looked down. "Oh." He *wasn't* the only one. I fidgeted with the hem as I considered why that was.

"Shall we?" He held out his hand.

"I—" Should I say no and try to navigate the island by myself?

Will was my best bet, and I was curious about who he was and how he came to the island. I ignored his hand and walked by his side, twisting my hair up to give my hands something to do.

Outside, the air had cooled, but the sky glowed with the sunset. I wrapped my arms around myself as a breeze blew. With it came a stench. I had smelled it earlier on the island, but the wind brought it on stronger. I shivered. It was the smell of mold. Of decomposition.

"Are you cold?" Will wrapped one arm around me and rubbed my shoulder. My stomach quivered at his touch. I frowned. I shouldn't feel uncomfortable at his kindness.

"I'm fine. Thanks." I lifted my shoulder in a shrug until his arm fell away. "Where are we going?"

"To eat, unless..." His gaze raked my body appreciatively before he quirked an eyebrow. "You wanted to do something else?"

"No, I could eat," I blurted out.

He laughed. "You can relax, you know."

I can? No, I didn't think I could. I couldn't afford to "relax". Things didn't turn out so well the last time I let my guard down to "relax". Until my people were back on Sirbiad safely, I wouldn't be able to *"relax"*.

We walked to the other side of the quad, to a building he had shown me earlier. A fork and knife were engraved above the doors. Will had explained on the tour that each building had a purpose. The one with the carving of the bed obviously meant lodging. This one, I assumed meant dining. My theory was confirmed as we strode into the building. A marble entryway separated a staircase from a large hall. Inside were rows upon rows of picnic-style tables. I walked toward them, hoping to find the prisoners.

"Where are you going?" Will caught my hand and pulled me behind him and up a staircase.

"Where are *you* going?" The noises from the hall receded as he led me up the spiraling stairway.

"Somewhere private."

When we reached the top of the stairs, it opened up into a small room. Silk rugs complemented the opulence. The floor-to-ceiling windows made it feel open yet private. A single table sat by the window that faced the sea. It was covered in white linen. A candle flickered on top of it. I squeezed my hands into fists. "What did you have to do to get this place?"

"You have no idea." There was darkness in his

voice I would have to address later. It didn't match the friendly boyish charm I had known up until this point.

I turned my attention to the table and he led me toward it, holding out the chair for me. At least his manners were consistent. Sitting down, I appreciated the remarkable view. On one side, there was the sea. On the other, it overlooked the majority of Asmodeus' island. You could see the complexity of construction from up here, and it unnerved me to know how prepared he'd been. I couldn't begin to imagine why someone like Will would be working for him, filing that question away to ask at a more appropriate time. I wouldn't let my curiosity jeopardize us getting home.

Below me, more people filed into the building. Something yearned inside me to join them. It felt odd to be up here looking down on them. I was no better off than they were until Will took me under his wing. Lifting my head, I gave Will a warm smile, grateful for his kindness.

"Asmodeus doesn't eat?" I asked. The man was beginning to seem immortal.

"He does. Just somewhere private."

"Someplace like this? I hope he doesn't need to use this table. Of course, he could always join us..."

"In such a hurry to meet Asmodeus? If I didn't know any better, I'd think you were fond of him."

I swallowed down my disgust, which was thick and bitter in my throat. As casually as I could manage, I shrugged my shoulders.

"No matter, he's not back yet. And how else was I going to woo you?"

"Why would you need to woo me?" Panic crept in, like tiny knives on my spine.

"It just seems to me like you need convincing."

"Convincing of what?"

"That things aren't always what they seem." The

way he said it came out as a reluctant warning.

I placed my palms flat on the table, the action a little too harsh. "Who have you been talking to?" I whispered severely at his parroting of Ahmed's words.

"Talked to about what?" He tilted his head in genuine confusion.

"Nothing. Sorry." I shook my head. *Stop being so paranoid, Lux.* What was wrong with me? I talked myself down to the point where I was able to relax my shoulders.

He gave me a courteous smile. "Let's eat, shall we?"

At his words, a uniformed waiter came from behind a curtain, rolling out a cart. A plate was set in front of each of us, and I was distracted for the time being just studying the food in front of me.

"Salad?" The heap of lettuce, crunchy croutons, and creamy dressing made my mouth water.

"A chopped cucumber and tomato salad, accompanied by a chicken broth-based soup, and stuffed clams for appetizers. For the main course, braised beef in a burgundy sauce with asparagus and potatoes, followed by a cheese and fruit plate, and finally, dessert." The waiter's voice was courteous yet patronizing, and he left before I could say thanks. Clearly, he had misinterpreted my amazed comment for indifference, and I made no move to correct him as I licked my lips at his descriptions.

"But that last bit will be a surprise." Will lowered his voice, being purposefully mysterious. I lifted my head to find a smile had lit up his handsome face.

I swallowed. "Do I even want to ask how you got all this?" *Yes. Yes, I did.*

"We have everything here. *Everything.*" He brushed it off. "Now eat."

Pushy, I thought, bemused, as we ate in silence.

"Do you have any family here?" I hadn't dared to ask what I had wanted to—why he came here with Asmodeus, but perhaps his answer could give me clues about that.

Will shook his head once.

I swallowed a piece of lettuce whole. That was all he was going to say about it, I guessed. Maybe it was a sensitive subject.

"I don't have any family here in the sense you're referring to." He set his glass down and winked at me.

"Oh." My head jerked back. His openness and casualness on the subject was vastly different from Draven.

"You'd think at least one of them would've survived," he said, surprising me again.

"You came from a big family then?"

He set his fork down and beckoned with his forefinger. The young man standing by the door approached. "Five brothers and four sisters."

I leaned back so the guard/waiter could take my plate. "Let me guess, you're the youngest," I deducted from his tone.

He chuckled. "Worse. The middle child."

I held a curious smile as I encouraged him to continue. I couldn't begin to imagine what life in a big family would be like.

"Do you have any siblings?" he asked, and my smile died.

"Only child." I paused to take a taste of my soup. "*Mm.* What were your parents like?" I'd mastered diverting the subject away from me.

Will narrowed his gaze at me. His eyes passed over me once. When his features softened, he started talking again.

"They were rich and we moved about every two months." A pained laugh came quietly from his chest.

How did they know Asmodeus and where were they now? But that was too insensitive. I felt sorry for him. "That must have been hard. What about your friends? And school?"

"We had a team of people caring for us. Nannies, chefs, tutors. We were enrolled in college by twelve. My sister became the youngest doctor in the US and opened her own practice at twenty-two."

"Really?" I was fascinated by this piece of information from my country.

He nodded, clearly not as impressed as I was. "There was this song my dad played whenever we were about to move. I still remember coming home from school and hearing it. You wouldn't find a single soul in our house that day. My brothers and sisters would be gone, saying goodbye to friends, breaking up with girlfriends, telling off the school bully..."

I looked down at my plate and shifted uncomfortably in the soft chair.

He tapped the table with his fingers, as if starting a beat. "The song was like, *da da dum dum. Da dum da dum—*"

My lips trembled with the need to smile.

His good humor fell. "Now I've gone and made a fool out of myself."

"No, not at all," I said in a fit of giggles. "I think it's... adorable. I'm just sorry I couldn't help you out. I'm afraid I don't remember many songs."

"You don't remember music?"

I shook my head.

"Chopin, Beethoven, not even Elvis?"

I knew who they were, but what their music sounded like was only a luxury afforded to the girls on deserted islands whose fathers hadn't forced them to leave all technology at home. I shook my head more fervently.

"Well then, you are in for a real treat later." A twinkle of anticipation sparkled in his eyes.

His good mood was contagious. I ate through the courses as much as I could between laughs. By the time the fruit came out, my stomach was sticking out in an unladylike way, and I didn't know if I could tolerate one more bite. The dessert, though, wasn't something I was going to pass up. I tried to not think it but there, in the back of my mind, was the truth. That no matter how many strawberries I ate, no matter how much I laughed at Will's jokes, no matter how much I told myself this felt normal... I was not *okay.*

Armored boots busted confidently into the room. My smile fell, and the blood drained from my face at the familiar sound. Will had called in each course, so when heavy footsteps busted in unannounced, it commanded his full attention. I looked up and was greeted with the face of the very last person I expected to see.

I gripped my stomach, which twisted tighter than any sailor's knot.

Words caught in my throat. I tried to say something.

He approached our table, keeping his focus on Will alone, not sparing even a single glance toward me.

My heart dropped to my stomach, the knot in my stomach unraveling from impact.

Stupid me for thinking, hoping, wishing, that this had to do with me.

Draven shot an anxious look in my direction. It was brief, but it was there.

My heart immediately resumed beating as hope returned.

I followed the direction of Draven's gaze—to Will.

Will didn't seem surprised at his presence. They

obviously knew each other, but Will's jaw twitched like he wasn't happy about it.

"Draven." Will's tone was scolding. "Why are you here?"

"Oh, I'm leaving, but before I do, I had business I wanted to conclude."

I worked down a swallow, but my throat was too tight.

"You should take that up with someone else," Will warned.

"I want to settle my debt. I won't expect any kind of payment, and I'm willing to add more years of service to my contract as well."

"What's all this in exchange for?" He swirled his hand in the air.

"All I want is Lux. Just let her leave with me."

My legs turned into jellyfish at his declaration.

Will laughed, and Draven followed it with a string of Arabic profanities. I touched my cool lips with the tips of my fingers.

"Why are you asking *me*, Draven?"

"You know why," he snarled through clenched teeth.

"No, I mean why are you asking me like she is my property? I don't own her. Lux is her own person and can make her own decisions."

Draven leaned toward him, his nostrils flaring. "What game are you playing?" he whispered through clenched teeth.

"I'm not playing any games. Why don't you ask Lux herself? She's right here."

Draven turned his attention toward me, and then his eyes darted back at Will in a sideways glance.

"Let's have Lux make the decision. If she wants to go with you, she can. If not, well..." He breathed contentedly. "She can stay right where she is."

"Fine." I wished he hadn't smirked. "C'mon, Lux. We're leaving." His head turned toward mine as if waiting for me to jump up and go with him.

What, no *'hello'*? No *'how are you'*? How about *'I'm sorry'* for starters. "Leaving?"

"I'm returning you to Sirbiad."

"Draven, you're the one who brought me here in the first place. Why do you want me back now?"

"I made a mistake, but I've returned for you now."

"You've returned for me now," I deadpanned.

"I'm sorry, Lux. Please—"

"How dare you!" I gripped the table so I wouldn't slap him. If Will weren't our audience, I probably would have done a lot more. "You made me believe I was worthless. That I was nothing to you. That I was *using* you. And you think you can just come back and apologize and I'll just give up everything? Risk the lives of my people—again. For you? What happened to your land being the most important thing to you? What has changed?"

"No, Lux. I didn't think it would be that easy. Nothing is ever easy with you."

"Do *not* turn this on me."

He squeezed his eyes shut. "We've both spent the last five years with only one thing in mind—going home again. And I was so close. I could go home again. My *crew* could go home again. But you were right, Lux. I was a coward. I couldn't let go of my past like you did. I've realized I'll get home and then what? I've realized I don't belong there. I've realized I don't belong anywhere. I've realized the only time I felt anything meaningful was when I was with you."

Every part of my body wanted to resist. Every beat of my heart assured me that I still had feelings for him, but could I go with him? *No.* I couldn't trust him. I couldn't let down my people again. Although, why would he be willing to give up the last thing he wanted in this world for me? He was fighting. Fighting for me. But then again, it was he who brought me here in the first place. My head and heart were unable to reconcile. "What kind of game are you playing?"

"This isn't a game. I'm in love with you, Lux. I don't care if you don't feel the same way. I can't leave you here with Asmodeus. If I can't be with you, at least I'll know you'll be with your parents, happy and safe. I'd give anything for the chance to be with my parents again."

He said he loved me, and I believed it with every part of my body. My heart felt whole again. My anger not as wrathful as it should be. I thought about how I felt when I learned going home again was impossible. Just then, the image of the shaman came to mind. Remembering the betrayal in his eyes was like a pail of cold water to my flaming heart. "I can't. I won't risk my people again. I don't trust you. You lied to me once, Draven. How do I know you're not lying again?" My voice rose.

"Lied to you?"

"You don't have to kidnap people to bring them here. Asmodeus doesn't force you; you do that on your own."

"Who told you this?"

"No one needed to tell me this; I've seen The Island with my own eyes."

"What have you seen, Lux? Your plush little bedroom, the acts of Asmodeus' loyal goons? You think anyone would come here willingly, once they knew the truth?"

Will made a chocking sound that briefly caught my attention.

"You're wrong, Draven. He's going to send us home, so I guess I don't need you anymore."

"And you believed that? What has changed you? I should have never brought you here. I should have hid you in the storage hold like I wanted and made it seem that I never even took you in the first place."

Will's chair crashed to the floor. "That's treason!" He shook a finger at Draven.

"Will..." I started to protest, shocked by his outburst.

"I don't care what's right or wrong anymore. I'm taking her one way or another."

"Draven Sabriye, as requested, the terms of your contract have just changed. Guards." Will's voice was sinister as he signaled to the men waiting by the door.

Draven's hand slipped into the inside of his outercoat, and he pulled out a gold-handled dagger.

"Draven, oh my God!" I pleaded. "What are you doing? Don't!"

His eyes were hooded like those of a hawk as he looked at me. "You really don't believe me?"

"I don't know what to believe anymore."

He pushed his lips together and slipped the dagger back as easily as he removed it. "Fine. But I'll return with proof. I won't leave you again."

He gave a challenging look at Will. "I'll be back for you, Lux." Then he turned away, not waiting for my reply. The tail of his leather coat flew behind him as he walked away.

"Go after him." Will spoke to the guard in a low, composed voice.

My forehead puckered and I faced Will, gripping his arms. "I don't understand. Why did you say it was treason to keep me hidden in the storage hold?"

"He admitted to the kidnappings..."

"Please. They have to let him go. It... it was a misunderstanding," I rambled on.

"I'll see what I can do, but I don't make those decisions. Treason is taken very seriously on this island..."

I stared up at him with pleading eyes. My heart felt like it was suspended in my chest with a fishing net. No matter what had happened between Draven and me, I didn't want anything to happen to him because of me.

Will's jaw clenched in defeat, and he left.

I covered my eyes with my hand and plopped back into the chair. My full stomach surprisingly felt like it had holes. And my heart—my heart would have hurt less if it had been stabbed with the dagger.

Draven had come back for me.

The whole situation was such a mess.

Someone stomped up the stairs, and I stumbled to a stand. It was Will.

I swallowed, wringing my hands together. "He's not going to be in trouble, is he?"

"He won't be punished as long as he leaves first thing in the morning and never returns to The Island." Will pulled his chair back to the table and sat.

"What about his contract with Asmodeus?" He needed Asmodeus' help to get back his land!

"As I've said, I don't make those decisions. However, I told him that if he complied, when Asmodeus returned, he would take that into consideration, as well as his years of service."

The air left my lungs in a huff as I sat in mine. "And he agreed?" I asked, breathless. My head was hoping he would take Will's advice, but my heart was hoping he wouldn't give me up again so easily.

"If you're thinking about trying to go with him..."

I was.

He shook his head, not bothering to finish his sentence. "I told you the decision would be yours. If you want to leave with him, then go."

I couldn't imagine how foolish the hopefulness

written all over my face was. Will put his elbows on the table and rested his chin on his entwined fingers. "I am only telling you this because I care about you as a fellow American." He took a deep breath. "But there are no American laws here. I was lucky to be able to let Draven leave here unharmed. I can't protect you if you choose to go with him. There were witnesses, a scene."

"What does that mean?" The warning in his voice prevented me from standing right that moment and rushing back to Draven's ship.

"I'm just not sure if your people would make the same choice considering he did kidnap them in the first place. Let him go, Lux. Stay here and enjoy yourself. In a few days, you'll sail home with your people."

I nodded in understanding. I had no choice but to stay if I was going to get them back to Sirbiad. That still didn't mean it didn't hurt. Was that why Draven was so determined to bring me here? That was why he was afraid? I knew how important his parents' land was to him. I met Treymore firsthand and knew how humiliating it must be to know he had it. As angry as I was for how he treated me, I didn't want to see him get hurt or punished. I didn't want him to be in any more debt to this place. I wanted him to find peace. If he thought he could find it through honoring his slain family by getting his land back, then so be it. Draven was free to leave. It was what I wanted, wasn't it? I tried to swallow again, but this time I couldn't. "Thank you, Will. You are becoming a good friend." I didn't bother lifting my gaze from my plate.

There was a pregnant silence between us before I exhaled. "I think I should get some sleep." Setting my napkin on the table, I rose halfway out of my chair.

"You can't; we haven't seen our movie yet." He reached across the table and put his hand over mine. I pulled mine back as if I'd been burned. I couldn't bear to be touched right now. "I'm sorry. I'll take you home."

"Home?" My heart soared.

His smile fell, and his face twisted. "To your room, sorry."

I nodded. Together, we stood and left.

There were no words exchanged. No small talk spoken. No comment on the weather as we walked back to my door.

"You owe me a movie." He flashed a sweet smile, the silence broken, his boyish charm rebounded, the incident with Draven forgotten.

I nodded, not sure how I felt about that, hoping Asmodeus would return soon and we could just go home. Though my stomach was filled with delicious food, it still managed to growl with worry.

I told myself I had made the right choice, but there was that cynical voice that was hard to drown out.

Hurrying inside the room, I closed the door behind me. I leaned against the cool lacquered wood, squeezing my eyes shut. Emotions swirled around me.

"Sweet dreams." Will's whisper drifted through the door. I twisted the lock before pushing away. Collapsing on the bed, I succumbed to sleep, and, with it, the luxury of unconsciousness.

Chapter Sixteen

*"The Light is in my heart between my ribs, so why would
I fear walking in the Darkness."*
-Abu Al-Kasem Ash-Shabi. Poet 1909-1934

"TELL ME YOUR DEEPEST DESIRES."
"Why? Who are you?"
"Tell me what you wish for."
"I don't wish anything."
"Tell me or I shall see myself."
*The memories of my past flicked before me like a
slideshow. My life was on fast forward and didn't stop
until the first night I started building the boat.*
"Interesting," the disembodied voice said.
"What? What is?"
*A scene played before my eyes. It was of my con-
versation on the beach with Leif. It was all foolishly out
before me, of how I had believed that the US had some-
how survived. Of how I yearned for friends and that life
of comfort again. That was when my memories shuffled to my time with Draven. Our first almost kiss, and
midnight chats and dinners together.*
*A red-colored haze clouded the memory and I
wished it would clear so I could replay the sweet scenes.
The red haze was now like a cloud until it became so*

thick I could no longer see those memories. "No," I cried.

The voice huffed. "He's gone. Make the best out of where you live now."

"I don't live here. I will find Asmodeus and he will send me home."

"You don't want to stay?" The voice was now vicious sounding, like a string of different voices layered on top of another.

"Never. I hate him!"

The red smoke filled my lungs, and I choked.

I woke up gasping for air, unsure if I had a dream or a nightmare. Guilt followed as I wiped the sweat from my brow.

Having the past replay in my dreams was a wake-up call. I didn't know what I was thinking by trying to leave Sirbiad. I had wanted to feel free, but being free was not what I'd thought it would be. I had only thought of myself and the things I would get as I made my plans to sail away. I didn't think of how it would affect my parents or discourage my people.

I had calmed down by the time I stood, but the guilt remained. Walking to the door, I made sure it was still locked. When I was sure nothing was out of place, I grabbed the first outfit I found in the closet and rushed to the bathroom to get dressed.

Bathroom routines were overrated: I swear, brushes could also double as torture devices. Wading in the ocean was much easier, but I wouldn't admit that to anyone.

Anyone.

As I made the bed, a thought passed quickly through my mind. Another Sirbiad-related thought. I missed my hammock. Finishing with a huff, I sat on the bed, thinking of how to handle what would come next.

This wasn't about me anymore. I would keep to

my plan—find Asmodeus and get my people home. The speech self-motivated me, and I was eager to follow through. Maybe Asmodeus was back.

I rushed out the door and smacked into a hard chest under a citrus-fresh chambray shirt.

"Whoa, Lux." Will was cheerful and his smile told me he enjoyed catching me. "Careful." He winked as he set me straight.

Warmth spread to my cheeks. "I'm sorry. I was just leaving. I didn't realize you had knocked."

"I didn't; I was just about to when you nearly ran me over."

"Sorry." I looked at my feet.

He pressed his palms to my cheeks and forced my head to tilt back. "Your blush is irresistible."

My eyes met his. I resisted turning my face toward his palm as I became mesmerized by the swirls of brown in his eyes.

"Where were you going, Lux?"

"Hmm?" I felt like I was pulled out of a dream as I tried to clear the unwanted thoughts that came when I looked into his eyes. "I was going to find Asmodeus." I found my voice.

"So determined to see the man. I'm afraid he hasn't returned yet. You'll meet him, just have patience." He dropped his hands from my face and grabbed my hand. "In the meantime, we're going to have some fun."

"Fun?" I was intrigued enough to follow him.

He glanced over his shoulder in a move that appeared appraising. "You don't have to wear your old dress. I filled the closet with new clothes for you."

Before, this would have been a dream come true, but now, it didn't interest me. I saw my old sundress for what is was—an old, outgrown outfit. I offered the sincerest thank you I could manage before we continued walking.

"Where are we going?" I followed Will down the staircase with anticipation. What could be his idea of fun on Asmodeus' island?

"You'll see. I hope you like surprises."

The people in jumpsuits still watched me, and I had a sinking feeling they thought I should be with the others.

"What if I said 'I don't'?"

"Well, you'll like this one."

We walked past a group of people who stood in a circle, talking. They weren't wearing jumpsuits, and their clothes were worn with Asian influences.

"Who are they?" I asked Will.

"Who?" he said, looking back over his shoulder. "Oh, they work here, of course. They've been here a while. Actually, I think they came from Sirbiad."

"Really?" I didn't bother hiding the surprise in my voice.

"Yes, really."

"I didn't imagine they would have such freedom. I'll admit, it didn't look the most humane when I first arrived."

He laughed at the memory. "*Cattle* did you call them? They were just getting assigned their roles. It's like any city here, except without a monetary system, of course. They work, and in return, they are provided for."

I stared up at him with disbelieving eyes. "Where are my people and the others who came here on Draven's ship?"

"As promised, I alerted the guards to the mix up and they are comfortably resting in guest rooms as we speak."

"And we will be able to leave? You will return us to Sirbiad?" I felt the need to make sure.

"Of course," he said for the third time. He pulled my arm to increase my pace. "Now, c'mon, we have a lot to do."

Will took me through the buildings until we arrived under the arches toward the sea. We walked toward the dock, and I automatically searched the horizon for Draven's ship. The goose bumps on my flesh had nothing to do with the breeze.

It wasn't there.

Nothing, not a spec of his ship was on the horizon, but in searching, I spotted a smaller boat tied to the docks. It was unlike any I had ever seen, and I examined it, determined to discover why.

As we approached, I had my answer. The boat wasn't pieced together; it was like a normal boat you'd find in the Old World. And it was in excellent condition.

Our feet squeaked against the dock as we drew level with it. "Don't you like to sail?" Will jumped on the boat with familiarity, and then held his hand out for me to join him.

"I-I wouldn't know," I stammered in bewilderment.

"Then I'm glad to give you your first lesson." He grabbed my hand and pulled me toward him. I stepped in time to make it on the boat without landing on my face.

Wincing, I rubbed my arm. "Do you just want a leash or something?"

"Now that you mention it, it has crossed my mind."

"Funny." My voice was droll. "How did you get this boat? Oh, right, *you* didn't. But Asmodeus could have. What I mean is—how are you just allowed to take his boat?"

He shrugged as he worked to release the rope from the dock. "I have flexible working hours."

The anticipation of going out on a modern boat made my heart speed up, but there was a sense of guilt that came with it. The awkwardness of enjoying something that belonged to Asmodeus eventually won out. "I don't know if I feel like sailing..." I pinched my bottom lip with my index finger and thumb, looking toward the dock.

"Sit. You'll love it." He pointed to a padded bench seat.

The boat was distancing itself from the dock, and I no longer had a choice. I took a look around. The sunlight reflected off the water, and I shielded my eyes from the brightness. The light breeze combined with clear skies promised a calm day.

The clinking of metal and the waves breaking against the shore were the only sounds as we were carried away.

Will freed the sails with the ease and knowledge of a mariner. I sat next to the railed edge. Curling my hand around the cool metal railing, the wind blew generously against my face. The slosh, slosh, sloshing of water against the boat was rhythmic. I felt free, like I was made for the sea.

"You look peaceful."

I opened my eyes and turned my face away from the sun. "I am."

"Me too. I love it out here. It clears my mind, lets me think straight. Out here, I can be my true self. I can forget."

I nodded, not wanting to be eager in agreeing but feeling the exact same way. "No chance you can drop me off in Sirbiad while we're out here, hm?" I asked, already knowing the answer.

"Then you wouldn't get to see the best part."

We sailed straight out, following the blinding reflection on the water. Relaxed under the sun's warming rays, I stretched out across the bench, one arm over my forehead, one dangling off the seat. My eyelids fluttered, fighting sleep, sun, and sea.

Maybe this wasn't such a terrible idea after all...

After a while, I felt the boat starting to turn. Sitting up and blocking the sun from view, I discovered we were heading back toward the island.

I took a slow breath, my body warm and rested from the afternoon on the water. Disappointment at returning was both unfamiliar and unwelcome.

Will probably had to get back to work or whatever it was he did.

"Are you feeling well?" he asked, breaking a silence I didn't realize was there.

"Yes." I cleared my throat, my voice husky from sleep. "Yes, thank you."

"Good. I hope you didn't think I was going to let you off that easily, did you? I want to show you the other end of the island."

I looked back to discover the island was now off to our left. "I thought I'd seen everything?"

"Not this. The only way to get here is by boat." His lips twitched to a smile. He had a twinkle in his eye that made me nervous.

We sailed close to the island's shore, passing the familiar buildings. There was emptiness as we reached the last building until a group of trees and cliffs came into view. We curved around the far end of the island, somewhere behind the White House. The 'city' had gone out of view. A small cove appeared at the southernmost tip. Will turned the wheel toward it. There was no dock, and I wondered what he was planning to do as we approached shore.

I was admiring the sails when the anchor cut the water, followed by another splash. Jerking my head, I peered over the railing. Will was knee deep in sparkling aquamarine water.

"What are you doing?"

"Jump in. It's the only way ashore."

"I..."

"I'll catch you. Don't worry; no sharks come up this far."

Crossing my arms, I gave him a look that screamed 'yeah, right'.

"If you don't come down, you'll have to stay there until I get back. That might be a while, and then you'd miss out on what I had to show—"

"Fine." Kicking off my sandals, I carefully put one leg over the railing, and then the other. I hesitated, but not long enough to show fear, then held my skirt down and jumped.

Laughter escaped as water splashed me. The warmth of the water and sand squishing beneath my toes was intoxicating. Will grabbed my hand, and we trudged to shore.

"I was never going to let you stay behind, you know."

"And *I* would never allow myself to be left behind anyway."

When I raised my head, I found him watching me. His eyes darkened with emotion, and a lustful smile spread across his face. I dropped my head and kept walking. "So what is it you wanted to show me?" The blood drained from my face as I thought again about the suggestive way he looked at me.

"Follow me."

I trailed behind as he led me on a footpath through thick vegetation. Tall trees formed a canopy, and they were plentiful with fruits.

The worn path showed signs of constant use. "Do you bring all the girls here to impress?"

"I'm glad to hear you're impressed." He glanced

back with a triumphant smile like a cat that just *devoured* the canary. I swallowed. "But no, no one has ever been here before."

"Except Asmodeus," I corrected.

"Yes, it is his island, isn't it?"

"You're not his son or anything, are you?"

He snorted. "No. Wouldn't that be weird?"

I laughed. "Yes, that would be *very* weird."

We reached a clearing and I stopped next to Will, wiping the sweat from my hairline with a sigh. He placed one hand on his hip. With the other, he directed my attention to a formation of flat rocks. From a wide crevice in the middle, water bubbled in a laughing spring. Palm trees dotted the perimeter, their branches hanging lazily over the surface of a deep, sun-speckled pool.

I sensed movement and turned at the precise moment Will removed his shirt.

"What-are-you-doing?" My heart involuntarily sped at the sight of him half-naked. His tan skin stretched perfectly over a flat, muscular stomach.

I had to look away.

"Cooling off. Join me?"

"No," I spat out.

"Suit yourself."

He jumped in. Cool water battered my skin. I watched with an envious gaze as he splashed around in the clear spring.

On our island, we retrieved fresh water from a lens under a well. We only waded in the ocean to bathe and attempt fishing; no one dared to go further.

To be fully emerged in water was enticing. To swim around, to be weightless, that was almost irresistible. To do so in a cool, crystal-clear spring, on a pristine beach, surrounded by flora, well, that was downright sinful.

"It's odd there is so much beauty in a place with so much evil," I called out.

Will became still in the water. "He's not evil."

"Says the one who's living off his transgressions."

"That makes a lot of people living off him then. Including you." He raised a mocking eyebrow at me that was a little bit teasing, but mostly trying to prove an irritating point. "What do you know about it anyway?"

I crossed my arms over my chest. "I know he was a scientist who worked for the government. He knew the Floods were going to happen, but instead of warning people, he prepared himself. Hence everything on this island, including the boat we sailed here on."

"You know nothing of the truth; you only heard what you were fed." He blew out a breath in what seemed like an effort to compose himself.

I pursed my lips as I debated with myself. "Then tell me the truth."

The teasing laughter was back. "I can't possibly tell you from there. You'll have to come in."

I rolled my eyes. "Fine. You would have made a great lawyer. You know how to charm people into getting what you want." I walked to the edge of the rocks and dipped half my foot in; the water was as refreshing as it looked. I bit my lip, trying to convince myself there was no harm in enjoying this. Before I could talk myself out of it, I pushed my feet off the rocks and dove in.

I stayed underwater until my lungs tightened in my chest. Only then did I break the surface. The water made the air outside feel cool as it touched my skin. I quickly went back under, longing for the feeling of being submerged. I no longer felt the exertion and warmth from our hike. My skin was refreshed, wet and glossy as I resurfaced. This time, I looked for Will.

He sat against a rock, watching me with a little

too much enjoyment. I swam toward him, joining him at the rock. His hair was damp and disheveled, water still dripping from his locks. The water made his hair darker, more intimidating. His skin was moist from the swim, and a bead of water hung on his lips.

"What?" His tongue came out to swipe away the droplet.

"Nothing."

"Do you like it here?"

The spring or Asmodeus' island? The question was lined with double meaning, and I hated that. I thought about how I should answer, but then he spoke again.

"We get all our water from this spring. It's filled with rainwater, but it's also replenished by an underground source. Almost like there is an underground stream that flows into it. Like magic."

I scoffed. "There's no such thing as magic."

"You don't believe in magic, Lux?"

I shot a sidelong glance at him. "Mmm, no."

"But you believed that Asmodeus had forewarning about The Floods."

"What does that have to do with magic? That was science."

"You believe in science."

"Well, yes."

"Magic is science. Science that works. I'm not talking about conjuring anything, just simple ways to bend the elements that already exist to your will. If one knows all the factors, it can be achieved. Neuro-magic, for instance. By understanding the simple science behind our brains, you can accomplish certain cognitive tricks."

It wasn't *not* possible. Who was I to be so close-minded? But the thought just didn't sit right with me. "Sounds like opportunism."

"Those are just the theories, anyway..." He let his last thought drift off as he ran an admiring hand through the water and changed the subject. "Throughout world history, water has been a source of tension because of its scarcity. You'd think now, since we were surrounded by water, that we'd be sick of it."

"I like the water." Whoa, where'd that come from? "I mean—I don't like this water that's everywhere, but I liked the ocean and swimming..." I willed myself to stop talking.

He studied me. "Me too. Water brings life; it's ironic it was also the one to take so many away."

A raw and primitive grief overwhelmed me. "Yes, well, most of them could have been saved if it wasn't for Asmodeus."

"A lot of them were saved because of Asmodeus. Does your island not get help from him?"

"People are still starving! If Asmodeus had given the government warning, we could have prepared. We could have saved people and been prepared for this water world! Do you know why I'm here? Why I survived and not any other girl in my school? I'll tell you why—because of chance. Because my father was a diplomat for the United States government, and we were in the South Pacific on vacation. Everyone I used to know is gone. "

He shook his head. "Now what kind of man would send nearly three-fourths of the world to their deaths?"

"An evil, selfish one."

He laughed.

"Why do you do that?" I frowned.

"Do what?"

"Laugh like you know something I don't."

He laughed again.

I put my hands on my hips. "Stop that."

"You're cute when you're mad."

"All right, I'm done." I pushed myself to a stand, regretting it as I felt my body leave the water.

He caught my arm to keep me down. "Don't you want me to tell you what I know and you don't? Maybe then, we can laugh together."

I slipped back into the water. "I'm not going to beg you to tell me about Asmodeus, mainly because I know he's evil."

Will's intense stare forced me to break our gaze. I stared at the ripples of water.

"No one ever wants to admit they're wrong. So, of course, he took the fall for something he didn't do."

My gaze returned to his as he continued. "Asmodeus was a scientist for the US Navy. He frequently studied oceanography and what effects the environment would have on water levels. He didn't just predict the floods overnight. It took months of research to discover the precise disasters that would lead to the flooding."

"Well, why didn't he tell anyone? Why didn't he share his research?"

"When the disasters started, he tried to warn the government. A young scientist with virtually no recognition? They didn't believe him for a second. He did what he could to help people survive. He didn't have the resources to save everyone. The government could have done more, but he knew his only chance would be this city. He prepared as much as he could, spending millions of his own money to get the materials he needed. When the Floods started, he used his ships to bring people here. For this place to succeed, he needed people to work. They helped build this place, they help make the food, but they also get to live here and eat the food. Even those who live on other islands, he provides them with as much as he can in return for their cooperation. It's simple really. He did what he could. For that, he got a bad rep. Wouldn't you do the same thing if you were in his position?"

"I don't know," I said. My face twisted in thought as I considered everything he had just told me. Were we really blaming the wrong person all these years? It seemed possible that we hated what happened so much we needed something, or someone, to blame. That it was a part of our grieving.

What would I have done? I hated the possibility that he could be right. I hated that all my preconceptions could be false. If this was the truth, why was this the first time I was hearing about it?

My dad knew Asmodeus, and he was a good judge of character. He appreciated the food and supplies, but knew they were only tools of submission. My father would have seen that he was a good man. But he didn't. Or did he just not say anything?

"I need to meet him."

"If you meet him, will you be able to believe me?"

"Yes." I nodded firmly, more to reassure myself than him. "I'll know if he would be capable of such a thing or if he is the person you claim."

He nodded, pleased with this. "Then you shall meet him." Without notice, he plunged back into the water.

"Really? When?" I asked when he resurfaced.

"Tomorrow."

"Are you asking me or telling me?" I splashed him.

"It doesn't matter. Either way, I'd know your answer." He splashed me back.

"Stop that!" I hit the water with my hand, scooping it up and throwing it at him.

"You started it." He slipped under.

I waited as the blurry vision of him underwater approached me, readying my hands to get him with more water as soon as he came up for air. Suddenly, I felt a presence by my feet, but it was too late. I had been pulled under.

I kicked free to the surface. "Hey," I shouted, but it came out more as a laugh. He was chest deep in water, and I was up to my chin. He stared at me, his eyes narrowing and his lips pursing.

"Come here." He pulled me out of the water to him.

I froze, incapable of making any movements of my own as we were locked in this intimate position. Too intimate. He didn't have a shirt on, and, too late, I realized my damp dress clung to my body. I tried to break away, but he pulled me tighter.

"What are you afraid of?" His seductive whisper sent gooseflesh all over my body.

What was I afraid of? Getting hurt, wondering why this felt wrong, wondering why the more time I spent with him, the more I realized my feelings for Draven. The last admission was dredged from a place beyond logic and reason.

Will, oblivious to my heart's revelations, tilted his head and inched a hair forward. His breath smelled sweet, and my gaze automatically shot up to his eyes. The look on his face mirrored that of Draven's when he wanted to...

"You want to kiss me." There was an alarm to my voice when I shouldn't have been surprised.

He chuckled. "Yes. Look at me." I did. "And you want me to."

His brown eyes seemed to warm and captivate me. My tongue slipped out to lick my parted lips as I slowly leaned forward, never removing my gaze from his eyes. The little flecks of honey swirled, causing me to push away. I blinked profusely, trying to regain my senses.

What was I doing? He was about to kiss me. And

I was about to let him? My weakness disgusted me. I was one to make rash decisions, but it wasn't like me to kiss a stranger. Especially when my heart was with someone else. Somehow, I had considered Will a friend, and this felt like betrayal on that trust.

I swam away and lifted myself onto the rocks. He swam over as I rang the water out of my dress.

"I'm not going to apologize."

I scoffed at him. "Well, that's good because I'm not sure if I would accept your apology."

"You can't deny our attraction."

Will was attractive, but I had *noted* rather than *noticed*. I wanted to like him, and why not? He would be a perfect match. An American like myself, he understood me. He had been so kind and open. Unbidden, my tortured mind picked that moment to filter back to when Draven comforted me that one night. My lips tingled in remembrance of his touch. I could feel him on my skin. I wanted him, but that didn't quite seem to cover it. Was it need? Was it love like my conscious so recklessly suggested before? All I knew was that I craved him, even for all that he was. And it hurt. It hurt like hell because he was gone.

I closed my eyes tightly at this intrusion. I couldn't help it. It was just the way it was. If only I had met Will weeks ago. My eyes flashed open. *Damn it, Draven.*

He managed to taint everyone else for me. I was amazed he could piss me off even though he was probably on the other side of the planet by now. *You should move on,* my conscious suggested, but even *it* lacked its usual enthusiasm.

"I know you're still getting over whatever happened between you and Draven."

'Still' meant I was capable of getting over it. "How do you know about Draven and me?"

"He did interrupt our dinner. Rather rudely, I

might add…"

"He was trading for me. That means nothing. Who knows where I would have ended up?"

"You're right. You made the right choice. You're not the first girl I've seen him bring here."

I shot daggers labeled "accusations" at him with my eyes. "I'm sure you're no better yourself. People look at me strangely when I'm with you, and I have a feeling it's because they'd expect me to be smarter than that." *Bull's-eye.*

"People look at you *enviously* because you're amazing. If I was Draven, I would have never relinquished you so easily." He turned me so I faced him. "In fact, if you had been mine, I would've never given you up in the first place."

That comment hit home.

"We should probably go."

He nodded. "Sure." We stood together. "Lux?"

I peered over at him.

"I'm sorry if I'm so forward with you. My circumstances have prevented me from pursuing anyone before, but you're the first person who is able to understand me, and how you look at things so objectively is refreshing. You are exactly what I need. I have all the time in the world to wait. I'll wait until you're over him."

I ignored him and tried to find the path we came in from. The sun was setting, and I was overcome with a sense of urgency to get out of there.

"Are you always this cold?"

"What?" Shock froze me at the familiarity of the words.

"You always seem to have your arms wrapped around yourself like you're cold."

"No, not cold." *Just uncomfortable.*

He came to me with a warm smile and wrapped

an arm around me. "The path is this way." He pointed, keeping an arm draped over my shoulder as we walked toward it. I shrugged him off to give one final glance at the spring before we made our way to the boat, side by side.

The water became different at night. It now bore the reflection of the moon. I couldn't believe I had only been here two days. It felt like weeks. But you knew what they said: time slowed when you were having fun. Well, that wasn't how it went, but whatever.

Despite the argument with Will, I felt completely relaxed after spending the entire day swimming and sailing.

The boat cut through the dark water easily as we made our way back around the island.

Would this be how it was here? This freedom? Sailing the open sea? Having a real bed, a real bath? A normal guy interested in me?

The lights from the island seemed far away while we were out on the boat. I thought again of the story Draven told me about the night coming from the sea.

"Do you want to steer?" Will's tousled brown hair looked touch-worthy in the moonlight.

"Are you sure?" My hesitance lacked conviction, and I didn't wait to hear his reply as I stumbled over to him. He stepped away from the wheel with a smile.

I did my best to contain my childlike excitement, but inside, warmth radiated throughout my body. Awake, rejuvenated by adrenaline, I was actually heading my own boat. Well, it wasn't *my* boat. *Semantics,* I shushed my conscious.

"You're a natural."

My lips tried to twitch into a smile. It took getting everything I always wanted and losing it to experience true freedom. I glanced over my shoulder at Will. He was leaning against the boat, his shirt loosely blowing in the night breeze. Lowered brown eyes burned into me with desire.

It was only a second after I let go of the wheel that his arms wrapped around me.

Chapter Seventeen

Love is reckless; not reason.
Reason seeks a profit.
Love comes on strong,
Consuming herself, unabashed.
Yet, in the midst of suffering,
Love proceeds like a millstone,
Hard surfaced and straightforward.
Having died of self-interest,
She risks everything and asks for nothing.
Love gambles away every gift God bestows.
Without cause God gave us Being;
Without cause, give it back again."
-Mathnawi VI, 1967-1964

FIGHTING FOR MY SENSES TO RETURN, I PULLED AWAY before Will's lips touched mine. I must have been an emotional mess to metaphorically jump into the arms of the first guy who was nice to me.

Only after I was alone in my room was I hurtled back to earth as reality struck. It was like whenever I was with Will, my thinking was clouded.

Then the guilt set in, which was really starting to get on my nerves. *Where was the off switch?*

I couldn't let Will think I was anything more than

a friend. I couldn't let myself open up to him. It just didn't feel right. I didn't feel things for him like I did with Draven. Was that normal?

Will was an attractive, charming guy. Any girl should be lucky to have his affections. *Why couldn't it be me? Why couldn't I like someone who could like me back? Why did I have to like the person I could never have?*

I wished my head and heart would reconcile, because I was tired of this back-and-forth uncertainty. Climbing into the high bed, I felt achy and exhausted.

Sleeping was easy; it was the falling that was the hard part...

...All my fatigue was washed away and I was wide awake again. Images of my day with Will replayed involuntarily through my head, but I didn't cringe away this time. It wasn't at all painful to remember. Had I really been that carefree? I seemed so... grounded. Like I knew what I was doing was okay, and was confident that I was with Will. The guilt was finally gone! The memory seemed so real, like I was back at the spring again.

Suddenly, I was falling through the air. A hundred butterflies beat their wings in my stomach. I landed feet first, cutting through cool water. Completely submerged, I kicked my way toward the surface. I shot out of the water to find Will laughing on the rocks. As I climbed out of the spring, a playful smile spread on his lips as he grabbed my hand to pull me out. He had pushed me in! I laughed and brushed a piece of hair off his brow before planting a kiss on his enticing lips. When he leaned in for another, I didn't pull away. Instead, I pushed him back and he tumbled into the spring behind him. I bent over laughing until he splashed me. That was when I jumped in after him. We laughed as we held our breath and sank underwater. He grabbed me and for as long as we had enough air, we finished where our kiss had left off...

...That girl wasn't me.

A knock on my door startled me. I threw the sheets off and flew to answer. Peering through a crack in the door assured me it was Will.

The memories of our time together encouraged me. I held the door open wider, an unspoken invitation. That girl was me, I thought as Will took one step into my bedroom and pulled me into his arms. He leaned me back, and I stared up into his eyes. Everything about him seemed real. He was here, and it was now. Something inside me wanted him. When he bent over to press our lips together, I made no move to try to stop him. I felt his lips move on top of mine and after a while, he didn't need to encourage me. He straightened me and my hands found his hair, pulling him harder into the kiss as my lips parted. His hair was thicker than I thought it would be, and my fingers running through it was better than I imagined.

It was almost like...

Well, it reminded me of...

I opened my eyes at the similarity and found I wasn't kissing Will.

Draven, I whispered with excitement. My heart soared at the thought of being with him again. As a noticeable red haze appeared, my heart sped up in nervousness. I clung to Draven tighter, but his hold on me started to loosen. Suddenly, his entire body sank away like sand blowing in a desert storm. A tingle spread across my body as my surroundings fell apart before my eyes. It wasn't just Draven who was gone; everything had disappeared.

"You like Wilson," an eerily familiar voice said. My voice. "I do?" is all I could say.

Why shouldn't I like him? He was kind and patient toward me. He didn't rush me or drive me crazy like Draven. Damn him for haunting my thoughts again. How did I let him ruin a perfectly good dream? I knew why. It must be... because... it was because I... knew exactly why...

Thoughts flooded my head along with voices. Some of them were mine, some were deeper, some laced with a sneer. I tried to find the ones that belonged to me, but the same phrases repeated over and over in my head. 'You like Wilson...'

My eyes snapped awake with a shocking realization. It was a dream, just a dream, and now it was morning.

I rubbed my hands over my face and through my hair. My palm lingered on my forehead to gauge my temperature. Thankfully, I wasn't feverish, but a thin, cool sweat covered my skin. I sat up, my body energetic and well rested. I couldn't believe I had slept through the night so deeply when it felt like I had only been asleep for minutes.

You like Wilson, echoed from my dream.

My dreams were getting out of control. Maybe I was losing it, but a weight had lifted from my shoulders. I felt lighter. I knew I had to leave this place, no matter how enticing The Island, or Will, was. Warning bells went off as I remembered a children's fairy tale my father used to tell me, something about a lotus flower, but I ignored them, not wanting anything to ruin the peaceful euphoria I experienced from thoughts of spending time with Will.

Racing through getting ready, I skipped to the door, feeling rather chipper. Why?

Will.

I opened the door to find him leaning against the

adjacent wall.

"Hey,"

"Hey," I said with a stupid smile over my face. I didn't know why something warm spread happily over me at the sight of him. I would miss this when I returned to Sirbiad.

"Looks like someone woke up on the right side of the bed."

"I did. I slept extremely well. Thank you."

"I see you decided to utilize the closet—purple is your color."

A blush stained my cheeks, and I needed to change the subject. "I just wanted to thank you for yesterday. I had a really good time, and it was nice to feel like things are normal."

"Things here are just like the United States used to be, and if you had fun yesterday, you should see what I have planned for us today."

Another unanticipated wave of eagerness mixed with delight filled me.

He put his arm around me, and I unintentionally sank into him. "Do you not have anything better to do than entertain me all day?"

"That's a foolish question. Do you really think so low of yourself? I guess I shouldn't be surprised with how Draven treated you. He tied you to the bed, for God's sake."

The thought of Draven was sobering. I stopped before my foot made it to the first step on the staircase. "How did you know that?"

He scoffed. "Who do you think had you freed?"

A chill seeped into my bones. I was pretty sure when I first met Will, he had no idea I had been kidnapped. I wasn't sure why that had bothered me. It was probably just a simple mistake. Draven hurt me. Draven lied. *Not Will.*

"What's bothering you?"

I wet my lips and shook my head. "Nothing. Just unwanted thoughts."

His lips straightened, not pleased by my comment, but his features softened in contrast. "I know it's going to take a while for you to trust me, but I told you before, I'm willing to wait. Just let me know if you ever want to talk about it."

You like Wilson. The memory resounded. Maybe I did like Will. Why wouldn't I, right? He was the opposite of Draven in every way. Even down to his appearance.

Slowly, the corner of his mouth pulled up and the playful look returned. "Let's go make you forget."

His hand slipped into mine. He parted my fingers as our hands intertwined. I didn't pull away this time, and with a quick squeeze, we walked away.

Outside, a blanket of clouds that covered half the sky dampened my good mood. I looked forward to a beautiful sunny day like it was yesterday. One side was clear, the other dark. It looked as if the sky couldn't decide its mood and was torn between a storm and a sunny day. The sun was caught in the middle, the cloud shielding more than half its light, giving the morning that eerie feeling of pre-dawn.

"Where are we going this time?"

"I can't let you starve, can I?"

Breakfast on Sirbiad was very light, sometimes nonexistent. Three meals a day were not a part of our schedule, but my stomach growled anyway.

"No, breakfast sounds great. Back to the lion's den or do we get to eat with the others now?"

"The Lion's Den?"

"Just a name I picked out for the private dining room on top of the world."

"I like that. I'll look into getting it engraved on

something." He chuckled.

"You could just have a picture of a lion in a cave."

"If I didn't know any better, I'd think you were being sarcastic."

"You don't miss much, do you?"

From behind me, he grabbed both my shoulders to keep me from walking. He turned me around slowly as the smile left my face.

"You know what I'm going to do to you for that?" His face was expressionless.

I swallowed. "What?"

"Tickle you."

I keeled over laughing while trying to swat his hands away. "Stop that. What are you, five?"

"I can be funny, too."

"I can see that."

"Again with the sarcasm? Did you already forget what happened last time or do I need to remind you?"

I held up my hands in mock surrender. "Okay, okay!"

We had stopped in the middle of the quad. That was when I noticed the sky had decided it would be a sunny day and the dark cloud was swept away. That was also when a Jumpsuit came barreling toward us.

"I think we better get out of his way," I commented to Will.

He turned in the direction of the man and touched my arm, "I'll be right back," he said with a hint of irritation. "It's work related." His eyes never left the Jumpsuit.

"What is it you do again here, Will?"

He ignored my question. "Why don't you go ahead and go to our table upstairs? I'll meet you there, all right?"

"I can come with you," I suggested, wanting to hear what they had to say.

"That's not necessary. Go straight to the table. I'll be right there, okay?" He gave me a reassuring smile.

"S-sure," I answered in automation, my mind going over what the man could want and why Will didn't want me to hear, all the while planning to eavesdrop as soon I could.

Again, my imagination ran wild as I arrived at the doors of the dining building. When I pushed, one of the giant doors opened. The sounds of chatter and utensils filled the air. I stepped inside, but didn't let the doors close all the way. I peeked out the opening to find Will scolding the man. I turned my head to try to hear.

"The ship is still on the far side of The Island. The guards found a few of the men who had come ashore. They are being held at the beach. They are waiting for you command, Sir."

Ship? What ship? Had Asmodeus returned? That made sense. Will had said I'd meet him today. Maybe he returned, but why would the guard make it seem like they weren't wanted, maybe even hostile? I needed to hear Will's reply, but the noise inside drowned out their conversation. Uneasiness advanced to pure dread. This was all wrong.

On a gut feeling, I shifted my gaze to the large hall. The smell of eggs and maple hit my nostrils.

There was not an empty bench space at the tables. People talked and laughed while eating. I sighed. Maybe it *was* just how Will said it would be here, and maybe I was just paranoid again.

In the corner of the room, four men were standing in a tight circle. The flailing of arms and tight hand gestures assured me they were debating. I recognized three of them from yesterday, the ones Will had said were from Sirbiad. My heart did a weird ticking thing as I wondered why they were wearing Jumpsuits now.

Who were they talking to? The fourth man was older with thick glasses and a comb-over. He was wearing a white scientist's coat over his jumpsuit. *And who did Will say we'd be meeting today?*

Shock tore through my body at the realization that the fourth man had to be Asmodeus. *Oh my God, Asmodeus!* This was it. This was my chance. Chance to go *home*—I meant to Sirbiad.

I didn't hesitate to think of a plan as my feet started toward the hall.

I was finally going to meet Asmodeus.

As I ducked my way through the standing crowd and scooted past those sitting, the group didn't notice me as I approached.

"Asmodeus." I blurted out his name in nervousness.

The man turned to peer at me over his shoulder, but then turned back around.

That was rude. Maybe I was the one being rude by interrupting their conversation, but I just couldn't think of anything else than to meet him after all this time.

I cleared my throat. "Asmodeus," I persisted.

He turned to me. "Are you talking to me?"

A nervous laughed slipped out. "Yes..."

"That's fine, but I'm not Asmodeus."

"Oh." I was taken aback. "I'm sorry." I felt foolish. But maybe he was a fellow scientist and knew where he was. "Do you know where I can find him?"

"Why, he's right there." He blinked at me, like I was insane.

Following the direction of his pointing finger, I stared at the window.

I turned back to face him. The only person there was Will. He was still outside in the quad, telling off the Jumpsuit. My head whipped back. Will! "Wilson?"

I whispered out loud.

"Wilson?" the man answered. "I suppose that's his first name, but I wouldn't advise calling him anything but Asmodeus. Are you new here?"

I was frozen, my body and mind benumbed, when one of the Jumpsuits in the group interrupted.

"That's enough, Clyde. Let's go."

I was still processing what Clyde had said when the men walked away. Will was Asmodeus? Wilson Asmodeus? The guy I spent time with, trusted, the guy I almost kissed?

No, there was a mistake. Clyde must have meant the man Will was talking to. That must be it. It was impossible that Will was Asmodeus. It was... It was just impossible.

I ran out of the dining room and straight to the door. My hand shook as it fumbled with the handle. When I pushed it open, the sunlight was blinding. I shielded my face as I prepared to be corrected on the true identity of Asmodeus. This was just a mistake. It would get cleared up in a matter of seconds, and then we could have a good laugh about it.

"Asmodeus," I called across the lawn.

Will's head was the only one that snapped in my direction.

Chapter Eighteen

EVERY OUNCE OF BLOOD DRAINED FROM MY FACE. IT must have gone to my heart, because that hurt, too.

"Oh my God," I sobbed.

He started toward me. "Lux!"

I had about two seconds to figure out what I was going to do.

Instinctively, I sought to cower inside the building.

I pushed the heavy door shut behind me and started running for the stairs.

It was only a matter of time before he followed me into the building.

Hiding was the only plan I could come up with. I just needed to get away. Needed time to figure out what this all meant. I needed to be alone with my thoughts. Adrenaline, pain, and anger flushed through my body. If I didn't channel it soon, I was sure to break.

The familiar wooden door was the closest to me. *If someone is disloyal enough to go in here, then they certainly deserve the unknowns that lurk inside.* A chill ran through me as I remembered what Will had said. I opened the door at the same time Will, or Asmodeus, opened the one to the building. I stepped inside the cool, damp closet and slammed the door shut behind me.

The smell of mold and mud filled my nostrils, and I had suspicions this wasn't a closet. I turned around to see a light flickering from further down a tunnel. A secret passage?

Before I could start walking, I mentally kicked myself.

Will *was* Asmodeus.

What was I thinking? How could I not see the signs? Why didn't I listen to the alarms going off inside me? How could I fall for that? It just seemed so real, everything about Will. He didn't seem evil. He was just so normal, so much like me. Yet, this whole time, he had lied to me. He had tricked me. *Why?*

When I first came to the island, he was taken aback when I asked him his name. Now I knew why. Why he dressed the way he did, why he lived in the White House, why we were able to take the boat out, why he never had to work, why we dined in Asmodeus' private room, and why everyone looked at me the way they did. How careless of me to not put the connections together earlier!

I couldn't imagine what everyone must have thought of me. My people must have thought I betrayed them. No wonder I had never met Asmodeus, never seen him around. It was because he was right in front of me the entire time.

And Draven.

When Draven came for me, no wonder he was bargaining with Will. No wonder he was surprised that I'd want to stay with *him.* Because *he* was Asmodeus.

I still couldn't get over it. *How could someone who seemed so good really be evil? Why? What was all that for?*

I couldn't trust anything Will had ever told me. Could never believe what he said now. Everything he told me about him trying to warn the government and preparing this island so he could help people was probably a lie. He tricked me once; he was almost certainly tricking me the entire time. He was worse than a liar.

Oh my God, and I thought I liked him. The thought made me sick to my stomach. I let him hold me, laugh with me, touch me, and almost *kiss* me. He was my friend. That all felt ridiculous now—like I was under a spell the whole time and now that spell was broken.

A spell. I thought about the dreams I had. The physical pull I felt around Will. No, how could that be possible? Did he drug me? *What was it that he said about magic and science...?*

I heard noises on the other side of the door and knew it would only be a matter of time before he realized where I had went. I tiptoed toward the light.

Danger, my mind shouted.

Turn back!

I was overcome by a terrible sensation. It was becoming harder to walk with each step. My survival instincts wanted me to run back. Maybe I had been wrong about Will. Something didn't add up. He didn't look *that* old.

I debated with myself to go back, that there had to have been a mistake. That Will couldn't possibly be Asmodeus. I laughed almost hysterically.

"Pull it together!" I cleared my throat and ignored those feelings. For all I knew, I could still be under his spell. Probably the only reason I hoped it was one big misunderstanding was more to justify my feelings for him than anything else. How could I have liked someone who did so many wrongs to the world? Shame seeped in and threatened to pull me under. Like fishing hooks, it tugged at my skin, my heart, my belly—I gripped my stomach at the onset of nausea. Deep inside, a small part of me also suffered a loss. Once again, something from my world vanished. I couldn't linger for long in here; I needed to get out.

If there was a way out, if this was somehow an escape tunnel, what was I going to do when I did escape? I was trapped on an island, but I knew I had to try even if my efforts were futile. Asmodeus never planned to return me home, and most likely, he never would.

Taking a deep breath, I continued down the tunnel. With one step, my right foot sank into the ground. A clicking noise came from the walls, followed by a hiss. My eyes dropped to the ground. My foot was in a hole. But it was a perfect square carved into the dirt. Odd that the shape was so defined. I leaned over to get a closer look. The corners made it appear to be man-made. *Why would someone*—the pieces came together in my mind.

There was a reason why no locks were necessary on this tunnel.

The hissing continued, and I squinted ahead of me to see a red mist coming from the walls. It appeared to be glowing from the light behind it. I whipped around to find it all around me. My heart slammed against my ribs and I ran straight ahead, trying to escape it. The mist filled my lungs with each ragged breath, and I choked. I stopped running, gasping for air. The cool air disturbed me, and I wrapped my arms around myself to stop shaking. I coughed again. The pain in my chest, lungs, and throat made it unbearable.

There was something unnatural in the air. It was charged, almost humming. It was magical. I didn't know why and I didn't know how, but I knew it was from Asmodeus. A voice whispered through my mind, telling me how to escape it. If I gave in, I would be free. *Sleep.* No. I might not ever wake up again. A new pain shot through me. My skin burned as if it were stretching.

Pressing my fists to the sides of my head, I bent over in agony. The sound of my heartbeat thrashed in my ears. I just wanted the pain to stop. Screaming, I was overcome by dizziness. Black spots appeared in the red haze, the huge, gaping holes becoming bigger until everything was dark. My knees gave out, and I crumpled to the ground.

Twitches racked my body. I could close my eyes and the pain would be gone, but so would I.

No. I would fight.

The shaking got worse as I thought it. I clenched my teeth. *Don't give in, Lux. Fight it!*

The hissing stopped.

My body relaxed, back to being warm again. All the pain was gone, and I was no longer shaking.

I lifted my head; the red haze was gone—like it was never there.

Pushing myself up, I stood.

Like it was never there. It never *was* there.

Something that Will had said at the spring resonated within me. *A trick of the mind.* It wasn't real. Feeling my body, I searched for any injuries. I pressed two hands to my cheeks. I was normal again. Nothing had harmed me. It was all in my head, and I had broken free of the spell by fighting it.

Why would he have a trap in this tunnel? How was it possible? Logic replaced panic as my mind went through the possibilities and the determination to find out just what was here that was worth hiding.

I took a deep, appreciative breath of fresh air when a glimmer of silver caught the firelight and materialized in front me. Kneeling down to examine the wire, I followed it from the middle to either sides of the wall.

The place was full of booby traps!

I was hurtled back to earth as the reality struck. I doubted Asmodeus would be coming after me. He probably counted on anyone who dared to enter to never make it through. It probably was a trick he set just to test loyalties.

Turn back. I shivered off the last of the magic, reminding myself that it wasn't real. *Mind over body, mind over body...* I chanted, and it worked. I knew what I'd face out there would be worse than what was ahead of me. My only option was to keep going and be thankful that I now knew what to look for.

I pressed my body flat against the floor as I squeezed myself under the trip wire. Even as I cleared it, I didn't want to get up again. I had almost made it to the light, but then what? How many more traps could there be? I knew nothing about Asmodeus' magic. Before this, I didn't even know it was possible. *What twisted, dark trap awaited me?*

I kept walking slowly, venturing deeper into the tunnel. My eyes widened, and I scanned the floor, walls, and ceiling. I avoided pebbles and uneven ground. Everything and anything could have been a trap. Maybe I was just paranoid; maybe those *were* the only two traps.

A spot on the ground appeared darker than the rest. I bent down to prove to myself that it was nothing. When I brushed the area lightly with my hand, the ground shifted under it. A thin brown cloth was swept aside, revealing a hole. My heart sank. I tried to reassure myself and instead just proved that I *should* be cautious of everything. Leaning in, I looked down onto a sharp spear protruding from the bottom.

My body shot back. How many other traps like

this had I missed just walking this far? This place sickened me. My chest tightened with the feeling of being trapped.

I positioned my body back toward the door; two oil lamps lit the way in a very appealing direction. Tendrils of whispers played across my mind. My head whipped left, and I stared deeper into the tunnel. It was darker and scarier. Did it actually seem more forbidding or was it the work of magic again?

I moved in that direction, my jaw tightening. As I continued walking, I noted that I now had to look out for pitfalls, as well as trip wires and uneven ground, which was becoming harder to do as the light behind me faded. There was no lamp, and it became more difficult to notice the little things. *Was that another pitfall or just a shadow?*

No, that was definitely not a shadow. Slowly approaching an object off to the side, I squinted my eyes in the dark as the outline of a flashlight appeared. I sighed heavily as I picked it up. *It's just what I needed!* I examined it. It was a little worn, and I hoped it would turn on. *Wait.* This *was* just what I needed. Why, in a tunnel full of traps, would there be just what I needed? The flashlight was another trap, and I had picked it up.

With a palpitating heart, I slowly set it down in the same spot.

I was still in one piece after picking it up, which meant I was supposed to turn it on. Whatever its purpose, it was worth walking in the dark without it, rather than risking losing an arm.

I rubbed the sweat on my forehead. *I can't believe this is happening.* Weariness enveloped me as I tried to concentrate. I took a deep breath and kept walking, feeling blind as there were still no more lamps to light the way. The thought of the unknown traps was terrifying. Tears threatened my eyes, but I threatened them back. I would not break down now.

Finally, there was a soft glow ahead to my left. If I could only wing it just a little farther, I would make it. As I approached, the light came from a bend in the tunnel. I was near enough now that I could see any potential dangers as I came around the curve.

A lamp shone above three white doors at the end of the tunnel. *No!* Just when I thought I would overcome one thing, another obstacle presented itself. Was one of the doors the way out? If so, what did the others hold? I rubbed my eyes, fighting the urge to just curl into a ball on the cold, unforgiving dirt.

With all the enthusiasm of gutting a fish, I tried to concentrate on the next challenge of the tunnel from hell. The doors had locks above the brass knobs. Again, if someone was able to survive all the traps this far, what was a lock going to keep them from, and which door did I choose? I walked up to the first door to test the handle. Turning it slowly, I listened for any clicks. When the knob couldn't turn anymore, I pushed slowly, but it wouldn't open. Of course, it wouldn't open. It had a lock for a reason. I moved on to the next door.

I slowly twisted the knob on the second door handle, but this time when I pushed, it opened a crack. Without thinking, I sighed and pushed it all the way open. The door seemed to lead into another dark tunnel, but something didn't feel right about it. I stepped away hastily, and at the same time, something clicked, followed by a swoosh of air. As I turned, something tore through my bare shoulder. I gripped it in pain as the arrow, or whatever the hell came out of that door, hit the wall.

I whimpered as warm liquid spread between my fingers, and I sank to the floor at the excruciating pain that followed. Once I found my breath again, I assessed my wound. The gash in my arm pooled blood; the sight of torn flesh and the smell of rust forced me to keel over. I'd mended wounds before, but the sight of my own injury sent me over the edge. My stomach was empty and had nothing to heave, but I managed to cough a few times before spitting. I cursed as I tried to bring my muddled thoughts together. I didn't know if my slight swaying was due to the sight of my blood or the loss of it.

"Get it together," I told myself.

I was a healer. I had treated injuries before. I was like my mother; I tried to remember that small fact. After taking a few reassuring breaths, I was able to question my intelligence. I should have never opened that door. It was probably the only door that was unlocked; of course it was another trap. If I had realized that too late, I would never have stepped aside in time and would probably have a spear sticking out of me. The thought made me want to heave again, and I swallowed hard. What kind of person would set up these traps? More importantly, why would they?

The thought of Asmodeus made me queasy again. What was he going to do? How long would it take for him to get through the door or was he just waiting for me to die?

Switching my mind into survival mode, I assessed the wound again and cringed. Hiking my dress with one hand, I brought the hem to my mouth, clenching it between my teeth and pulling until the satin tore. I tied the fabric clumsily around my arm with one hand and my teeth. It was a temporary fix, but at least it would stop the bleeding. If I ever got out of here, it would need stitches or worse. I shivered at the thought of those on our island who were limbless because of such infections.

Now what? I couldn't dwell on my injury too long. I'd done all that I could for it. The only option for me was to go forward and to choose a door. It was luck that I made it this far without setting anything else off. I doubted I could make it back to the beginning, and I definitely didn't want to. I threw my head back and clenched my teeth, trying to hold back the pain and nausea that pulsed through me.

I let my head fall forward. I had two doors to choose from. *That's a 50/50 chance? Right? No, it would be 2/3. Or would it be 1/3?* Just because the door I opened was not the right door, didn't mean I had increased my odds. I took a breath. *Think, think, think.*

The first door. I had to just go for it. I was already dirty, scraped, and bleeding. What did I have to lose? I laughed, a little hysteria in my voice. That didn't cheer me up at all.

I slammed my left side into the door. Nothing budged. Fear prevented me from putting any real strength into it.

Should I have considered that maybe all of these doors were traps? Too late. I started with a little run and put my shoulder into breaking the door open. Hitting the door, I fell through the air. I twisted my body, trying to land anywhere but my wounded shoulder. When I landed flat on my back, the breath was knocked out from my lungs. Groaning, I lifted my head to stare at the door I just came through. The latch lock was swinging from its hinge, and I pushed myself up on my good elbow to glance behind me.

Guess I picked the right door.

The tunnel seemed to continue, and my chest quivered in a sob. *Would it ever end? Maybe it didn't lead anywhere.* The thoughts chilled me.

I stood, brushing the dirt off my hands. Small cuts

on my hands burned, and I realized I was just rubbing it deeper into the scrapes.

With the last ounce of will I had left, I walked forward, finally able to make it around a curve when the tunnel split off. To the right, the passage was better lit, but I chose the darker path, not trusting the easier way out. I was shocked to discover the tunnel I chose ended, but it wasn't a dead end. Three or four cells lined both sides of the wall. My tired feet shuffled dirt, followed by cries from the previously silent cells. The agonizing moans answered my question; they were not empty.

My horror could not persuade my curiosity to stop me from going further. The first row of cells I came to were empty. But I knew my relief wouldn't last long. The moans had to be coming from somewhere. When I got to the second row, I didn't know which was more horrifying, the old man on my left whose rib cage was visible, or the boy on my right who was missing an arm.

I ran to the bars and knelt.

"Boy," I whispered. The idea of dungeons having guards came into my head. "Are you okay?" Of course, he wasn't okay. He looked sick, his arm infected.

"Boy," I whispered again. His head lifted this time and then swayed. He squinted at the light coming from behind me.

"What?" he rasped.

"How long have you been in here?"

A ghost of a shrug. "Days, weeks." A cough rattled him. "Years."

I hoped he was exaggerating.

I turned my attention to the man in the other cell who had risen from the dirty ground. One bony arm reached out to me. The space between the cells was just wide enough to stand in the middle and avoid being touched.

"I will get you out of here." It was a wish to myself and a promise to the boy.

"I'll be back," I told the other man who was still trying to reach for me, his mouth open yet soundless. Continuing down the line of cells, I was relieved to find one of the cells empty while the one next to the boy's had a strange smell coming from it. A lifeless lump on the floor propelled me quickly past it, and then I reached the last row of cells.

I set my hand against the wall, gaining my breath and hoping I wouldn't vomit. The smells, my arm. I swallowed down the taste arising in my throat. Standing erect again, I swayed on my feet. The world became a million little dots in front of me. Had I lost too much blood? Maybe I better rest, just for a little while. Regardless of the possibility of not waking up if I fell asleep, I sank to the floor against the wall. Drained, hollow, lifeless. My head rolled to the left.

"Draven?" Was I dreaming? Did I really see Draven in the cell next to me? "Draven," I cried, refusing for this to be a dream. When I dragged myself to the bars, I saw the familiar black hair was limp and crusted with blood at his forehead. *Please, don't be dead.*

He looked at me with a scowl. No, not dead! My heart soared. When his eyes focused on me, his expression cleared. He let out what sounded like a sob and a curse.

"Lux?" His tone was disbelief. He pushed himself up in forced ease and made his way to the bars. I stood, my happiness overriding the pain.

My hands gripped the rough, rusted bars as he studied me.

"What are you doing here?" he asked. "You're hurt."

"So are you." I thought about how long he had been down here. *Since the dinner most likely, that first night.* That would have had to be at least three days. How horrible I felt at that moment. I was enjoying myself while Draven lay rotting below my feet.

"I will get you out of here." I reached through the bars to touch him, but he flinched back.

"You need to leave, Lux." His voice rose, turning rougher than sandpaper.

I shook my head, unmoving. "I'm not. I'm going to find a way to get you out. There have to be keys somewhere." I searched the wall behind me.

"Leave," he growled.

"You didn't leave me." I choked on my words. "I'm not going to leave you."

His face was pained. "I should have—then I wouldn't be half-dead in prison hell right now. Now leave, I don't want you here."

His words cut me. "You are being cruel because you are trying to protect me."

His features twisted at my words. "I want you to get away from me. How arrogant you are to think it has anything to do with you."

Draven's eyes were cold and he clenched his jaw before continuing. "If you go back the way you came, there will be another fork in the tunnel. Go left; do not go right. Take a left and follow it out. You'll come to an alcove. Ahmed should be waiting around the east side with a ship. Go with him and sail far away. Never look back. Tell Ahmed, *Ma'a salama.* He'll know the significance."

I gritted my teeth at his stubbornness, his willingness to give up. "No, Draven. I will not tell him good-bye for you. Tell me what is to the right of the fork in the tunnel."

"The left is the only way out of here. Follow it if you value your life—"

My hand shot up to his lips to shush him. "Don't—"

My eyes widened when he lightly kissed the tips of my fingers. I pulled away my hand in disbelief, my fingers burning as I curled them into a fist.

As my gaze lowered, I saw something familiar tucked into the sash at his waist. "What is that?" I reached out for my necklace. "You're a terrible liar, Draven."

"Get out," he shouted.

Wordlessly, I turned, my feet pattering on cool stone as I ran.

Chapter Nineteen

*"The Revolution of souls sever ropes, and the Revolution
of minds removes mountains."*
-The first Arab Poet Laureate, Ahmed Shawqi.

LIKE DRAVEN PROMISED, I CAME TO THE FORK IN THE
tunnel. *Left or right?*

I'd already made my decision. Draven should
have known I wouldn't listen. What would I encoun-
ter on the right side? Were there more traps? My only
hope was that somewhere down this route would be
the key to Draven's salvation.

I didn't have to walk far, and I knew exactly why
Draven wanted me to go the other way.

There was another simple wooden door at the
end of the hall. Fire lit the lamps along the wall. Why
was there no electricity here, when it was so common
throughout the rest of the island? This door, like the
one I came through before, had no locks. What fresh
nightmare would this one open to? The sinking feeling in me told me I already knew.

I was in the heart of the island—Asmodeus' lair.
The door revealed a wide-open cave. Inside were more
candles. In fact, hundreds of candles were magically
ablaze. Bright reflections shining like diamonds cov-

ered the walls. The light was wavy like reflected water. When the realization dawned on me, I searched the room to see where it was coming from. Along the wall to my right was a row of desks. Papers were scattered carelessly over them. That would be the first place I should look for keys to the dungeon. The other side of the room was more homely, with elegant couches ladened with pillows. Nothing was in the center of the room; everything seemed to be pushed to the walls. There was no water that I could see or hear. Until my eyes followed up the hundred-foot vaulted ceiling.

Suspended in mid-air was a waterfall. But the water didn't flow down like it should; it seemed to flow up, going into the ground above.

"Who are you, Asmodeus?" I whispered.

Before I could make any sense of how it was possible, I felt a sense of urgency to my discovery. My eyes drifted down to search the room for an explanation. A bottle on the desk caught my eye. Inside was a ship similar to Draven's, and suddenly, I wasn't as interested in knowing how it was possible, but rather getting Draven and me out of here.

Running over to Asmodeus' desk, I pushed past the papers, feeling for any keys. The desks on the end were wooden and had ancient Oriental influences. I pulled the dainty brass handles on the drawers and pushed my hands through more papers. A set of skeleton keys lay in the second set of drawers. Relief shook my hands as I grabbed them and turned to leave, but I froze when a familiar armoire caught my eye. Dad used to have one just like it, salvaged from his childhood home. As a little girl, I had endless hours of fun hiding things in its secret compartments.

Walk away, Lux. But I had no free will when it came to my curiosity. Feeling the spaces between the drawers with my fingers, I pressed on the sides until I felt a little movement. A rectangular false door popped out. I reached inside, completely blindsided as to what I was going to touch. My good arm was elbow-deep in the desk when my hand hit something. My fingertips traced the edges of what seemed like a box. I picked it up with one hand and slowly pulled it out. It was wooden and as small as a music box. Carved into the top was a familiar drawing—a hand. The same hand I'd seen carved in Draven's cabin and tattooed on his crew. *What did it mean?* The box had a small keyhole lock. I tucked it under my arm and tried to rush out quickly to regain the time I had lost.

I ran back the way I came, but the throbbing in my shoulder slowed me. The area around the wound was turning gray, and I stopped to adjust the tie.

When I returned to the cells, the old man in the first row was back to lying in a supine position on the floor. Clearly, he didn't have hope I would return. I used the keys to unlock the boy's prison first. His head shot up, and he cringed before he saw who I was. I placed an index finger to my lips. His face beamed and I had no doubt he wanted to cry out in his relief, but I tapped the finger on my lips again, reminding him to keep quiet. I didn't know who was listening, and I felt uneasy that I had been so lucky this far.

I unlocked the last three occupied cells and finally made it to Draven.

"Draven," I whispered.

He was leaning against the far wall with his back to me. When I spoke, his head cocked to the side, as if he only imagined I called his name. Then he dropped his arm from the wall and slowly turned. His eyes widened as he watched me stick the key into his lock. Chest heaving, he let out a scoff of disbelief and anger.

I pushed the door open with a creak.

"You are the most stubborn, hardheaded..."

Draven strode toward me.

"Do you have a list of my faults memorized or is it written down somewhere?"

The corner of his mouth turned up as he pulled me against him. His body pressed against mine felt better than I remembered. He stopped inches from my lips. His eyes searched my face, resting on my lips. He smirked, revealing teeth that looked whiter against the dirt.

"Draven, I—" Draven swallowed my words as his lips came crashing down on mine. When he gripped me tighter, my body cringed away. I had momentarily forgotten about my shoulder.

"We need to go." Draven seethed as he studied my wound. I nodded, and he put a hand on my waist to lead me out, but not before his eyes darted to the box in my hand, a strange gleam lighting his eyes even though he made no comment.

The cells were quiet, and I discovered they were empty as we walked past. I had hoped, like Draven, that the prisoners knew where to go. Draven took us into the tunnel, and when we came to the fork, we went left. That must be the other—and safer—entrance to the dungeons and Asmodeus' lair.

A knot of unease sat low and heavy in my stomach. It didn't lessen with each step toward freedom. Something just didn't feel right about this. Why had Asmodeus not been able to stop us yet? Would we really be able to leave the island, sail off into the sunset? Draven had once said he didn't believe in happy endings—that there could not be one for him. Was that true? If Asmodeus knew the things I had seen, and taken from his den, would he just let me leave? I didn't want to think about what was going to happen if Draven and I did make it off this island alive. Staring up at Draven, I longed to touch his midnight hair. He suddenly turned, meeting my gaze.

"What is it?" he asked. The uncertainty must have been written across my face. I'd thought about voicing my concerns, but he was the one who told me not to come back for him in the first place.

"Nothing." I gave him a weak smile.

When the first rays of sunlight appeared as we approached the end of the tunnel, I hadn't realized what relief sunlight could bring, what good it did to the soul. The sound of the waves crashing against the sand and the smell of salt told me we were free. This was the same beach Will had brought me to, the one that could only be accessed by boat—

"If it isn't Romeo and Juliet. You didn't think it would be that easy did you? Oh, you did? How pathetic, Draven." Asmodeus greeted us before we took our first breath of open air. Beside him was a group of Jumpsuits, complete with menacing expressions and weapons to match.

I searched the beach around us for the others who were in the cells. A small rowboat was pulled ashore. Ahmed, the prisoners from the cells, and several pirates were next to it. Why were they not guarded? The grim expression on Ahmed's face told me there was a reason for that.

Draven put his arm out in front of me, shielding me as I slunk behind his back. Out of sight, I took the small box and tucked it into the back of his pants. Draven tensed at my touch, but he made no other move to incriminate me.

"You can do what you want with me, just let Lux go."

"I couldn't care less about you. It's Lux I want." Will or Asmodeus or whoever he was, his voice dripped with venom.

"You can't just have her, and you'll take no more

slaves if I can help it." Draven pushed me farther behind him.

"If it wasn't for that babbling idiot who said I was Asmodeus, I would *still* have her."

"She was never yours." Draven took the words right out of my mouth. "Why do you care so much? Why do you want her so much?" He yelled the last part. I couldn't help but wonder what Asmodeus could want from me.

"Do you think so low of your *girlfriend* that you can't understand why I would want her?" I couldn't see Asmodeus' face from behind Draven's strong shoulders, but I could imagine what his sneer looked like. Though, his words were layered, and I suspected that there was another reason that had nothing to do with me.

Draven ignored him. "I said you can't have her," he repeated, enunciating his words.

"And how are you going to stop me?" At this, his guards took a step forward.

Draven reached for a weapon at his belt out of instinct before seeming to remember he was defenseless. His fist clenched at his side, not fazed by the fact he had no weapon.

"If he doesn't, I will." Before I knew what I was doing, I closed the distance between Asmodeus and me, skidded in the sand, and swept my right leg under his. Asmodeus fell on his back. I jumped on top of him, aiming for his neck. My hands wrapped around his neck, but my upper body swayed from the movement. My vision flickered to black and I blinked my eyes, fighting the pain in my shoulder. I renewed my grip on his throat. "Run, Draven," I yelled. As Asmodeus choked on air, a cool, metal object pressed against the base of my skull.

"Don't shoot her," Asmodeus snarled, trying to

fight my hold.

Draven stepped forward, but then another guard came at us, aiming another silver object toward me. He froze.

I'd seen guns, but the barrel of this weapon was too large to hold a bullet. Whatever the ammo was couldn't have been good.

I released my grip on Asmodeus and eased off him, backing up toward Draven.

Asmodeus stood, running a hand through his disheveled hair. A menacing laugh shook his chest. "You think I wouldn't come prepared?"

I stepped out from behind Draven, preparing to fight alongside him for our freedom.

"It's funny. You didn't put up this much protest when I asked you to kidnap her a month ago."

I gasped. Draven scowled before turning toward me with pain and apology all over his face. My eyes darted to Asmodeus, whose expression was the exact opposite. He was very pleased with himself.

"It doesn't change anything," Draven said.

"She's injured. Let her come back to get treated and cleaned up. We can settle this after she is taken care of."

"We'll settle this now, and then she can get treated and cleaned up on *my* ship."

"If that's how it's going to be, fine. Now, I am good to my word. I told you before it would be Lux' decision. If she wants to go with you, she can. If not, well..." He laughed at his repetition of words. "She can stay right where she is."

What was he up to? I doubt he would just let me go, not after all this. Draven's eyes narrowed like mine, but in them was a little too much hope. I didn't know whether to answer, but Draven spoke the same words he had used the first time Will made the offer.

"What game are you playing?"

Asmodeus let out a delighted laugh. "No game." His voice was anything but reassuring. "Just Lux's decision."

Draven scoffed, but turned to me anyway so I could declare it. "Well?"

"Wait." Asmodeus interrupted my reply. "Of course, it wouldn't be fair to let you make your decision so hastily. Let me give you something to think over before you decide."

"And what's that? Threatening Draven? Because I'm pretty sure he is no longer working for you."

Asmodeus held a wide smile. "Just when I thought I had you figured out." He shook his head. "And I have been trying so hard to impress the *ever-elusive Lux*. I forced the cooks to whip up the most delicious, most exotic dishes. Yet, you barely ate. I had brand-new clothes put in your closet. Yet, you still wanted to wear that tattered old sundress. I took you out on my private boat to show you the beauty of the island. Yet, your mind still remained far away. Well, I think I got it now."

"Do you?" was all I could muster up for a response to his assessment of me.

Again, that wide, amused smile. "You care about your Sirbiad, do you not?"

My expression fell. Beside me, so did Draven's. Because we both knew where Asmodeus was going, and we both knew I wouldn't be able to turn away.

Asmodeus snapped his fingers. One of the Jumpsuits stepped forward and placed a piece of paper in his hand. I recognized it; it was the official paper used for correspondence with Asmodeus and—and the Islands.

"And look, here's a letter from your father that came by ship this morning." He feigned surprise.

I stepped toward him, horror and longing combining over a simple slip of paper.

He held the paper away, as if he thought I was going to grab it. "Let's read it, shall we?"

"*Asmodeus,* blah blah blah, *daughter is missing. Please help me find her. If you could spare one of your ships to help locate her or use your contacts on the other islands, I would forever be indebted to you.* Blah, blah, blah. *Sincerely, Mayor Aiello.*"

He folded the letter with a deliberate slowness. "And look, I have found you. I guess that means your father is indebted to me. Oh, and let's not forget the rest of the Sirbiadians who are safely locked away in the executioner's room, just waiting for my signal."

I shook my head in wordless denial.

"Don't look at me like that. Please, don't make me be the bad guy. Don't you understand how much better your life will be, how much better *their* life will be, if you stay with me? I will give them whatever they need."

"No, you are threatening to take away what they need. What they have to survive. And you *are* the bad guy. You are a coward by making me choose between Draven and the well-being of my parents and the people on my island."

He shrugged. "I never said I played fair."

"If I stay, do you promise to return my people and leave my father alone?"

"That was the plan all along, wasn't it?"

Turning, I let out a grunt of frustration. I had not spoken an answer, but the look on Draven's face said he already knew what it would be.

"Don't believe him, Lux."

"I have to..."

I stepped closer to him, to give us privacy from the impatient eyes of Asmodeus.

"Lux..." He sighed as we touched. "I know you feel bad about trying to leave Sirbiad, but you were only missing your true home and not wanting to grieve for everything you lost. You can't carry that with you forever. Listen, I'm sorry for ever calling you selfish. I'm sorry for taking you away that night. I'm sorry for not letting you go. I'm sorry for bringing you here, and, most of all, I'm sorry we couldn't have met under different circumstances. I wish we could have met at a different time so you wouldn't have seen the person I have become, this monster as you called me."

I placed my palm on his chest. "The good and the bad are what make you." I shrugged. "Besides, your bad side has kinda grown on me."

He put a finger under my chin and tipped my head back. "Don't. I know that face. It's the same face you made when I tied you to the bed and brought you here. I will not let you resign yourself to this." Raw hurt glittered in his eyes.

"Enough whispering. Let her go, Draven!"

I stepped away, the apology written in my eyes for what I was about to do. Just as Ahmed had said, I might have been Draven's weakness. And if I really had let him onto what I was thinking, he would never let me go through with it.

I had already put distance between us.

"Ala Mahlak!" *Wait!*

It was the first time Draven had willingly spoke Arabic to me. The tingling in my heart spread throughout my body, and I ignored Asmodeus' sudden urgency.

"You don't have to do this. I can help you; I can help them," he continued in Arabic.

"You can't possibly go up against the whole world."

"We can. *We* can, Lux."

"How?"

"Come home with me."

"Do you trust me?"

He drew one side of his mouth up in a smile. "You've tried to kill me, turned my crew's loyalties, and refused to obey me at every turn, but yes, Lux, I trust you."

"Then you'll have to trust this." A tear escaped, rolling down my cheek as I quickly gave Draven's lips one last kiss before turning away to Asmodeus.

Asmodeus smiled triumphantly; nothing of the person who was Will shone through.

"I don't care what's right or wrong anymore. I'm taking her one way or another," Draven said behind my back.

Asmodeus took hold of my arm, and I turned around to see Draven's usually bright blue eyes turn murderous.

"Don't. Touch. Her."

"Take him to his boat and make sure he leaves this time," Asmodeus said to his guard.

"Lux!" Draven's roar was deafening.

Two of them were on Draven in an instant. One he easily threw off and the other he elbowed in the nose. With a crack, blood shot in every direction. That didn't stop another from coming at him or more from moving in behind us.

Asmodeus grabbed my wrist to pull me out of the way. That was a mistake.

Draven's arms grabbed my waist as he pulled me back against his body. He punched one of Asmodeus' guards with one hand before something forced him to lose his hold on me. I stumbled out of his arms, whipping around to face Draven. He was on his knees, being held back by two guards. A few more stood behind him. His hair, his eyes, everything about him looked wild and dangerous. I instinctively took a step back when he called my name. His head drooped and his chest rose and fell with each forcible breath. This was the side of Draven I hadn't seen before. The one I had wanted to fight for me. To fight for us. As I looked at the unleashed passion in his eyes, I knew I would never be able to doubt his intentions again. A shimmer of silver flashed behind him and it drew my eyes to one of the guards, who held a syringe in his hand.

I gasped and looked back to Draven. His head lowered further, his breathing evening. He took one last look at me before his chin hit his chest, the glorious dark hair on his head spilling down.

"No." I stepped forward, but Will caught my arm.

"Leave him," Asmodeus told the guards.

I shot him a disgusted look. "Let me go!"

Ahmed and some of Draven's crew stepped forward and drew their swords.

"Oh, wait." Asmodeus held up his hand to stop the guards. "Looks like we'll have a fight today after all."

"You'll have a fight all right." The coldness in Ahmed's tone chilled me. *I can't let him do this.* The weapons the guards had were far superior to the pirates. It would be suicide. I couldn't let anything happen to Ahmed, or Sokum even, because of me.

"Lux, are you going to call off your guard dogs or shall I instruct my men to dig five graves?"

Asmodeus would pay for this. "Ahmed," I pleaded. *Help Draven,* I mouthed.

Ahmed's brown eyes bore into me, searching for something in my gaze. His shoulders slumped before he gave a tight nod. He turned to the crew and sheathed his sword. The rest wordlessly followed. Draven's crew was upon him, dragging him back to the boat.

Asmodeus pulled me away as I watched helplessly, wondering if, yet again, I had made the right deci-

sion. "We'll take my boat; it's the quickest way back."
He looked back at Draven, and then quickened our
pace into the water.

When my legs met the water, the coolness sent a
chill up me, causing a sharp pain in my wound. I cried
out as I hunched over.

"Don't worry, Lux. I will take care of you." Asmodeus took my other arm and wrapped it around his
neck to support me. I tried to take one more step, but
I couldn't.

"I'm not... I'm not feeling well." My vision was
blurring to the point objects no longer had colors. It
was as if all the energy I had used to save Draven had
been sucked out of me. All the adrenaline that was
coursing through my veins had left me shaking, and
sweating, yet cold. Oh so cold.

"Lux, you're burning up!" My feet lifted out of the
water, and I no longer had to support myself. I was in
Asmodeus' arms, and he was treading quickly toward
the boat.

How ironic would it be if I died right now? I tried
to laugh, but the sound seemed far away, like it didn't
come from my throat.

"Lift her in." I didn't know whom Asmodeus handed me to, trying to blink my heavy eyelids to clear the
picture. I was laid horizontally. My last waking thought
before I drifted into unconsciousness was that I was
laying in the same spot on his boat that three days
earlier I thought would lead me to my freedom.

Chapter Twenty

I WOKE IN MY BED AT THE WHITE HOUSE. THE GOLDS and whites shimmered from the sun shining through a cracked window. My eyelids shut tightly at the brightness. *Go back to sleep,* they seemed to urge. My body agreed, in no hurry to sit up—too exhausted and drained. At least my shoulder didn't feel as bad. I managed to open my eyes long enough to look at my arm, which was now wrapped in a clean white cloth. I wore an unfamiliar cotton tank top and silk pajama pants. Tubes came from my arm. *What is this?* I ripped them out and tossed them over the bed.

Pushing myself up, I closed my eyes from the dizziness that followed. I was so empty inside. *Thirsty.* I looked toward the nightstand and was relieved to find an untouched glass of water. My hands shook when I reached for it, and I greedily finished it all. *More.* I needed more. I couldn't seem to recover from waking. Had I been drugged? *If he drugged me, I swear!*

I hoped I hadn't slept until the next day; I didn't have time to waste. A noise at the door caught my attention. My heart briefly fluttered with a gullible hope, but the last face I wanted to see right then came unannounced through the door. He entered quietly and took his time closing the door behind him. He turned around, focusing on me, and his expression changed.

"You're awake." His voice dripped with relief and delight.

"Of course I am," I spat out. Was he worried he had drugged me too much?

"How are you feeling?"

I snorted. Suddenly feeling vulnerable in bed, I threw off the covers and attempted to stand.

Asmodeus rushed over to my side. "You should lie down. Take it easy. I'll call for a bowl of broth."

I pushed his arms away. "I'm fine. Now let me dress."

"You are not fine; you've been out for three days. You have to take it slow."

Like he cared, like he— "What do you mean I've been out for three days?"

"With the wound and the fever... you've been sleeping for three days now."

No! That was impossible; I shook my head. It couldn't have been three days. But just as I thought it, I remembered. Through my disbelief, the memories— which I thought were dreams—came back to me. Pieces of information through the fog. I could recall waking up several times to hear people talking about me. I was half-asleep, unable to move or speak, but I could hear everything *they* were saying. I remembered hearing Asmodeus threaten them if I didn't survive. Then when he left, they said I was already dying. *No!* I wanted to scream at them and tell them I was alive, but I couldn't.

Tears stung my eyes; I had been at Asmodeus' mercy for three days. That feeling, and the one of losing so much time, left me ill.

"I will get you something to eat; you must be starving. All we could get down you was a few spoonfuls of water and broth at a time."

Oh, wonderful. Now I had to feel indebted to him?

Asmodeus left the room, leaving me alone with my thoughts. Someone must have been waiting outside the door as I heard him speaking from just the other side. *Guards?* I swallowed. Or would have swallowed if I had enough spit.

Asmodeus came back with a bed tray, hesitating before setting it over me. I didn't have any pride left to refuse.

He watched me as I ate, and again, I didn't have the energy to protest.

The tray held some sort of fruit juice, soup, and bread. I went for the bread first, tearing a piece off with my teeth.

"Slow down," Asmodeus urged. I speared him with my glare, murderous thoughts filling my brain.

It didn't take long for me to finish everything. I leaned back against my pillows with a groan. My stomach ached so badly. The soup was barely better than a broth, yet I felt like I was exploding at the seams. I really *must* have been starved for days.

As I squeezed my eyes shut, something cool connected with my forehead. I shot up, my heart pounding from the cold, wet shock. Asmodeus stood over me, wide eyed.

"I'm sorry. This used to help you when you were out." He tried to dab me with the wet washcloth again. This time, I pushed his arms away.

"Well, stop. I am *fully* conscious now, and I don't need or want you doing that."

He pressed his lips together and nodded as he set the washcloth back in the porcelain bowl on the nightstand. I should not feel bad for him. He did this to me. I did not ask for him to care for me like a child, and I certainly didn't want him to be this... this human.

"I don't know why you came with me so easily. It was a smart choice, no doubt. But know this—if you leave, I will find you. I will *never* stop." The humanity was gone now.

We stared at each other, and I was careful to remain emotionless.

"Asmodeus?" I said after a while.

"Yes?"

"I think I should rest now." I broke our stare by turning to my other side.

With my eyes still open, I listened to him leave the room and quietly shut the door behind him. I stayed awake a while more, wrapped in the feelings of entrapment and solitude, before I unwillingly fell asleep.

———

It took a few more days before I fully recovered. Handicapped by my condition, I thought I would never feel normal again. But today, I had woken up, physically like my old self again. I had no choice but to get dressed in the clothes he gave me, but I wouldn't be stuck in this room.

I couldn't believe I was back here. Except, it was as if I were seeing everything for the first time. The clothing the others wore, which I hadn't realized before, was used to segregate people and indicate position.

What was my plan? Now that I was here, it seemed Draven was so far away. Where was he now? Had he recovered? Was he back home? *I asked him to trust me.* Closing my eyes, I relived the pain of that final scene. I thought I could beat this—beat Asmodeus. But now the reality had set in, and I had no idea how I was supposed to do that. Ice spread through my stomach at my failure, my inadequacies.

Relief was little condolence when I left my room

and Asmodeus was nowhere in sight. I ignored the people at my door and headed outside, leaving a trail of stares behind me. The sunshine warmed my deprived skin. I walked through the quad, going toward one of the only places I belonged—the water.

I walked onto the dock. The same dock where I was brought by Draven, and the same dock where I went sailing with Will. I stared into the rippling water, entranced as it gently beat the edge of the wood. My chest heaved, needing to cry, but the tears wouldn't come. What was wrong with me that I couldn't even cry? *Empty.* I was empty inside. Even when we were first taken by pirates, Lilou was never as down as I was now. Because she had hope. That was all I needed now—hope.

"Lux."

The voice behind me filled my stomach with pins.

Asmodeus took a seat next to me on the dock. He glanced at me and then to where my stare was directed.

"You're not happy here."

I scoffed. *Was he serious?* I lifted my head toward him. The sun shone through his hair, making it look golden. He looked like the vulnerable one right now.

"So, I thought we could take a trip. I thought... I could take you back to Sirbiad."

Hadn't I just asked for hope?

"Well, what do you think?"

"I'm hardly in a position to say no," I said, trying to contain my excitement. Why should I believe him? He was a liar.

"Right." He pushed his lips together. What had he expected? That I would be grateful? It wasn't like he was serious. Unless he was and he meant I wouldn't be going there alone. Speaking of...

"How long do I get to stay?"

271

"A week or so. And then we'd have to return here." He emphasized the word *we*, as if I didn't understand that he wouldn't be letting me go that easily. Oh, I understood.

He waited so his point could sink in before he continued. "I already had a boat sent to the island to prepare for our arrival. We can leave whenever you are feeling well enough to make the journey."

"I'm better. Let's go now."

"You've just recovered; we can wait a few days."

No, I couldn't wait a few days. I had to get off this island *now*. Needed to go home *now*. "I am fine, Asmodeus. I want to leave today, unless you've changed your mind."

He sighed. "I just want you to be happy. Does that make you happy?"

"Yes, Asmodeus," I grudgingly answered.

"I want things to be the way they were between us. They will be; you'll see."

I got up, having had enough of this conversation. "I will never pretend to understand you or your motives, but know this, whatever you are trying to get out of me or from me, you won't find it."

I walked away before he could say more.

Chapter Twenty-one

A FEW LONG HOURS LATER, SPENT WAITING IN ANTICI-pation, someone knocked on my door. I had taken a few things with me, but nothing more than I need-ed. After all, it was the hope I was given that had me thinking I would not be returning to this place.

I had expected another guard to escort me to the boat, but I was never that lucky. Asmodeus stood out-side my door. He was dressed more formally. Wear-ing white shorts, he also wore a matching crisp white shirt under a navy blue blazer and an ascot tie that complemented the blue. His hands were wrist deep in his pockets, revealing a brown leather belt and a chunky wristwatch. Though his stance was casual, he had an air of excitement to him.

"Are we leaving now?" I asked before he could get a word in.

Some of the excitement deflated. "Yes." His eyes briefly fell. "I'll have someone grab your things."

"Not necessary. This is all I need." I slung the bag over my shoulder and stepped out of the room.

Asmodeus didn't protest.

Side by side, we walked in silence. When I didn't sense him next to me anymore, I turned.

"The ship is this way." Asmodeus held out his arm

in the other direction.

"I thought this was the way to the docks?" I questioned.

"That port is for smaller cargo ships."

Of course it is, I thought as I followed him to the west side of the island.

An automatic door opened as we walked toward another building. I jumped as if fire crackled at my feet. I had never been inside this building. The differences between it and the common areas were apparent. My head swam with unasked questions.

We walked up a single staircase and entered a small room. At the other end was the opening to a covered walkway. Next to it, a guard was sitting at a desk. They nodded at each other as we walked by. I stepped onto the walkway, becoming skeptical for a minute that we were actually getting on a ship to go to Sirbiad.

I took my last step off the walkway, into what seemed like another house. Except, now I could feel the slight sway of the ocean under my feet.

Asmodeus walked me down the hall of the huge ship and murmured that he would be taking me to my rooms to get settled. When he pushed back the mahogany door, I understood he *had* meant *room* in the plural form.

The suite was bigger than Draven's cabin. It could have only been built before the Floods. There were so many questions I wanted answered, but could I ask Asmodeus? I didn't think I could stand hearing his reasons and excuses. Glancing back toward the door, I found he had left me alone.

I took a moment to familiarize myself with the suite. It had a separate living area, and through the bedroom, there were floor-to-ceiling windows. I opened the sliding glass door and stepped out onto the large, wraparound balcony. One side faced the lower deck while the other half looked out onto the vast ocean. I sat in a high-backed chair on the ocean side. It was almost peaceful, and there was hardly any noise, except for the faint rummaging of the crewmen on the deck below me. It was just before sunset, and the sky was glowing with the colors of cooked shrimp and turquoise. The temperature was a perfect match for bare skin, as I felt neither chilled nor too warm. Yes, it was serene, but nothing was what it seemed. And this ship, and the 'freedom' that came with it, came at a hefty price.

The sliding glass door opened. At first, I was alarmed that someone would be able to enter my room freely, but then I realized it was from the balcony next to mine. Asmodeus stepped onto the adjoining terrace. I sighed. *Couldn't he leave me alone for just one minute?* I ignored him, all the while waiting for the inevitable comment he would make.

To my surprise, he didn't say anything. He didn't comment on the beauty of the evening. Didn't utter one word of greeting. He just sat in a chair identical to mine and stared at the horizon, just as I had. *Odd.* He breathed a sigh of contentment and awe. Something that sounded so innocent and appreciative; it almost made me see him like he was another human being.

I turned away and tried to continue rejoicing in the silence.

After the sun had gone and the last flash of green as it set, Asmodeus got up from his chair to return inside. He hesitated at the door, and, in a voice that was neither demanding nor threatening, told me there would be dinner served outside on the lower deck.

Back inside, I finished exploring the suite. Guilt nagged me for being excited about the bookshelves. I finally found the bathroom, not sure if I was surprised or not that there was a full working shower and separate bath. I turned on the shower to the hottest setting before taking off my clothes in a slow, automatic motion.

Steam fogged the glass as I stepped in the shower to prepare for dinner.

~~~~~

I walked onto the lower deck where Asmodeus sat at a linen-covered table. Artificial lanterns hung around the railings, providing more illumination than the moon or firelight could ever do.

Asmodeus stood as I approached. "You came."

"I had to eat, didn't I?"

His face fell. "I would have had something sent up to you."

"I wish I would have known that sooner..." I said.

His face fell more. A twinge of guilt shot through me so I gave him a small smile as I sat. But what did I need to feel guilty for? *He did take good care of me while I was an invalid, more than a crazed, power-hungry scientist should have...* God, I hated this.

Asmodeus remained quiet until something was set down in front of us. Again, the meals would be served formally in courses, but I was glad for the distraction. He couldn't—and shouldn't—expect me to be good company.

"I hope you have everything you need to keep comfortable on our journey."

"I'll be fine. I've suffered through worse."

His lips twitched at my comment. "Let me know if you need anything at all. I brought the Healer with us, so if your shoulder is bothering you and you need something for the pain—"

"I said I would be fine," I snapped. Closing my eyes, I added a grudgingly muttered, "Thank you, though."

"Wait a sec—"A thought popped in my head that disintegrated any thanks I may have temporarily felt. "Why do you care if I'm in pain now? It's your fault that I'm in this condition. You couldn't have known that I would have survived your twisted traps."

"You wouldn't be the girl I thought you were if you didn't survive."

"Well, I almost didn't!" A server leaned to take my untouched soup bowl just as I yelled at Asmodeus.

When I could see him again, Asmodeus had steepled his fingers and appeared detached. "I warned you to stay away from that door. By the time you entered, there was nothing I could do. If I had the door unlocked and came after you, it just would have rushed you and possibly put you in more danger. I told you not to go in there. I told you it was a test for anyone who dared to enter it."

A plate of delicate white fish smothered in a creamy sauce and garnished with crab was set in front of me. My tongue wet my lips by its own doing as a small plate of crusty bread was set next to it. "Thank you," I told the man who served me, not sure if he worked for Asmodeus out of his own accord.

"You know, when I opened that door, I actually thought for a moment I must have been mistaken. That you couldn't possibly be Asmodeus. I mean, you're not much older than I am. But now I've seen you for who you are. A liar. A manipulator—"

He shook his head. "I never lied to you. I never told you I wasn't Asmodeus."

I rolled my eyes at *Wilson* Asmodeus.

"Then you lied by omission. And I *hate* liars. Besides, it's pretty obvious that you are—" I threw up my hands. "—trying to rule the world."

"Someone has to," he said as simply as one would note the weather conditions. He held up a finger. "But what I told you at the spring was true."

"You're absolutely right." I let that sink into him for a little bit. "No, I don't think you let the world be destroyed. I think you caused it."

"And how would I do that, Lux?" he flippantly said.

"What's the word you used for it? Magic?"

His smile faded. I couldn't prove anything, but the look on his face told me I had gotten close to the truth.

"And the lies continue. You told me, after I begged you to help him, that Draven sailed away, back to his lands, but that was a lie. Not to mention the others in your prison. You must have thought I was such a fool because I didn't realize it was you. That you were able to..." I blinked profusely. "Seduce me, all the while knowing I despised your true identity."

"No." He put a hand on the table, and I retreated. "I don't think you are a fool at all. Quite the opposite in fact. When you first came to my island and didn't know who I was, it was refreshing. Here was someone who could finally get to know me, and like me for who I was, not tainted by what others said about me. As for Draven and the others, they were traitors. That's why they were in the cells. You were mine first. I sent him on orders to collect you from Sirbiad. If you had heard the things Draven has done, the things he's capable of, you wouldn't have thought it possible that he would fall for you. Who knew the devil himself would be my competition?" He took a sip of dark liquid from a crystal glass.

"Why did you order him to kidnap me? What do you want from me?"

He set his glass down. "As I've said before, Lux, someone needs to rule the world. I have the power and the land to do so. The people obey me, but I don't have their hearts. That's where you come in, my little darling. Our unity could change that. They *adore* you."

I shook my head. "They don't adore me. I was so selfish before."

He raised both eyebrows at me. "You have not heard what I've heard. Besides, with our new alliance, I think your father would think twice about a revolt."

"Revolt? Our tiny island stuck in the middle of the Pacific? You're kidding."

"Kidding? The famed warriors of Sirbiad? No, one does not kid about rebellions. What did you think you were training for, Lux?"

"To protect ourselves from pirates."

"Well maybe that, too, but your father had other plans for when a shipload of supplies and men came back to Sirbiad."

My father? There was no way. He would have told me about something like that. Wouldn't he? I started seeing the training on Sirbiad in a different light. *Oh, God.* I hated life right then. It was like everything I ever knew never existed. Lies. Betrayal. Hurt.

"How did you know I would be on the shore that night?"

"I didn't. They were prepared to do whatever it took to take you. Luckily, you were on shore, and I didn't have to risk things getting messy. But that's why I had the pirates do it in the first place. Even if things didn't go as planned, the fault would fall on them. Honestly, when you first came to the island, I hadn't realized you wouldn't know who I was. I wasn't trying to deceive you. It was fate. But now, it worked out so much better. I won't even have to use you as leverage. With our alliance, we'll rule the world."

"Your plan isn't going to work because you don't have Draven's land under your control."

He scoffed, but I noted he looked a little worried. "What he doesn't know is that his uncle Treymore *is* under my control. I have everything I need now, and

Prince Draven is free to *attempt* to reclaim his throne."

"Excuse me?"

"Well, his uncle is ruling his country, as Draven lacks the proper documents to prove he's the rightful heir. He can only *attempt* to stake his claim, although something tells me it won't be easily won," he finished with a knowing smile, oblivious to the shock that tore through me.

My mind reeled as all the puzzle pieces Draven had shared with me fit together. "*Prince* Draven?" I repeated, the syllables breaking on my tongue. "He's a bloody prince. That's why he wants..." I let my last thought drift off as I gaped at Asmodeus.

His brow arched and his mouth puckered at the realization of his error. "You didn't know he was a prince," he said, nodding. "That's very noble of you. Falling for a pirate, not a crown. Maybe that reveals a lot about your character. Not the morally superior girl we've all come to know and love." He cocked his head, a sinister smile on his face. "I have hope for you yet, Lux."

I wanted to scream at him, but quickly changed my tactics. "Would this proof, these 'proper documents'...?" I swallowed down laughter that threatened to bubble up. "Would they be in a wooden box with the Sabriye crest carved on top?" The crazed, victorious laughter I tried to hold back spilled from my lips.

His lips twitched, but he neither confirmed nor denied what I said. He picked up his glass and melodramatically swished around its contents. "You and I are a lot more alike than you realize, Lux. In time, you'll see this." He blinked. His eyes opened, and they were looking straight into me. "After all, time is what I have."

My revelation didn't faze him as much as I hoped.

I stood, needing to be alone with my thoughts and needing to be away from the person who constantly reminded me of my poor judgments. He caught my arm as I huffed and tried to make my escape to my room.

"With this ship, we will arrive at Sirbiad by tomorrow. That should give you the time to..." His eyes raked the length of me in a threatening and seductive way. "Reconsider your attitude. I expect by the time we arrive, you'll remember the position you are in and act like you are overjoyed to be with me. Both publicly *and* privately."

Chapter Twenty-two

THE EARLY MORNING RAYS APPEARED THROUGH THE sliding glass door of the balcony. I pushed myself off the couch and walked to the window. The ship cruised through the water at a pace that seemed alarming compared to Draven's ship. *Draven.* I closed my eyes.

I knew he'd been hiding something. He was more complex than I first believed. My heart knew all along he wasn't evil even though it took my head quite a bit longer to jump on board. But a prince? I had not expected that. I had no idea that a whole other continent survived. No wonder when he talked about his home, it was never in past tense. Maybe that was what Draven had meant on the note he left on my pillow when he had said other lands survived. Maybe that was what he was going to tell me before our heated argument. Maybe—no—obviously, that was why he had wanted to go home so desperately. So he could rule his people and not leave them at the hands of Treymore.

All this time, *that* was what he was willing to give up for me. My nose and heart tingled. I pulled at my nightgown, feeling inadequate. Draven was a *prince?* No—now, he would be a king. I had given him the box with the deeds to his lands. He could go home;

he didn't have to rely on Asmodeus. No wonder he always acted so superior, so regal. I tried to smile. Now he wouldn't have to give up anything for me. I should be happy for him, but why was that so hard to do?

My eyes burned with fatigue. I was too afraid to sleep that night. I wouldn't risk dreaming again. Even though it seemed impossible, the thought of what Asmodeus had said about magic repeated over and over again in my head. Magic? Really? No, I just couldn't believe it. There had to be some kind of natural phenomenon that could explain what I had seen in his lair.

I went to the bathroom to attempt to wash away my fatigue and get dressed. Sorting through the bag of clothes revolted me. It had come from *him*. I tried not to think about it anymore as I picked out the modest outfit he'd provided me—a simple pair of flowing pants and a tank top.

Brushing my hair after showering, the strokes slow and methodic, I stared at my clear reflection in the mirror. I never stopped to study myself in the bathroom at the White House, and I looked much different from the reflection of myself in the glass on Sirbiad. The skin under my slanted hazel eyes was puffy. My lips just a little swollen from chewing them all night.

When I emerged from the bathroom, the waters outside my window had become a bold aquamarine. I ran out to the balcony, overjoyed to see the clear, blue-green waters and sugar-white beaches of Sirbiad. The sun shone down on my island, making the sand look impossibly bright. The timing of the bird's calls seemed to agree with me. "*Home*," I said on an exhale of breath. How did we make the journey here in such a short amount of time? It was at least a relief. Asmodeus' modern ship had traveled five times as fast as Draven's.

We anchored a good distance from the shallow waters around the shore. Below me, crewmen prepared motor boats to go inland. A smile spread across my face. I was home.

"It's quite beautiful here."

My body stiffened as I slowly pivoted to where Asmodeus lounged in the minimalist metal and mesh chair on his balcony. He stood and walked to the railing. "Are you ready to go ashore, my sweet?" His voice wasn't mocking, and he almost seemed genuine. His mood swings ebbed and flowed more than the ocean's tide. Maybe his act as "Will" really wasn't an act. Maybe he really did have two different personalities. *He really is insane.*

I nodded and ducked into my room. Will was waiting for me when I exited the door. *Oh God, I called him Will.* Perhaps I shared in his delusions. Perhaps he was right. I *was* more like him than I knew. What other kind of person could fall for a pirate and befriend a psychotic dictator?

We walked in silence through the grand halls, lined with silk rugs, and back down the curved staircase with brass railings. It was elegant and refined, but I didn't appreciate a single inch of it.

I stayed two feet behind Asmodeus as we walked. Halfway across the deck, he turned around and arched one brow at me. I kept my eyes down at my sparkling slippers before glancing over at the swimming pool that was built into the deck. It was large enough to fit a smaller ship in it, but I could smell the clean scent of chemicals. Although the blue of the water was pretty, it was not as profound as the sea.

We arrived beside a handful of crewmen who had two dinghies prepared. I stepped with Asmodeus toward the first one when he suddenly spun around. I ran into his soft, citrus-scented chest.

He caught me before I could pull back and wrapped an arm around my waist, pulling me in a rough jerk against him. "Don't think I didn't notice your purposeful distance this morning. Consider this your last warning and do not forget what I told you." He let go to coil a slender hand around my wrist. With a tug, he pulled me behind him over the deck and into the motorized boat.

I sat next to him, and he peered down at me with that boyish smile I had seen in Will. Thinking of how close I was to seeing my parents again, I pasted a smile on my own face. The dinghy was lowered into the water. My heart sped with the roar of the engine. The smell of petrol and exhaust were behind us as we zipped across the clear water. I blinked, the wind whipping my face so fiercely I could hardly keep my eyes open. We flew across the water, weightlessly bouncing.

I rose off the bench with a gasp as people ran to the shore. Asmodeus pulled me back down. I squinted to see who I could make out. As we got closer, I spotted my parents. My father, standing tall and proud, had an arm wrapped around my mother. She was wearing her usual faded tortoise-shell brown dress. Her hands were steepled against her naturally red lips, and I could see her eyes sparkle even from the distance. The boat came ashore and the engine died. Flying to a stand, I fought the urge to push my way off first. I chattered my teeth together impatiently as the handful of Jumpsuits leaped off, followed by Asmodeus, who courteously took my hand to help me down. I tried to pull free to run to my parents, but Asmodeus held on tightly. I ended up dragging him with me.

"Lux!" My mother ran toward me, pulling me into a tight embrace. "Oh my God, my baby. Are you all right?" She gripped my head between her hands, and her beautiful warm eyes searched every inch of me to make sure I was unscathed.

"Yes, Mom. I'm fine."

She gasped. "What happened to your shoulder?"

"I..."

"Pirates. They're ruthless creatures. I was lucky to rescue her when I did. She didn't go down without a fight though," Asmodeus said, coming between us.

I tried not to roll my eyes.

"Hello, I'm Asmodeus." He held out a hand politely to my mother.

My eyes widened as my father approached. "Father!" I pulled free of Asmodeus and flung myself at him. My father gripped me in a tight hug that was contrary to the controlled emotion on his face.

"Lux." Sighing, he pressed his cheek to the top of my head. He pulled back and checked his emotions once again. His thick, chestnut hair seemed to have more silver than before.

"Asmodeus." He nodded at him and then grabbed his hand to shake it firmly in appreciation. "I can't thank you enough for reading my correspondence and saving my daughter."

Asmodeus smiled charmingly and pulled me into a sidelong hug. "Trust me—the pleasure was all mine."

My mother's eyes widened at the meaning, and her jaw dropped open despite the curl of a smile on her lips. She winked at me knowingly and almost— approvingly. Pins and needles filled my stomach. *Oh, no...*

My father shifted uncomfortably.

I scanned the beach. The other villagers who had come to greet us watched with a smile on their faces. The prisoners were there, like Asmodeus promised they would be. They never knew the truth that

Asmodeus was behind the kidnappings. They hadn't warned my dad. No wonder my father was acting like Asmodeus was a hero. I caught the back of Shaman Tamati's head before he disappeared in the crowd with the others who were returning to their duties. Where was Lilou? My eyes caught on Leif.

"Come, let me show you our island," my dad said heartily as he gestured for Asmodeus to follow. They walked together toward the village. "We can't express our gratitude enough for your generous donation of supplies. I can assure you that you will always have Sirbiad's cooperation and compliance in whatever you need—"

Asmodeus stopped and turned back toward me. "Won't Lux be joining us?" He held up an eyebrow at me in warning.

"You go ahead. I need to catch up on a few things, *my sweet,*" I added, not one bit mockingly when his eyes darkened.

My father picked up, like the diplomat he once was, and guided Asmodeus toward the village in a business-like manner.

As I turned back toward my mom, she brushed her honey-colored hair back from a warm breeze that had ruffled it. I stared into her hazel-green eyes that were identical to mine, or so my father had always said when he cursed them because they were the reason he couldn't tell us *no.* I smiled at the memory and hugged her again. "Oh, Mom." I pulled back. "Everyone looks so happy. What happened?"

"They're happy to see you, dear, and things have changed since you left. Before you arrived, Asmodeus sent a ship filled with supplies, along with the villagers who had been recovered from the pirates. His men have been working all night to repair the structures and the well so that we can properly irrigate the water. He also sent livestock, though I was amazed any had survived the floods. The villagers are practicing sustainable use of the new resources, and he's given us stores of grains, fruits, and vegetables. The weather's been beautiful on top of it." She threw up her hands. "I don't know what else to say; things are going so great!"

I smiled at her before I felt my throat start to close up. So much good had been done because of my decision to stay with Asmodeus. I knew now that I would never see Draven again.

"I know that look." My mother's voice blended in with the sounds of the waves lapping against the shore.

"What look?"

"That lovesick look."

I rolled my eyes. "I do not have that look."

"You'll be with him soon enough," she said in a matter-of-fact voice.

"What?" My heart stopped, and I whipped my head toward her.

"He just went with your father. They'll be back soon."

I closed my eyes at my idiocy. When I opened them, I noticed Leif still stood on the beach even though most of the others had went about their business or followed my father and Asmodeus.

"Just one second, dear. I know you want to catch up with Leif, but I wanted to talk to you before all your attention is on a certain someone again." She winked, and my stomach rolled.

"What is it, Mom?"

She turned me, indicating she wanted to walk. "Leif told me everything."

"Oh." My face fell, and I glanced back to narrow my eyes at him.

"Now, don't be upset. He was very worried about you."

I turned my head away in shame.

"I'm not mad." She turned my chin. "Look at me. I don't agree with your unsafe methods of leaving and without saying goodbye." She shook her head to scold me. "But I understand. That's why I want you to know the villagers told us everything about Asmodeus' island and what they have there."

"They did?" So she knew the truth about Asmodeus...

"Oh, yes. Down to the very last detail of how Asmodeus' ship ambushed the pirate's and rescued everyone. It was very unexpected, really, after the things we all knew about him. But they said only great things about The Island and how it functions. It's everything you've always wanted, everything you deserve to have. That's why your father and I want you to know that it's okay if you go back there. You can make a difference there—you can do something for the other surviving islands. I know you felt caged here and didn't enjoy the simple life we have, but now you don't have to."

So they didn't know the truth. What did Asmodeus have to do in order to get them to share in this mass delusion? "I'm not sure it's what I want anymore."

"That's very mature of you," she said seriously.

"I think I've changed."

"I know, Lux. And I hope you can see now that your father and I are content here. So if Asmodeus and his island are what you want, then go for it." She nodded, pushing quivering lips together.

I blew out a breath. I would be leaving, but not for the reasons my mother suspected. The worst part of it all was that my parents were okay with it.

"Asmodeus' ship can get us here in a day."

"Really?" My mom stopped walking, intrigued. "That's wonderful, dear. Tell me all about it."

For the next few minutes, we fell into our old roles until my mother left me to make sure Father wasn't boring our company.

I eagerly jogged to Leif, stopping in front of him. He remained in the same spot, stone faced. Biting my lip, I hesitated to speak. I nearly died inside when he shook his head at me.

"You crazy, hardheaded... C'mere!"

My surprised yelp was muffled by his bear hug. I curled my arms around him, gripping his shoulders. "I take it you missed me?"

"If you ever pull something like that again, I will personally come after you."

"Yeah, like it was my fault." I laughed. "I'm so glad you didn't blame yourself for leaving me alone that night. In fact, so many things wouldn't have happened if you hadn't."

"I did, Lux. I went home to my hut to sleep; all the while, you were being jostled by pirates. We had no idea you were missing until the next morning. Your parents were panicking, and your father made us search every hut. I thought maybe you had left, that you somehow finished that night and were so upset with me that you left without a goodbye. I went back to the other side of the island, and that's when I saw it. The satchel left exactly where you'd thrown it and the boat deserted. I ran back and had to tell your parents everything. I'm sorry." He hung his head.

"Don't be. It was for the best." I let go of Leif to plop down in the sand.

He joined me. "So I was told you were rescued by Asmodeus."

I shrugged while running my fingers through soft, white sand. "Uh, yeah, that's what they say."

Silence passed between us as I drew patterns in the sand.

"Right before you came, another of Asmodeus' ships came with other people who had been taken prisoner."

I nodded.

"But the day before *that*, another person came. A young, traveling fisherman. He came to trade with us, I suppose, not realizing the predicament we were in. I thought it was something else, especially since you weren't here to see it. The last one who came had been a dozen moons ago when... well, you know, when you got the map." He drew up his legs, dangling his arms over his knees. "Well, anyway. I didn't tell anyone else this, but I just thought him strange."

My head snapped up to see Leif shiver while looking out over the ocean. "Really?" I encouraged. He always knew how to entice my curiosity.

"He looked as though he were in awe of our island. He took turns getting to know a lot of our villagers, so I thought he was a friendly sort, but when I introduced myself, he..." Leif tilted his head up in thought. "It was almost... as if he already hated me. Strange, I know."

My heart beat a wild rhythm. "What...?" I swallowed. "What did he look like?"

"That's the thing; I couldn't tell you. The entire time, his face was covered with a scarf, but one thing you couldn't mistake was his eyes. They were this bright blue."

"Go on," I spoke in automation. "And he left, you say?"

"Yes, he left quickly thereafter. But the reason I'm telling you this is because right before he left, I caught him doing something strange."

"What was it?" I clenched fistfuls of sand with

both hands.

"He... I found him in your tent."

I jerked to my feet. "My tent?"

"You don't have to worry, Lux. It's not like he took anything. He was very well off."

"Did you tell anyone?" I paced.

"Well, no. That's the thing. He was very kind to everyone, and he gave us a lot of things. In exchange for nothing. I didn't want to spoil that with any suspicions I had. That's why I'm telling you now, to see what you make of it. I just thought it strange that he came to the island, when no one had in months, and was in *your* tent right before you returned. What do you make of it?"

I took off without warning and sprinted into the village.

"Lux! Lux, wait!" Leif's words trailed behind me.

"I'll talk to you later," I yelled over my shoulder. I dodged palm trees and the fire pit until I reached my family's tent. Throwing back the canvas door, I stepped inside. I searched around frantically for any clues. Passing my parents' partitioned side of our house, I went to where I slept. Everything seemed to be in the same position I left it. The hammock with the straw pillow hung still. The books below were still discarded like I remembered when I snuck out that night.

My luggage trunk was locked and closed in the corner. A shawl was folded neatly on top of it. I threw my head back and closed my eyes. Draven had been here. I clenched my hands over my heart as I tried to imagine him on my island. Seeing where I lived. *Meeting my parents.* Why had he come? Had he left me some kind of clue? Some plan to escape? My eye flashed open, and I scanned my things again.

Of course. I ran over to the stool next to my hammock. There, lying on top, was my charm necklace. The one I had left on Draven's bedside. The chain I had seen him keep even while imprisoned.

Oh my God. I scooped it up and examined it. Nothing new there. I searched around the stool, hoping to see a note that might have fallen to the floor. Nothing. *Why had Draven come here, damn it?* Why had he left this here? *Think, think, think.* When I had left it on his bedside, it was for closure. Or, maybe if I were honest with myself, so he'd have something to remember me by.

When the reality struck, it was a cold splash of seawater. Of course. I had given him the key to getting his land back and to reclaim his... *Ahem.* Reclaim his throne. He had work to do. I brought my entwined hands to my forehead, the compass on the necklace digging into my palms.

That's it? Seriously? No. It had to be sign. A message.

The ebb and flow that was getting my hopes up, just to have them dashed again, left me feeling sick. What was Draven trying to tell me?

"There you are. And here I thought you'd forgotten our promise."

I turned with a start. "Asmodeus." I hid my hands behind my back. "Of course not. I was just getting settled back in."

He walked toward me. One smooth hand stroked my bare upper arm. "You don't have to live like this anymore. I had a tent set up for you next to mine. It's fully furnished. And despite your assurance that you've packed everything, I brought more clothes for you."

"Thank you," I managed.

"Stop that, Lux."

"Stop what?"

"Stop acting like you're my prisoner. Stop acting like I'm forcing you to behave this way."

I licked my lips. "I'm just hurt, Asmodeus. My shoulder may be healing, but I don't think my heart ever will."

He gripped both my arms at the elbows and gently shook me. "It will. And I will wait however long it takes. I just want you to look at me like you used to."

"I do," I lied.

"Tell me—what has changed? Is it because you found out my true identity or because you lusted after that pirate? Because I know you will have no problem looking past my transgressions if you've done it so easily with his."

I sucked in a breath. "How *dare* you?"

"That's it, Lux. That's what I want to see. I want to see your emotions. Your passion." He pulled me flush against his chest. Tilting his head, he leaned forward. His breath was like velvet against my throat, and his lips grazed bare flesh that prickled under my skin.

Clenching my fist, I longed to slap him. I closed my eyes at his touch despite panting, angry breaths.

"Hate me, Lux. Hate me all you need to."

I pulled back and turned my head away from him.

He huffed. Out of the corner of my eye, I saw him adjust his clothes. "Your body betrays you, Lux, and that is all the hope I need. Remember, my sweet, love and hate *do* stem from the same place."

I closed my eyes. *No, they don't.*

"Now, come on. I want you to give me a personal tour before the celebration tonight."

My eyes cracked open out of curiosity, "Celebration?"

"Of course. Your island is throwing a celebration for us. For the ruler of the New United Territories." He smiled like the cat that ate the canary. "And his new queen."

Chapter Twenty-three

WE SAT AROUND THE ENORMOUS, IMPROVED FIRE PIT. The flames and the proximity warmed my skin. I stared at the plate in my hand, proper porcelain from Asmodeus' island. My dinner sat untouched, and I glanced over at Asmodeus to see if he'd noticed. He sat closely next to me, his own plate forgotten as he chatted with villagers.

Small arms wrapped around my neck from behind.

I choked on my laugh from the tightness of her grip around my throat. "Lilou!" Putting my plate down, I turned in order to give her a proper hug. "I wondered when I would get to talk to you. I didn't see you on the beach with the others."

She sat on the bench next to mine. "Papa said I had to give you time to get settled in. Are you settled *now*?" She pouted.

"Yes, of course. I've been so worried about you. I thought—never mind. You're here. You're safe." I beamed at her. "And your sister is here as well?"

"Yeah. She's around here somewhere. Probably off talking to Harou again." She slumped, and I let out a sole laugh and gripped her arm with affection. Lilou appeared healthy and in no way traumatized.

"I tried looking for you on Asmodeus' island, but I couldn't find you."

Lilou busied herself by digging her feet into the sand. "That's because we didn't come back with—" She looked up at me, eyes wide. "I mean..."

I peeked over at Asmodeus again, who still chatted away, oblivious to the turn of our conversation.

Scooting next to her on the bench, I kept my voice low. "What do you mean, Lilou?"

"Nothing. I didn't mean anything."

"Lilou, you can tell me anything."

"Well, I suppose it's okay if I tell *you*. Since the crew said the reason you fought all the time was because you really liked each other."

I laughed. "Did you come with the captain, Lilou?"

"Yes, but we promised to only claim he was a traveling fisherman who found us at sea and pretend we had no idea where the other prisoners went. They're really nice, Lux. Meddy treated us so nice and gave us whatever we wanted. They can't really be pirates. But Meddy said they wouldn't understand, and no one could know they were here."

"Meddy?" I was barely able to keep the laughter from my voice.

"You know, *Ahmed.*"

"Oh, Lilou." I pulled her into another hug. My heart soared.

"You're acting strange." She brought two index fingers to her lips and looked at me sideways.

"I am? How?" I teased.

"Like my sister, when she talks to Haruo. 'Haruo this and Haruo that.' And she has that same look on her face like she's in the middle of a happy dream."

My laugh sounded like a cry.

"I'm gonna go get more to eat." She got up to leave, but turned around and pointed a finger at me. "And when I come back, I want you to be back to normal."

"Yes, Your Highness." I nodded in mock obedience.

My smile faded as she left me to my musings. I turned back to the fire, watching the flames lick the driftwood. Hot embers flared before turning to ash. The dim blue part of the fire entranced me.

Despite everything, Draven had kept his promise and returned Lilou and her sister. That was why he had come. Even though I knew the reason he had come wasn't for me, I felt peace knowing he was finally capable of kindness.

And I would never see him again.

My sense of loss was beyond tears. *Just say it, Lux.* I shook my head. *Why can't you just say it? Why can't you just admit it?*

I was in love with Draven.

A flash of wild grief ripped through me. It froze me for a long moment, but not in horror. Peace washed over me as all the questions to my many frustrations and sleepless nights were answered. My body drained of tension as soon as my mind accepted that truth. I flew to a stand. I needed to be alone. My wound felt like it was out in the open for everyone to see.

I took off toward my family's tent.

Out of the corner of my eye, Asmodeus stood. I swallowed down my misery as I turned to face him.

"Where are you off to?" His tone wasn't accusing, only concerned.

"I was just going to get some rest." I hoped he hadn't seen my lips quiver as I tried to smile.

"Are you feeling all right?"

"I'm fine. It's just my shoulder has been bothering me."

"I will send the doctor." He set his plate down on the bench and lifted his arm to motion to a guard.

"No!" I held up my hand to stop him. "No, it's fine. I just need to lie down." My eyelids fluttered as the permanent sorrow started to weigh me down.

"Are you sure?" He stepped toward me, almost tenderly, and ran a thumb down the line of my jaw. Oh, this must be the Will side of him. How odd that I wished I could forget everything that had happened with him. How easy would it be if I could step into his embrace and just pour out every emotion into him. To have him understand and tell me everything was going to be all right. Maybe I just needed someone to talk to. My head perked up as I thought of Leif. He was my best friend; I should be able to talk to him about these... feelings. But then, I remembered he had no idea of the truth.

I dropped my lashes to hide the hurt. "Yes. I'm sure. And I think I'd rather just stay in my parents' tent tonight."

"Of course. Wherever you're most comfortable. I will inform them."

My smile was wistful and appreciative. "Goodnight, Will."

"Lux?"

I stopped walking and turned around. "Hm?"

"You called me Will." His face seemed more animated, and I realized my mistake.

"Oh." I frowned. *Damn it.* Why?

"No. I like it. I want you to think of me that way again. You are the only person I would allow to call me that name. And you haven't addressed me that way since. Well—"

"Goodnight."

"Yes, goodnight."

I turned back around and squeezed my eyes shut. Then I pulled together what little composure I had left to walk a coconut's throw to my parent's tent. I peeled back the opening, and longed to throw myself in my hammock. But then I slowed as I remembered how painful that would be on my shoulder. *Finally, I was alone. I didn't have to bottle everything up—*

Unfurling from the clinging shadows, a hulking figure strode toward me. "Good evening, Lux."

Chapter Twenty-four

MY HEART JUMPED IN MY THROAT. AHMED WAS STANDing in the center of my tent.

"Oh, my God. Ahmed. What are you doing here?" I didn't wait for him to answer, but ran to throw my arms around him. I pulled back. "Seriously, how are you here right now?"

"I see you've found the necklace the captain left for you."

"Is he still—?"

"No. He had to go back home and usurp that goat of an uncle."

"Oh." My emotions crashed just as much as they soared at the thought of Draven still here. "I don't understand. Why are *you* still here?"

He shrugged before his lips twitched into a smile. "My loyalties might have shifted."

"I knew that all along," I managed to tease, but then my eyebrows furrowed. "But I still don't understand."

"You didn't think he would actually just leave you, did you, Lux? Especially with *him.* Not after you risked your life to save Draven. After you gave up for your freedom for his. Gave him the key to what he's been longing after for years. And most importantly, not after he fell in love with you."

"Ahmed, just stop it." I couldn't keep the agony out of my voice. "Just tell me what this means because I can't keep hoping for something just to have those hopes dashed. It's killing me inside."

"Are you prepared to do anything for him?"

"You know that I'm not exactly cautious..."

"Are you willing to leave everything behind?"

"Yes," I answered without hesitation.

"The journey isn't going to be an easy one, and who knows what we will find when we get there."

"Okay..." This suspiciously sounded like something from a book I read. Ahmed, always the one to be so mysterious.

"You agree then?"

"Of course I agree." I was done wavering. I was more certain of this one thing than any other decision I'd made.

"Okay, good." Ahmed wiped his brow in relief. "Because if not, Captain's orders were to manually remove you if necessary, and Sokum told me what trouble you were last time they had to do that."

I covered my hand with my mouth and stifled a laugh. "So we're leaving? I get to see Draven again?"

He pointedly stared at me. "For someone so optimistic, you sure are doubtful when it comes to him."

"It's easy to be pessimistic when it's something you care so greatly about losing."

He gave me that wise, appreciative smile. "We leave tonight."

"Where? How?" I tried not to jump with joy.

"Meet me well before dawn at the same place you were taken captive the first time."

"You want me to sneak out?"

"It would be beneficial if no one knew you were leaving, yes."

Alarm ripped through me. "But Ahmed, as soon as the sun rises, Asmodeus will know I've left and come after me. His ship isn't powered by wind. It can travel ten times as fast. If he catches me, and he knows I left willingly, not only will I suffer, but my island will also as well." I took a step back.

"Don't fret, Lux. I have many allies on his island. They will ensure his ship won't be able to deport for several days. With that as a factor, plus the time it will take to track us, we will be well on our way to the Middle East. If you make sure it looks like you left unwillingly, he will have no choice but to keep up the pretenses until you're found."

"Are you sure? I can't risk what my people have going for them here."

"Do you trust me?" His words were as cool and clear as the ocean water at night.

"Yes."

"Then I'm sure. But how will you ensure that Asmodeus doesn't know you left willingly?"

A plan hit me, and I crossed my arms. "Done. What else?"

"I'll explain everything later. Be discreet, Lux."

Pulling the hood of a cloak over his head, Ahmed ducked out of my tent.

〜〜〜

It was a gruesome few hours as I lay awake in my hammock. I experienced joy, fear, and anxiety. I was experienced in sneaking out as I had accomplished it for months while building the boat with Leif. If you were to be skilled with stealth, you couldn't be impatient, and patience was not something I had when it came to Draven.

My parents had tumbled in very late that night. As much as it pained me, I pretended to be asleep. I knew I wouldn't have the chance to say good-bye, but I had prepared for that by tearing a page out of my father's favorite book and tucking it into my well-concealed satchel. Soon, my father snored and my mother's breathing seemed to slow in time with his. I smiled as I sat up.

Melancholy washed over me as I prepared to leave the only home I had known for the past five years. I was leaving anyway, whether it was now or when we returned to Asmodeus' island. This just seemed so rushed, but I was ready. My courage and determination were like a rock inside of me.

Quietly setting the stage for what looked like a kidnapping, I scattered my books across the floor, doing as much damage as I could without making noise. Then, just like I had two weeks ago, I pushed back the fabric door and stepped out into the humid tropical night.

I shook as I took every precaution to make it to the path in the rainforest. Everything was at risk this time if I got caught with a bag full of clothes and supplies. Asmodeus' tent was opulent and required a lot of space. I was thankful it was a good distance away from the village. He had stationed guards in front of his own tent, for his safety. Our lack of resources, or his ultimatum, must have made him confident enough to not put them at our tent as well. And my father would have been suspicious if he had. It would have been a slip in his perfectly crafted image.

When I made it to the path, I broke into a run. My heart pounded in my chest, and the sound of blood rushed through my ears. Fanned palms slapped my skin as I cut through the overgrown rainforest. Just when I thought I would have to slow from exertion, the path opened up to the beach. The full moon hung overhead, accompanied by a million dazzling stars.

The fullness of the moon made the beach look impossibly bright. How ironic that it was tonight that I was supposed to be on Fiji, starting my journey back to the US.

Ahmed stood by the shore. Behind him, a boat was anchored in the water.

I jogged over to him, letting the satchel slide from my shoulder. "Ahmed!" My mouth hung open, and I wasn't able to articulate any words from the sight of my boat completed and bobbing in the water.

"How did you...?" I slid my hands to the back of my head.

"I know you're shocked. I do hope this is a pleasant surprise, but we don't have much time."

I nodded and blew out a breath, trying to get a hold of myself. "So we're going east then? We're going to Draven?"

"Of course. Now, don't go getting all teary on me."

"I'm not! I don't cry," I huffed. "How far away is it?"

"With this boat, it will take a week if the conditions are right."

I bit the nail on my thumb. "You've completed my boat? It's truly ready to sail?"

"Yes, it seems to keep afloat." He smiled. "We did, however, make a few improvements."

"*We?*"

"Draven insisted that the vessel be completely safe for you to travel on. The whole crew worked on it to get it completed within the day. "

Warmth spread through me.

"And, by the way, Draven wanted to make sure I informed you that the condition it was in prior wouldn't have made it a hundred yards before it capsized." Ahmed fought a smile and his brown eyes twinkled in the moonlight.

"His arrogance hasn't lessened, I see." I shook my

head, but the mirth in his face was contagious and I couldn't help laughing.

"Lux?"

My body jumped at the voice of an uninvited visitor. Ahmed pushed me behind him, removing a knife from his belt.

"It's okay, Ahmed. He's my friend." I recognized the familiar voice and stepped out from behind Ahmed. "Leif, what are you doing here?"

"What are you doing, Lux?" His tone was so disapproving that I felt shame.

"It's not what you think."

We walked toward each other, meeting at the middle. "I don't understand."

I took a deep breath. "I should have told you the whole truth from the beginning. I just didn't want you to be haunted by it. Where do I start?" I ran a hand through my hair. "I was kidnapped, but Asmodeus' was the one behind it. The pirates worked for him. Asmodeus didn't rescue the others and me; we were sent to his island. Asmodeus is a tyrant. He's moody, manipulative, and, for some reason, he wants me by his side. He's trying to use his influence over the island to make me do what he wants."

"So who's this?" He flung out an arm toward Ahmed in accusation.

"This is Ahmed, the captain's first mate." I pointed my thumb behind me.

"He's a pirate?" Leif's eyes widened.

"Well, yes. But only because they were under contract with Asmodeus. You were right to be suspicious of the traveling fisherman, Leif."

"What does that have to do with anything?"

"Because that was the captain."

"Why would he come here, and why are you sailing away with his first mate?" Leif glanced at me sideways.

"Because I'm in love with him."

Leif's jaw dropped open. He turned away, speechless, and then turned back toward me again.

"I told you once that if I ever got the chance to go home again, I would. Well, this is my chance. I'm going to my father's homeland. I'm going to the Middle East."

"You were jus' gonna leave without saying goodbye?"

It pained me to see the hurt in his eyes. "I didn't want to, but I couldn't risk Asmodeus finding out. If he knew I left willingly..."

"Lux, we really should be on our way," Ahmed said. "If he followed you, who knows who else did."

"No one followed me," Leif snapped. "I have known Lux way longer than you have, and we know how to sneak out properly." He turned back toward me, trying not to be irritated.

"I'm so sorry, Leif." I gripped him in a hug. "But I'm so glad you came."

"What about your parents?"

"They will understand, I think. Will you tell them everything in confidence? I don't want them to believe the next part of my plan."

"Sure, Lux. But what's the next part of your plan?"

I dug through my satchel, pulling out the torn page I was originally going to leave behind on the beach.

"Give us a few hours, but when you return to the village to report me missing, say you've found this." I handed Leif the scrolled paper. "Oh, and Leif? Asmodeus has a special interest in this island. Be careful."

His hand coiled around it, and he swallowed. "Will I see you again?"

I smirked. "You didn't think you'd get rid of me

that easily, did you?" I pulled him back into a hug. "Thank you for being such a good friend to me all these years despite everything."

"It was you who was a good friend to me. Even though you seemed so put together, I could see that your soul was suffering. And how I longed to see it shining and blissful like I see it now." His voice was muffled as I pulled him down tighter into my good shoulder.

"Good-bye, Leif." I blinked away tears as I turned away from my best friend.

"Good-bye."

When I looked up, Ahmed stood stiffly with his hands clasped at his torso. He nodded once at Leif.

"And if anything happens to her, I'll hold you personally responsible."

I smiled as Leif made a threat for the first time in his life.

"I'm under the captain's orders to protect her with my life." Ahmed swiveled toward me to gather my belongings.

We waded through the water the short distance to the multi-hulled boat. Ahmed boarded first, and then turned to help pull me in. I pulled up the anchor as Ahmed prepared the sails. Moments later, the boat was carried away like a shooting star.

I thought once again about the legend Draven had told me about how the night came from the sea. As I situated myself on the netting between the vessel and the outrigger, I realized I had the answers to the all the questions I had about the story. Lemanja's daughter left, but she wasn't missed because her family knew that was where she wanted to be. They knew she was happy.

I watched Leif until I could no longer make out his figure on the shore, imagining him unfurling the note as soon as I disappeared over the horizon and reading it with wide, gray eyes.

Help, I've been captured by pirates.

The End.

Acknowledgements

There's a place on every word processor, where you can view the document's properties. There, you can see the "total editing time" on your manuscript. Writers, don't do this. First will come amazement, then shock, and perhaps grief. The amount of time spent on writing, researching, editing, and revising is amazing and shocking. If you write to make money, this may cause some grief. But if you write because you have to and can't imagine living without being able to write like I do, then this is insignificant. There were quite a few different versions of BLUE TIDE, so I can't give you exact numbers, but here's what I think a break down would look like and the people who've helped shape BT:

63,898+ Minutes: To myself. But not really myself. To my family, and all the other people and things in my life that were sacrificed to make 63,898 minutes of editing, rewriting, and revision possible. I hope you are proud. I love you.

21,485 Minutes: To the critique partner who I really owe it all to, Mary Cain. She first saw something in Blue Tide back when it only had, oh you know, 10,000 minutes of editing. Blue Tide wouldn't be where it is without her. I'm so lucky to have her in my life! Not only is she an excellent editor, but she is wonderful and patient and smart and funny and my best friend.

5,617 Minutes (or a month of intense editing): To Lara Willard. Freelance editor and blogger extraordinaire. She hosts writing contests like #Pg70pit and she was a judge in Pitch to Publication, where I snagged my agent. She chose Blue Tide out of tons of amazing entries and then spent the next month editing to prepare it for the agent round. This decision literally changed my life. I'm lucky to still have her guidance and friendship well after the contest is over.

3,284 Minutes: To my lovely agent, Rebecca who helped make BT shine. And also spent hours on proposals, talking me through the submissions process, easing my worries, answering late night texts, and so much more. Thank you for being a wonderful agent, and friend.

2,600 Minutes: To CTP's editor, Cynthia, who polished BT to perfection and probably read it so many times her eyes hurt.

240 minutes X 5: To all my wonderful beta readers who encouraged me and inspired me. Cheryl, Jennifer Austin, Daphne Rosario, Tera Barrera, and JD Burns.

Books take a lot of work, time, and people to make it happen. But everyone has a chance to be a part of an author's "minutes". Pre-order books, share on social media, leave reviews. It doesn't go unnoticed and we appreciate it. So, if you are reading this, thank you. You are supporting an author. You are now a part of my minutes.

xoxo,

Jenna-Lynne

About the Author

JENNA-LYNNE DUNCAN LIKES TO WRITE HEART-STOP-ping, page-turning, haunting romance in all YA genres. With a love for travel and special connection to the Middle East, she explores different cultures and different languages. Her current Young Adult releases are titled Hurricane, Tempest, Aftermath and the forthcoming Blue Tide. Jenna graduated with degrees in Middle Eastern Studies, Political Science, and International Studies. BLUE TIDE was the recent winner of RWA's Romancing the Lake contest. She welcomes those to contact her on Twitter, @JennaLynneD, or her website: www.Jenna-Lynne.com

CPSIA information can be obtained
at www.ICGtesting.com
Printed in the USA
LVOW11s0927271216
518815LV00001B/1/P